An Organized Panic

A Novel

Also by Patty Friedmann

(Titles in parentheses are for e-versions when changed for re-release)

—

Too Smart to Be Rich (Too Rich to Be Smart)

The Exact Image of Mother (Green Eyes as part two of *Too Jewish* trilogy)

Odds

Eleanor Rushing (Through the Windshield)

Side Effects (Pick-Up Line)

Secondhand Smoke

*A Little Bit Ruined (*sequel to *Eleanor Rushing)*

Too Jewish (part one of *Too Jewish* trilogy)

Do Not Open for 50 Years (part three of *Too Jewish* trilogy)

Taken Away

No Takebacks

An Organized Panic

A Novel

Patty Friedmann

An Organized Panic
By Patty Friedmann

Published by Old Stone Press
an imprint of J. H. Clark & Associates, Inc.
Louisville, Kentucky 40207 USA
www.oldstonepress.com

For information about special discounts for bulk purchases or autographed copies of this book, please contact Old Stone Press at john@oldstonepress.com or the author Patty Friedmann at afreelunch@aol.com

---

ISBN: 978-1-938462-29-0
Library of Congress Control Number: 2017910762

Published in the United States

DEDICATED TO
Bernie Sanders

“*What is religion really if not an organized panic about death?*”

—Quiet Company’s Taylor Muse

From an interview in *The Humanist*

March/April 2012 issue

CHAPTER ONE

I SLIPPED INTO THEIR family room where my mother sat staring in disbelief at Gracie and Levi playing a video game. Well, Levi was playing, and Gracie was patiently waiting her turn. Unlike their father and me, they were very close in age and forced to get along. The game looked violent, with a blue robotic creature attacking a red one. My mother liked to read but had nothing to flip through, not even *Good Housekeeping*. That's what I expected in an Anita Bryant kind of house. Since Ronald's rebirth, which Mama claimed came with a business deal with Jesus, the only reading material I ever saw in that house was the open Bible on the coffee table. My mother had no particular use for the Bible, though we had had one in our house when Ronald and I were children. It was full of yellow highlighter marks from when she had taken a course in college, the heaviest concentration of yellow in the *Book of Revelation*. I'd never wondered why. I peeked at the Bible. It was open to where Proverbs 6:16 had an ivory pointer laid underneath it.

"Is that our daily message?" I said.

"Could be," Mama said. "I put it there." I looked her in the eye to see if she was kidding. She grinned. "Unlike your brother, I read this book once upon a time."

I asked her if she wanted to join me in my car.

She stood up without saying a word, as if to say, *I don't care if you're asking me to come smoke weed while police cars cruise past, I'm coming*. She always had been the mother my friends coveted. Even now, she looked no older than any of us, slender and agile, with her hair colored a casual brown. I knew she shopped from Victoria's Secret catalog, but reasonably.

I actually had a blunt in the glove compartment, which a person can do if she's just past forty and drives an E-class Mercedes, because she would have to run a red light and slam into a person of even more respectability before her car would be searched, and even at that the odds were against the New Orleans police having suspicions. But I was thinking about the bottle of Chardonnay I'd bought and lost my nerve about bringing as a hostess gift. Ronald and Elizabeth were eclectic in their rules, which was Ronald's privilege in having his own orthodoxy, and I wasn't in the mood for an extra reason why I was going to hell. Ronald had enough reasons I couldn't see or touch. For years now, Ronald had been wielding an eternity of damnation the way my mother had wielded Santa Claus before we each turned six and learned the truth. Only Ronald never was going to sit anyone down and say, "Okay, I think you're old enough to know."

"We're not leaving, are we?" Mama said, with too much hope in her voice.

I shook my head, no. We were all together for dinner because *she* saw Thanksgiving as a valid non-sectarian holiday, never mind its cruel origins, and I wasn't going to do her the favor of saving her from the difficulty of it. Mama didn't believe one word Ronald said. Not only that his religiosity made no sense: she was sure he was a complete phony. She could not imagine herself as having reared such a person. A few years back she had made a bet with me: "I'll put up one of my Rodrigues against one of your own paintings that your brother's a fake." I loved her Rodrigues, but so far I hadn't done any sleuthing into Ronald's life as a man of God. I found it fun to watch in a peculiar way. It seemed genuine to me. But putting up a Rodrigue meant Mama was serious. "You know I'm not wagering the value of the painting," she'd said. "I'm wagering the joy of it." We'd gone off on a long tangent on that one.

I leaned across her. The wine bottle was in a paper sack on the passenger side floor by her feet. "Oh!" she said. "I hope it has a screw-cap."

"I'm way ahead of you." I'd known when I bought it that I was going to be opening it without a corkscrew. Ronald threw away their corkscrew years ago. He didn't even give it away. I'd wondered if giving a corkscrew to charity was a Christian thing or not.

I extended the bottle to my mother. Not getting backwash was the privilege of parents with adult children. "I know, just a tiny sip. Or not," I said.

"Probably not," she said.

She behaved only when she saw no ideology behind her choice. That was her basic approach to life: go with pure science.

She had dangerously high blood pressure. She believed only what she could see or hear. The doctor stood behind her when he used the cuff, but he told her the numbers, and he told her what they meant, and generally she behaved accordingly. She said she believed him, and by "believed" all she meant was that she knew he was right.

"All those flashes and bleeps from that video game probably were worse for your health than this entire bottle," I said. I wasn't trying to coax her to drink. I was trying to let her know I'd saved her. "You think Ronald knows they're in there killing people?" I said.

My mother patted my arm. "Honey, I doubt your brother's really worried about that." I tipped back the bottle and took a long drink. I didn't like wine. I didn't like any alcohol, really. For me it was just a legal drug that worked fast.

"Levi's saving Paradise," she said. "Bet you can't guess what the demon is." She said it like we were playing a parlor game. I had twenty questions.

The wine was hitting me.

"Money," I said.

My mother laughed. "I stepped right into that one." She liked to talk about the way Ronald was getting rich. She loved us both no matter what.

I tried to dredge up the Seven Deadly Sins. They were harder than the Seven Dwarfs. I wondered if they overlapped. Sleepy? Sloth? Grumpy? Wrath? Doc? No, nothing wrong with doctors. I was feeling the wine. “There should have been a dwarf named Greedy,” I said.

My mother had known me all my life. She could track my thoughts through any path. In spite of herself she started laughing as if she’d been drinking, too. I loved her so much.

“The demon was lies,” she said.

“Oh, dear,” I said.

“That’s why I left the Bible open.”

I knew lying was not a deadly sin. Deadly sins were not acts against other people; they were acts you wallowed in. Seemed you could be an angry, horny fat pig as long as you told the truth.

“See, Ronald and Elizabeth say that lying is evil, but they don’t have a clue what else is. I just thought I’d give them a little menu. Though lying about all this God stuff would be enough to send them straight to hell if there was a hell.”

I disagreed with her. I thought Ronald believed deep, deep down in what he was doing. He was in the business of cleaning up murder scenes, but he charged a fortune for something besides mops and chemicals and labor, which gave him a high profile in what I guess you’d call his industry. He’d started out creating a business niche no one else had thought of in New Orleans, and I’d secretly thought it was kind of excellent because it was flat-out macabre. But he struggled, and that wasn’t good for a man who tried to move proudly around uptown New Orleans with a waist bigger than his chest and a desire to send his kids to Newman School. In this city most men who had wealthy mothers had claimed their birthrights, then had gone to lunch at Galatoire’s. But Ronald had learned a big lesson in disappointment when our father died leaving our mother as usufructuary.

Now, just when he had found Jesus, he had something to show. To whom I didn’t know, because I didn’t understand what he believed was floating around in the sky—or the uptown streets. One day one of his crew had cleaned up a site where a child had been killed in a drive-by, and the man had spontaneously stood over the spot and prayed. Word got out that Price Services also did Christian cleansing after murders, sanctifying people's homes and spaces as pure and holy, and before he knew it, Ronald had JesusCleanup operating in a seven-state region, and he was rich as Croesus. He also was godly. Jesus was his salvation. Mama always said that he did a Jesus Cleanup on his house when he knew he was having visitors, plopping that Bible on the table and burying Grand Theft Auto under the sofa because it would mean he was still rational. But that couldn't be true because Elizabeth and his kids didn't look like part of a cover-up. After all, the word epiphany didn't come about in the twenty-first century. His was one of the old-fashioned kind. Jesus had saved him. He wasn't like those men I saw on television whose epiphanies came when they saw their spreadsheets.

The demon was lies! Poor little Levi, who was fourteen and wasn't so little anymore, was in there fighting a red-costumed demon because he, Levi, was the Truth Teller. Levi believed he was a truth-teller. Even his birthday told the truth, falling as it did seven months after his parents' anniversary, though he never knew that. He would save the world because he knew the truth, even in his video game, even through his avatar. In his regular life the truth was what his daddy told him. That was natural. It seemed that for Levi most of the truth was in that one book that stayed on the coffee table even when school books came and went. That book would imply the world was created 6000 years ago. That book made dinosaurs hard to explain when he was four and science class hard to pass when he was ten, but Levi believed his daddy.

I leaned over and hugged my mother. "I love you so much," she said.

"Please don't eat the poor turkey," I said back, still hugging her. The turkey would be shot so full of nitrates and nitrites that a person's navel would pop out if she ate it. I could feel my mother chuckling as I held her. She was the world's best laugher.

IT WAS OVER A forkful of string beans.

"Drop that," Elizabeth said. Her tone was the one she used only with her dog when she was in college. But a lot had changed with her since they started cleaning for Jesus. Or Jesus started cleaning for them. I guess they cleaned *with* Jesus. For instance, Elizabeth wasn't really her name as far as I was concerned. I knew her long before she was Elizabeth. We went to school and cut up together; I knew her when she could tell me to *drop it,* and we both would laugh. I shoved the fork into my mouth, my eyes extra big. I tasted pork and spat it into my hand. She was acting on rigid principles, but I had rigid principles, too. Mine were about pain, so I usually felt all right about myself.

Losing a friend didn't make me happy. But usually losing a friend meant she would go away and hide from me so I didn't have to wonder. Elizabeth was here in front of me, married to Ronald. Deeply married to Ronald. The way he'd been in recent years, I had to let her go. I had no choice, and I missed her.

"You've ruined the entire meal," she said.

Oh, no, please, no.

"Just don't tell him," I said.

"I assume you mean Ronald, because God would know," she said.

I whispered, "God's not watching me." I tried to catch her eye, remind her.

She got quiet. She remembered she was talking to me.

RONALD CAME INTO THE kitchen a few minutes later. Really, he shambled in like an inspector, looking this way and that, trying to put no offer of usefulness in his posture. It was a polo shirts and slacks day, but Ronald was wearing a dress shirt and pants—and a tie. I was sentimental about him in those kinds of clothes because he'd looked like a little businessman when he was ten, too, and he'd had Alex P. Keaton ways to match his looks.

"She ate out of the casserole," Elizabeth said.

Ronald looked at me with something of a paternal expression. It didn't work. I was five and a half years older than he was, and until I died, and he waited five and a half years, he wasn't going to catch up with me. That was the privileged perspective of birth order. "You're not supposed to eat before the food's been blessed," he said.

So there was the principle. Principles had become confusing since they started being clean with Jesus.

I apologized. It was his house, so I was going to go by his spoken principles. For our mother's sake I was there for Thanksgiving. I was going to tamp down my own principles. I'd tasted Elizabeth's recipe using pork fat for seasoning in the beans, which undid my vegan sensibilities. And canned fried onions on top, which went against my belief in good health.

"I didn't swallow," I said.

"We're not Jewish," Ronald said. "Jews are the ones who base everything on technicalities."

He said it with admiration. Ronald always had had a respect for Jewish people. I thought it had something to do with the dog named Baruch that Daddy gave away when it bit me. "A bite like that could really harm a child Ronald's size," Daddy had said, but only my mother and I had accepted his reasoning. Baruch had not been the first being with a Jewish-sounding name that Daddy had dismissed. And the loss of "Ruke" was only one of many times that Daddy had left Ronald grief-stricken. He'd been furious when Daddy died. Especially after the will was read.

"I'm not going to argue with you over whether you swallowed a few molecules or what your intentions were," he said. "You did the wrong thing, and since I know you won't pray for yourself, we'll all pray for you at the meal."

I sighed as slowly and quietly as I could. Poor Ronald.

I pulled my salad out of the refrigerator. Then I remembered that eating from my own salad right then had to do with my needs and not Ronald's. I was terribly hungry. For me hunger usually had to do with having nothing else to think about. I could go into my studio first thing in the morning and be surprised to learn it was two in the afternoon when I first needed to sit down to eat. I put the salad back. I looked at Ronald for appreciation, saw what might have passed for pride. And not the sinful kind.

"The table needs to be set," Elizabeth said. Since becoming Elizabeth, Tizzy had grown very fond of the passive voice. She animated a lot of inanimate objects that way. I pulled open the flatware drawer in front of Ronald. "Your bathroom needs to be visited," I said to him. I hoped he would laugh. He gave me a tolerant little smile. I was surprised. But he didn't reach for the forks.

Elizabeth ignored me. She'd announced I'd ruined her dinner. She'd upheld the principle.

WE HAD TO HOLD hands around the table. That meant I had to hold Ronald's hand, and I hadn't had enough to drink to make that pleasant. No matter how much I wished it wasn't true, I didn't like touching my brother. As an adult I once had told a psychiatrist about it, and she'd asked me if I had some unresolved sexual issues about anything, and I said, no, I had some unresolved aggravation issues. As a child Ronald had resembled Kevin's friend Paul on *The Wonder Years* on television, skinny and chinless with black-rimmed glasses and greasy dark hair. He looked like the sort of brother a girl should have protected, but not one of my friends blamed me for not keeping a close eye on him. It was his style of being an earnest little hustler, too independent for whatever pure strength a big girl could offer. At the time it didn't seem to me that he was trying to make up for anything the way some small boys did. Rather, he seemed to think he had smart ideas. And he actually did. Other boys didn't beat him or isolate him or in any way bully him. Mostly he got plaintive arguments, so he would talk other boys down or sometimes trick them out of their money, and they would walk away, heads down. The week before Mardi Gras, when he was in second grade, he bet a group of boys two dollars each that he could start a brawl on the playground from ten feet off. He then threw a fistful of doubloons onto the blacktop and caused a free-for-all. He made twelve dollars and said he'd put the blame on anyone who turned him in. He had used no Rex doubloons.

Time had placed a different mask on him. He still had answers, and now I had to respect those answers even if I couldn't define them. Levi was a truth-teller. That meant everyone else at the table was one, too. Except my mother and me.

Ronald droned on and on. He took far too long. "Please, God, forgive my sister Francesca for her indiscretion. She acts from pure ignorance." Francesca? I supposed I was on formal terms with God. Was I on some list? "Yes, it is ignorance, for she has not been saved by giving her heart to our savior, your son, Jesus Christ. She does not know that we must bless our food before it can be eaten." I waited for a special prayer for unholy string beans, but none was forthcoming. He simply blessed all the food, grandfathering in the string beans, or maybe saving all the dishes I had ruined; I had no way to know. "Thank you for allowing all of us to partake, even though she has failed to find salvation." He didn't preach like anyone I'd ever heard, but most of my preaching had come from Flannery O'Connor stories and a few black funerals.

"And as the Lord said in John 17:17, sanctify them through the truth," Ronald was saying. "I thank you for blessing Elizabeth and Grace and Levi and pray that my mother Patricia and my sister Francesca achieve grace through faith. Amen." His hand was so sweaty. I thought about a polygraph, which measured perspiration on a person's finger to gauge truthfulness. But truth-tellers didn't play by the same rules as criminals. I wiped my own hand on my skirt, but I was discreet. Maybe my own wet hand said I was lying about something in my silence. Ronald probably wasn't all that happy about touching me, either. According to everything he'd been saying all those years, and even today with all those string bean molecules, I carried the contagion of sin.

My mother was always incredulous that he believed what he said about me. She reasoned that he grew up in the same house I did so he should believe what I believed. We had the same mother. We heard the same emphasis on science and reason. We heard faith being mocked, and while she had waited until we could handle it, eventually she told us in no uncertain terms that dead was dead. We grew up with no worries about an afterlife. "An afterlife's a gift I have no problem giving up," I'd told her. I'd zoned out often enough on nitrous oxide at the dentist to know that nothingness was well worth waiting for. Ronald was doing everything in his power to float into eternity on a temperature-controlled cloud.

I thought our age difference accounted for much of our ideological difference. We had shared a home without sharing a history. We'd had parallax views. Of values, of moments. Except once. He was the one who named me. When he was two, in his mouth Francesca had become Cesca. My mother had told me to spell it Chesska, but my second-grade self had said that was wrong. It was the best favor Ronald ever did.

The names we carried did something to us. My father wanted a Ronald, Junior, so much that my mother acquiesced. She'd wanted a Giovanni to go along with a Francesca. Being a Cesca and a Ronald alone could have drawn a line. We also saw our father differently. Especially our dead father. A father can be a big deal.

My mother didn't buy my arguments. To her, children with the same mother should have the same religion or lack of it. If they didn't, one was a phony.

We had to go around the table and express our thanks for what was most important in our lives the past year. It was a Ronald ritual, and not a bad one if it could tell the truth about itself. I knew it was coming. I had no spirituality whatsoever, but I'd decided days earlier that I was going to let whatever moved me at the moment determine what I said. That wasn't a way of transcending reason. It was just a way of being lazy. I was hearing a lot of "Jesus" around the table. If I'd been those children, who were in two powerful stages of puberty, I'd have been thinking about boys whose names I might very well have blurted out, but they were saying that having Jesus in their lives was what they cherished most. Poor sweet truth-tellers. My turn came, and I had the salad bowl in my hands. The room was silent, full of ready condemnation.

"I'm grateful for the food I eat," I said.

Ronald started to smile, started to open his mouth and agree with me. My mother started to speak, as if it were her turn now.

"No animals suffered and died for the food I eat," I said. "This is beautiful food. No turkeys were penned and slaughtered. No hog was killed just so the string beans could be a little greasy. I get my protein from broccoli and spinach and soybeans. I'm a good person."

"You're being a spoilsport, sweetie," my mother said, and Ronald gave her a grateful look.

I saw the blank expressions around the table, except on Gracie's bemused little face. "I'm sorry," I said. I meant it. I didn't want to be the self-righteous one. And I knew from years of being so extreme in the way I ate that I really had become difficult to be around at eating times. Even at shoe-buying times. No one needed to be reminded about dying animals. I was more annoying than PETA, and I knew it.

"I'm thankful to have my family together today," my mother said. "All of us Prices. Except, of course, my dear Ronald Senior. I'll always be grateful for him." For a fraction of a moment, the face of Ronald Price Junior lost all peace of the holiday.

My daughter Klea, who wasn't a Price, wasn't home from school, but I saw no need to mention that. Klea was up in Massachusetts and beyond happy not to be home for Thanksgiving. She was a sophomore, and all sophomores had great certainty about everything they'd ever learned. That was the nature of having a year of college under one's belt. I hoped she retained her certainty. Klea felt she had escaped her family. She could come back and visit her cousins, but she would proselytize to them before they could proselytize to her. In college Klea had found reason everywhere. She was named after a wonderfully abstract painter, not the heroine of an obscure literary trilogy, she would tell everyone she met.

My mother usually knew what I was thinking. It was simple logic, she'd say if I asked.

"Maybe we can call Klea later," she said. She knew as well as I did that Klea had gone home with a boy she liked who lived in Connecticut.

"I'd be freaked out to bring him there," Klea had told me.

I'd asked her why.

"Uncle Ronald might make him say something he'd regret," she'd said.

"Oh, by all means marry him."

"That definitely makes me want to bring him there."

When Elizabeth's turn came, I tried to catch her eye, hoping I could transform her back into my kind of truth-teller, the same thoroughly honest girl with whom I'd talked about Jerzy Kosinski and Charles Bukowski before I introduced her to my brother. I knew when I first met her that she'd been reared in pure religious apathy. Her parents' full philosophy of life had been, *Nothing is worth getting up on Sunday*. It had been part of our bond.

She would say she was thankful for humor, for irony, for anything she and I once had shared. Oh, I'd even settle for her being thankful for the truth. I just wanted her back. My mother was different. My mother always was looking at Elizabeth as Ronald's point of weakness, the one who might give her a coded message that she was pretending for the sake of getting along, that Ronald believed and she didn't, or Ronald didn't believe, but she had to front for him, either way, but that she really was still Tizzy, that surely everyone knew how the easiest way to live with Ronald was not to argue. "I'm thankful for my family and our health," Elizabeth said. I couldn't disagree with that. I had to admit that wasn't what I'd called Cloud Nine Philosophy when Klea was growing up. "Not very Jesus-fied," my mother whispered to me. "But Jesus-y," I whispered back.

Food silence at that table wasn't comfortable the way it was with some hungry families. I knew from experience that most of us wanted to be the next to speak. Each of us wanted to find the perfect thing to say that would win the direction of talk for the rest of the meal. I would have thought Ronald had planned his out long in advance. I also would have thought that something would come to me without my trying.

Then I noticed the plates. Only I had taken salad, and all I had taken was salad. The rest of them ate from Elizabeth's collection of recipes off soup cans. Vegetables covered in thick cheese. Those string beans that were worming their way through a salty mire of mushroom soup and pig fat. For the potatoes, thick brown gravy that surely came from beef stock. And that turkey, that poor, poor turkey, not from a soup can, but just as mediocre and sad and dangerous. My mother was no better than the rest. Her plate was piled high and wide with as much of everything as she could fit. I turned in her direction and made sure to catch her eye. "What? What? I'm starving. It's three in the afternoon."

"It's a balanced meal," Elizabeth said. "It's got fiber and nutrients and protein."

But she alone had taken very small portions of everything. Elizabeth was no longer the easily slender girl I first knew; she was pretty chunky. So either she'd packed it in before she sat down, or she knew better than to eat this garbage. Since eating before the blessing was a ticket to Ronald's condemnation at minimum, I figured she was saving herself for dessert. Very few desserts were full of sodium.

"Mama has high blood pressure," I said.

My mother elbowed me just below the table. "One meal won't kill me," she said. "I'll take a water pill tonight."

My mother was a fiercely intelligent woman. She understood everything her doctor had told her. But her mind and her behavior occasionally disconnected because she liked to believe only what she could see, and a time or two she didn't refill her prescription for blood-pressure medication. Or sometimes she cheated on what she ate and drank. She was a thoroughly rational woman, but that didn't stop her from moments of irrationality. She was even willing from time to time to discuss her irrational behavior rationally.

I told her she was right. I wasn't there to ruin her day. I was there to make her day. When she had a second cup of coffee, I went right along with her. Caffeine was good for me, and she looked terrific. Coffee made both of us chatty and exuberant, and that was all that mattered. "Tizzy," I said, "I'll have a small slice of pie, please," and I grinned when Elizabeth reached for a plate before Ronald said to her, "You're way past that now."

"Elizabeth, pie, please," I said.

CHAPTER TWO

ONE GOOD THING ABOUT a pious family is that watching football after a heavy Thanksgiving dinner isn't a natural choice. That day Ronald and I had that one point of agreement. For our separate reasons, it was a colossal waste of time, energy, and money. He would find so many deadly sins in the game. I saw a thorough lack of mental acumen and, of course, a lot of dead pigs.

I was going to have to sit around their living room until my mother wanted to go home. She lived only four blocks away, but she was not going to go to her house on foot, no matter how much she insisted. I was going to drive her because I was going to leave when she did. That was my gift to her, to stick it out until whatever time she considered to be the end of the holiday. Not that Thanksgiving was a time for gifts, but to me it smacked of loving in the family and forgetting its origins; the holiday season was upon us. All the public service announcements gave Thanksgiving that aura of generosity. Ronald probably didn't sense deep love for him in my presence. I didn't think I had deep love for him. I might have at one time, but my love had been a child's love. For me, as for my mother, love was an intangible. It annoyed us both because we knew it existed. We were willing to be humanists, but we wondered why.

At least we didn't have to be proper. Gluttony clearly was a relative term, and Ronald had no *biblical* reason to keep his pants buttoned and belt buckled or both feet on the floor. He was all limbs and belly, like an insect. We lounged, most of us overstuffed. I didn't mind too much. Ronald's house was very comfortably uptown, and I knew it was because of Elizabeth when she was Tizzy. She'd overseen the renovation, the lush furniture and cathedral ceiling and pool for the 120-year-old Victorian. Ronald prayed for good backstreet people, but he lived like an avenue man.

"I don't feel so good," my mother said, and everyone except me agreed that Thanksgiving was a time of overdoing it, and a lot of overdoing was going to make us sick for most of the rest of the afternoon.

"I mean, I don't feel right in the head," my mother said with a crooked little smile that looked apologetic.

"I won't touch that line," Ronald said, trying to sound good-natured.

I sat up straight. Surely my mother was loaded with sodium and caffeine, and it was my fault. "Do you need to go to the emergency room?" I said.

"What are you trying to prove?" Ronald said.

I looked to Elizabeth for backup. She was a mother, and mothers knew symptoms. Elizabeth had loved my mother before she knew Ronald. Her face showed nothing, no alarm, no annoyance, nothing.

I knelt down in front of my mother and looked into her eyes. I'd have thought sodium and caffeine would bloat her, push her toward exploding, that her eyes would be pulsing and popping. But they looked normal. I felt the pulse at her neck. Strong, if a little fast. I'd gotten one of those e-mails with an acronym listing the three ways to recognize a stroke, but I couldn't remember a single one of them.

"I'm all right," my mother said. "I'm being a bad guest. I usually don't eat so much. It must have gone to my brain." She took me by the wrist and gently shoved my hand away. Her hand was dry. Maybe all that salt had sucked the moisture out of her like living, loving jerky.

She dusted off her knees with her palms as if to signal, *Well, that's all over with!* and I backed away, relieved.

"You need to quit babying her," Ronald said. "You're being a little obvious."

"Will you two cut it out?" my mother said.

I HADN'T NOTICED, BUT Gracie had been sitting off to the side of me, trying to draw my portrait in pencil on a sheet of computer paper. It wasn't good paper for erasing, easily pilling and ripping, and lucky for her, she had some natural family talent that let her draw lines that were dead-on the first time. She had my face in half-profile when she asked if she could show it to me. I whooped with praise and hugged her and thought but didn't say that she might be the descendant to keep my eye on. Klea was my treasure, and at least Klea wasn't channeling her uncle's irrationality, or her father's dry pragmatism. My ex-husband William was a financial genius, always using the opposite side of the brain from the one I used, so I knew Klea carried a counting gene. So far Klea didn't care much for the world of imagination. I wasn't above stealing my brother's child while keeping my own for other joys.

"We've talked about visual representation," Ronald said disapprovingly, in a tone that sounded just like, *We've talked about pre-marital sex.* "Gracie knows that drawing anything that resembles a person or object is like building a religious icon."

"Aw, come on," I said. This was the Ronald who had pissed off so many other boys. I'd never slugged him, but I'd also never taught him to talk like a regular person.

I was a painter. In fact a painter of national repute. It isn't bragging to say this now. I just know that buyers and critics appreciated how I communicate on the canvas—even if I'm cryptic—what I think and feel. I had classical training so I could draw and do oil portraits and still lifes and landscapes if forced to, in other words be a representational artist. I had my own idiosyncratic tastes in art. Some of them jibed with my own extreme abstract style; others less so. After all, I had named my only child after Paul Klee. But I wasn't a snob. I just didn't like being judged for the way I lived my life. And the media didn't do that. I was having a big one-woman opening soon at the Getty in Los Angeles, and the advance promotion saw me as a woman whose work and life made sense. With Ronald, my work was a childhood hobby that had gotten out of control. He was baffled.

"I know I'm still very strongly a post-Renaissance rebel," Ronald said with great cheer in his voice. "I object so strongly to the way in which Renaissance artists tried to paint images of biblical figures by using contemporary models. It was deeply sacrilegious, and eventually I evolved into someone who for a long time rebelled against any representation of holy images."

Who talked like that?

I didn't say a word. I just gave him the same kind of look I gave him when I was nine, and he was four, and he had wet his pants out on the front sidewalk with five other neighborhood kids standing around. That frown through the smile. Or smile through the frown. His choice.

"We've thought this through carefully," Elizabeth said. "Those Catholic churches with all their holy families and angels, well, it's just too much. We don't want anything to distract us visually."

We? This was what they discussed?

That explained why they'd given me the Walter Anderson my mother had bought them when she bought one for me, too. I had been terribly excited, and I hadn't hidden it from anyone. Walter Anderson was an artist I'd loved as a child, with his Gulf Coast motifs, water life spun into colorful abstractions that belied his sadness but glorified his craziness. My mother couldn't believe what Ronald had done in the name of piety, especially, she said, when monetary value was involved. "He must have struggled with that one," she had said. I cherished the painting even more now because Anderson's studio in Ocean Springs had been damaged in Katrina. After the storm my mother had said Ronald probably thought about its increased monetary value, but there was no way a man who said he was godly could profit in the wake of a disaster. She wondered if it crossed his mind: "If he sins in that funny little heart of his, he surely figures no one can tell," she said. "Except *God*, of course." She put air quotes around "God." She'd tried to convince me that Ronald was going out of his way to seem pure of heart. "Come on, how can that kind of belief exist in your closest blood relative?" she'd said. "Religion's not in the DNA," I'd said.

"There are good Christian artists now, though," Ronald was saying.

This interested me. I was going to Los Angeles next week to do a major PBS interview, and I needed to have some fresh ideas. Even if I was going to say, "This is what I'm not," it would be good. On the other hand, maybe I would be able to say why I could qualify as a good Christian artist in spite of Ronald, and that would stimulate an interesting discussion, as long as I brought it back to reality. Maybe I could say that my brother thought I wasn't very visually arresting, that my work was wallpaper as far as he could tell. But he'd approve of the fact that I definitely didn't have cherubim floating anywhere. I enjoyed controversy sometimes. I wasn't sure that this particular time in the national spotlight was a good occasion for uttering outrageous thoughts. I saw no harm in having ideas. No deity was monitoring what was inside my mind.

Ronald announced that they'd bought a very expensive piece of art, very Christian art, and it was hanging in the bedroom, over the bed, if we'd like to see it. I had no fear of going into their bedroom. I knew it would not reek of sex. I knew the bed would be made, smooth and tight, as if the house were going to be photographed.

Thomas Kinkade.

I couldn't believe it. I'd seen Thomas Kinkade paintings in magazines and flipped past them. I'd seen them on infomercials and fast-forwarded. I'd also seen a feature on him on "60 Minutes" and had had a few moments of philosophizing about what constituted art. Those silly pointillist cottages in dells with cozy lights and fog and overarching leaf-laden branches. With light. Lots of light.

I wanted to whisper to my mother that only a true Christian actually would hang something so awful in his house. I was thinking about being charitable.

"We feel so sacred when we look at it," Ronald said. "His works show the mysterious presence of God."

I made a mental note. Mystery. Maybe I would have to think about mystery.

"What did you pay for it?" I said before I could think.

My mother was standing behind me, almost leaning against me, as if I were going to protect her from the painting. They'd installed a little track light over it.

"A lot less than that Walter fish guy," Ronald said.

"Well, it was less than one of your paintings," Elizabeth said to me. "And look what we got. This guy is world-famous. It's a real painting, not a print or anything."

"Cesca's world-famous," Mama said. "We're going to Los Angeles next week to be on PBS."

I was glad she didn't tell them it was Tevor Souriante. Ronald would have asked what kind of name that was.

"PBS?" Ronald said. "But nobody watches PBS. This guy was on '60 Minutes.'"

WE'D BEEN OFF Daylight Savings Time a few weeks, and surely we'd start sensing the arrival of nightfall soon, but the house stayed full of late-afternoon light, and I thought I never was going to get out of there. I suggested Scrabble, and Ronald said they didn't have a set. His children weren't being reared to be competitive. My mother gave me a wide-eyed stare that said, *But everywhere they go, life is competition over money; they even go to Newman.* That's the message I read. I gave her back a winsome little smile that I hoped said we had an interesting little discussion ahead of us. In spite of myself, I was going to have to reconcile piety and excellence. Or else my mother was going to say what she was saying far too often lately: "If anything happens to me, promise you'll find out the truth about your brother." I didn't think that meant he'd kill her. I thought it meant that, lacking an afterlife, she wanted a posthumous life.

I suggested Charades, and Ronald chuckled and said, "I won't dignify that with a response."

"Oh, please, dignify it," I said. I knew the way I would play it with adults could be filled with innuendo, but I wasn't going to do that with children who surely longed for innuendo. Since they were sitting right there, I wanted to see what Ronald would say.

"I don't need to do this," he said. "Elizabeth and the kids know that people who play Charades do it so they can be dirty-minded."

"Come on, Dad," Levi said. He was more animated than he'd been all day.

I tried to give Ronald a conspiratorial smile, which he had a hard time fighting. "Oh, no one needs to know you were a bad boy once," I said to him. He gave me a look that said, *Not in front of the kids.* His version of being a bad boy had been having premarital sex for five minutes, but he took it seriously.

"We know how to play right," poor Levi said.

"Okay, watch what your aunt does with this one. Here's the phrase," he said to me. "Old Testament."

"You'd do 'sounds like testicles'!" Levi said.

Ronald turned pink. He'd probably been thinking of "breast" anyway. "I don't want to hear that word from you again," he said to Levi. "Or there will be consequences."

"'Sounds like testicles' is hard to do when you don't have them," I said to Levi, and even Ronald struggled to keep a straight face. He tried to glare at me.

"Come on, son," my mother said to Ronald. "We can set rules, you know."

Ronald suggested a walk in the park.

Not a bad idea. Out of that house. A full circle of Audubon Park surely would bring us to the onset of darkness. It was over two miles, a circuit between Tulane and the Zoo. Six people would have to split into two threes or three twos.

We were only six blocks away. We could have walked there, but we didn't. People uptown like Ronald didn't walk to the park unless they lived right next to it. Ronald was one of those white people who thought he had the bearing of a rich man with a Rolex and a lot of cash. All he had done was change shoes and take off his tie.

We set off at a leisurely pace, three twos. Ronald led with my mother, then Elizabeth with Levi, and I went last with Gracie. "You're a brave man," I'd said to Ronald, "trusting your little girl with her evil Aunt Cesca."

"Levi, you want to walk with Cesca?" Ronald said.

"No!" Gracie said, and Ronald laughed.

We stayed in a close pack, one of many comfortable families working off the bounty. I was far enough behind and working the air stream, so I could say whatever I pleased to Gracie. Our words would drift behind us. "I really love your work," she said. "There's a little of Kandinsky in you. Well, in the work you were doing the last time I was in your studio."

Kandinsky? I loved Kandinsky, though what I mostly had in common with him lately was what looked like exuberance. But what thirteen-year-old knew who Kandinsky was, let alone a little girl whose father might have thrown away an original Kandinsky if she had bought one for a dollar at a garage sale?

How did Gracie know about art? She had a secret mentor at school, and she knew I wouldn't tell her daddy. Her daddy, she said. That was her worry. Just him. Newman ran all the way from pre-kindergarten through high school, so she could go into the studio even though she was in middle school, and the high-school art teacher saw her for what she was, hungry to know. Sometimes she hid in the studio during her study hall. She read books. She painted. She drew. Even though seventh-graders only came once a week and all did the same thing. Last week it had been a still life. She had discovered Kandinsky in September. She had told her teacher about me. The teacher knew who I was. I said I'd come to school with her one day if she wanted. "Oh, no," she said, "he'd be scared to death."

I started to tell her that I hoped she and I could e-mail about art when I noticed we had picked up the pace. Skinny-legged Ronald was up ahead, power walking despite his fat reserves around his middle, and all of us were supposed to keep up with him. I told Gracie to follow me, and we jogged to catch Ronald.

"What do you think you're doing?" I said. I was trying not to sound breathless. I worked out at the Reilly Center at Tulane, but cardio wasn't a big part of my program. I probably could have bench-pressed Ronald, but I didn't know how long I could run alongside him. He kept walking in double-time, and my mother struggled to keep up with him. When she thought about her health, she wasn't worried about cardio so much, either. She worked out with weights because she was concerned about bone density. She was sure she was going to die from a hip fracture. She was such a small woman, five feet two and not much more than a hundred pounds. I imagined her bones being school chalk.

"Slow the fuck down," I said.

Ronald stopped in mid-pace. He put his hands on his hips. I hoped no one I knew would pass by. "What is your problem?" he said. He probably hoped no one he knew was passing, too. Expletives weren't good for his image, even if "fuck" didn't take the Lord's name in vain. And even if the choir to which he preached rarely slipped into the fancy streets of Uptown.

"My problem is that you're turning a nice walk into a miserable workout," I said. "Not to mention that some of us aren't fit enough to walk this fast. And it's not just me, it's your mother."

Ronald looked at Mama, who was accustomed to being caught in the middle between her two very different offspring. Her only way of dealing with us when we went at it this way was to make an exit.

While I knew that I was the one she believed, I also knew that she worked hard to keep Ronald from knowing how much she questioned him.

"How about compromising?" she said. "Not too fast, not too slow?" Compromise was not a trick she had tried more than a handful of times. Ronald and I rarely had had disagreements that could be settled by measures.

Ronald grinned at me. I was eleven, and he was six, and Mama had leveled the field out of a very wrong sense of fairness.

"But you set the speed," I told her.

At that Mama set off at a clip almost as fast as Ronald's had been, four steps for his every three. Gracie and I dropped back, and we didn't talk much because both of us were breathless. Even Gracie, a slender child who took physical education three times a week, was just as happy not to talk. I was glad I didn't have to see Ronald's expression. Technically, we were still at his house. We were on his terms.

My mother started veering right and left, almost as if she were drunk. Everyone else took this to be a follow-the-leader gambit, and mimicked her, but I didn't like the looks of it. I jogged up to her just as she said, "Something's wrong. I can't walk," and she collapsed onto the ground.

Ronald stood over her like a small boy lost in a grocery store, his arms hanging straight and rigid at his sides, his hands clenched, his eyes full of what looked like fear. He seemed too paralyzed to bend down. "Mother, get up," he stage whispered. "Please?" He looked up at the sky, as if something might be written up there.

"Ronald!" I said. "Call 911."

He looked at me as if this were 1960 and there were no such thing as cell phones. I looked around. No one had a cell phone. Ronald hadn't brought his; Elizabeth didn't own one. The kids of course didn't have cell phones because too much could go awry with them. Mine was in the car. I'd left it because I was wearing a skirt and had no pockets, and I wasn't going to carry it in my hand or shove it into my bra and radiate myself.

"How could you not stay connected at all times?" I said to Ronald, hoping he was not going to give me a mystical answer. Cleaning up murder scenes was a 24/7 operation, since most people didn't kill during working hours.

"I keep the office staffed around the clock, and all I personally need to do is console people," he said.

Grief was never an emergency. It wasn't going anywhere fast.

"Mother, please get up," Ronald said, ignoring me. Calling 911 wasn't going to be necessary if Ronald used the power of his word and nerves.

Elizabeth and the kids were pacing on tight curving paths that seemed unnecessarily close to my mother. I thought if I was lying on the ground with a stroke, I wouldn't want the stress of whooshing feet in random patterns that close by. I could imagine blood vessels popping in her head. I could feel blood vessels popping in mine.

"My...leg...won't...work." My mother sounded drunk.

No one passing had a cell phone.

I told Ronald to give me his keys and for Chrissakes not to touch her. "You don't have to talk like that," he said softly as I ran off. I could run just fine. I could run half the circle of the park without thinking about it. I could grab my cell and call and give the location and run back and not be winded. A true miracle.

CHAPTER THREE

I ONCE DID A PHOTO shoot for an art magazine in which I posed half naked, draped in rags, with a gun in my hand, pointed at my head, standing on the steps of the New Orleans Museum of Art on free-admission day. I had to admit, I was enjoying myself immensely. I knew that without the cameras and director I could have been arrested. I was hoping men I knew from high school would come past and be sorry, but people with whom I went to high school did not go to the museum when it was free on Thursday. Not one person stopped to look. That is the way it is with people in New Orleans. We are accustomed to the bizarre and the badly behaved. We give privacy to celebrities and the mentally ill and mentally ill celebrities.

That is why I was surprised that a crowd had gathered where my mother had fallen. Crowds only gathered around dead people. Usually in dangerous neighborhoods. Usually with a bad boy on the ground. Usually with his mama already summoned finally to lose her mind over him. The only time dead bodies were ignored in New Orleans was after hurricanes. My mother surely was dead. One more time I broke into a run I didn't know I had in me, even though there was no point in speed when it was too late.

I saw why there was a crowd when I came closer. There my mother was, lying on the blacktop, no one at her side, with Ronald's family standing over her—standing—in a circle of four people, hands clasped in prayer, heads bowed, as if over a dead person. I screamed, "No!" and kept the pace. My mother's head turned the slightest bit in my direction, and I knew she was alive, that the spectacle was not a dead person. The spectacle was Ronald's family, standing over her, with Ronald praying, his voice trembling, "Jesus, Lord, deliver her, to live another day, so that she will learn the error of her ways, that she will find salvation and be filled with the Holy Spirit--"

The runners around her weren't pious. They were incredulous. Sweaty and jogging in place, some of them, they could not believe what they were seeing, and yet not one was kneeling down to comfort my mother. When I came up I understood why.

There was panic in the crowd.

"Somebody needs to do something."

"He says she's breathing, so an ambulance is coming, and we need to pray with him."

"That's in-fucking-sane."

"He says he's Ronald Price."

"Who the hell is that?"

"JesusCleanup. He's on late night TV."

"Well, I don't watch TV, and my husband's a doctor, and what she needs is somebody to put a jacket over her."

Ronald's family was almost in a trance, swaying ever so slightly, their tight circle blocking onlookers from helping, and my mother lay there, possibly hearing their prayers that meant nothing about her prognosis, but possibly also hearing that an ambulance was coming and that she might survive. Especially if a doctor's wife was nearby, getting angry enough eventually to play Red Rover and break through the prayer circle.

I slipped in by separating Gracie's and Levi's hands, knelt down, and cradled my mother's head.

"She might have a neck injury," a young woman said.

"She had a stroke," I said.

"We don't know that," Ronald said. It was more a question than a statement.

I could hear a siren coming from Magazine Street, the demarcation line between the front part of the park and the Zoo and river. The crowd dispersed, satisfied. I asked the family if someone would please go out and guide the ambulance in. No one moved. "For God's sake, will somebody do something?"

Levi said he would go, and Ronald said, "For your grandmother's sake, son, not for God's sake." Levi hesitated a fraction of a valuable second, processing, then ran off. Ronald wasn't pretending. He was serious. He had no audience now, unless I counted Levi—or God and Jesus and whoever else was hovering over the oak trees.

Then I realized he had someone else in his audience. I wanted to tell him his mother might die right there and then, but I was six inches from her, and she probably wasn't in the state of mind to understand that I was only being hyperbolic, so I said nothing.

I WONDERED BRIEFLY WHAT would have happened if all of us had not gone to the park in one vehicle. Right away Ronald made the offer that I drive his car, drop his family off at his house, and go to the hospital by myself. I didn't even need to stop to grab the keys to my own car. He sounded scared to death. Really, he sounded scared *of* death, which was odd given his chosen career. And his deep comfort in an afterlife. Maybe he feared my mother wasn't a candidate for one yet.

"I think we need to follow the ambulance," I said.

"It's sitting in the middle of the park," he said. "I can't drive the car into the park."

The EMT could hear us. He could hear Ronald's plan. He was putting an oxygen mask on my mother. "Come out to Magazine and head downtown, and you'll see us coming out of the park," he said to me. He had no use for Ronald. It made me wonder if I was reading Ronald wrong. Over time I'd probably heard a lot more of his fear than I realized.

Levi rode shotgun, making no effort to conceal his fascination with watching his grandmother through the back window of the ambulance. He had not been allowed to pay this much attention to her when she was in terrible danger, lying on the ground. Elizabeth and Gracie were crammed in next to me. I should have ridden in the ambulance. Or shotgun. I wanted not to think. As long as the lights were flashing on the ambulance, and we were running nonstop through intersections, I knew my mother was still alive. But that did me no good.

At the emergency room we didn't have to wait. Ronald thought it was because he had made his impatience known. He knew administrators at the hospital, he said more than once. To us, to the woman at the admit desk. I didn't point out that triage at emergency rooms gave top priority on a different basis.

Once the CAT scan revealed that in fact it had been a stroke, Ronald took his family home. A hospital, even one still called Baptist by everyone in the city despite several name changes over the years, was nowhere for children to be, he explained. I agreed, but now I wasn't sure why Ronald didn't return by himself. Fear had explained his wish not to follow the ambulance in the park. Maybe fear was keeping him away from the hospital, too. But I was frightened, and I was there.

Part of me was grateful, because being alone with Ronald was always a struggle, but part of me was resentful. I didn't know if it was because once again he left me with all the pain, or because I thought Mama was sick after eating his food. I probably never quite had gotten over his behavior when Daddy died. He wasn't as hard to read back then. It was before JesusCleanup took off and Ronald became a deep Christian. Back then Ronald just was desperate to hold up his head in New Orleans. In New Orleans either a man had crafty ancestors who left bad old money, or he needed nasty new money. Ronald needed to be like all the boys he went to school with, callow and rich. I watched and wished he was not the former while suspecting he wasn't going to be the latter.

The day Daddy died, Ronald behaved as if it were just another day in his life. He went to work. Even my terribly practical husband had stayed home despite the market being open and fluctuating wildly. In the weeks that followed, my mother had a great deal of sorting to do, of accounts and clothing and feelings. Ronald never even saw paperwork until the day at the attorney's office when I found out what my father had told him in his last days in the hospital: the entire estate was in Mama's name, including usufruct of our inheritances. Finally that day Ronald could be loud with hurt. He'd never deserved a nickel, except because of childhood disappointments, but evidently he'd expected at least a million to do with as he pleased. He came right out and said so. "That's what happens to everyone else." He'd said nothing to Daddy in the hospital room and thought himself a good person.

Since Daddy died he'd been waiting.

Jesus came along as some sort of substitute. Ronald had learned somewhere uptown that money was love. Daddy left him no money, so Daddy didn't love him. Jesus gave him love. Jesus didn't hurt his feelings. Jesus made him rich. But Ronald was still waiting.

While I sat passing time too slowly in the Emergency Room, I found myself blaming Ronald for damaging Mama. This stroke was his fault. His and Elizabeth's, and her small portions at the Thanksgiving dinner table made me wonder which of the two of them was guiltier. It was as if Ronald had figured out a legal, Christian way to kill his mother and get his inheritance. It wasn't a ruthless, conscious, hands-rubbing-together plan, of course, but it was working in the farthest reaches of his brain all right. He'd been the one to compliment Elizabeth on those terrible recipes. Surely he'd suggested them, and while he hadn't said to himself, *Oh, excellent, this recipe will amount to 700 mg. of sodium per serving which is dangerous to someone like Mother*, when he read the label, he had been aware subconsciously.

But then when it had worked, he realized he couldn't let her die without finding Jesus. So he had to stand over his mother in the park in front of witnesses and pray that she survived to find Jesus, but at the same time, deep down inside, he was thinking, *Oh, if the old woman bleeds out her entire brain and dies I'll finally get all that money which I should have gotten such a long time ago, and that's not greed or dishonor of my mother or murder; it's simply letting an overdue debt be paid but she needs to find Jesus first because first and foremost I am a man of God who loves his mother and wants her salvation.*

I knew what Ronald and Elizabeth did for a living, and I knew their Christian cleansing of death scenes made them do so well, but I also had heard Ronald say he had his eye on an empty church building in Kenner. Ronald had sinned in his heart and in the string beans, but he didn't see it that way. If Jesus loved him, Jesus would bring him more money. Love was money. Or rather, money was love. Ronald was a true believer.

I admitted that my mother in a court of law would have had to answer to charges of contributory negligence. She knew what she was doing. She ate wrong. She often ate wrong. But that day she was forced to wait until three in the afternoon for blessed food. How much was she supposed to restrain herself? Okay, I restrained myself. But my food was an acquired taste. One Mama could have acquired. Low salt was a good acquired taste. Oh, this was all a matter of motivation. Who wanted my mother bleeding in the brain? I didn't. Mama didn't.

Mama was still in the Emergency Room. Not in the waiting area, but in the back in a bed. I could sit with her, and it was difficult, because it was the first time she ever looked old to me. She was a trim woman, and she colored her hair, and to me she didn't look sixty-seven—until that day. She was so small in the bed, with so many tubes and lines connected to her. Despite what the doctors had practically promised me, she was having a hard time speaking, even though they had started an aggressive treatment right away. There was a window of opportunity, they had explained, and she had come to the hospital within twenty minutes of falling down, so that meant the prognosis was good for her recovering completely from the stroke. But there was some risk. The treatment would break up clots, but it would break up all clots in her body, and she had a risk of bleeding out somewhere beside her brain. They thought it was worth the risk. Mama could sign a paper. She wasn't shaky on her left side, and she was left-handed.

Alone with me, Mama said, "Oh that headache. It was horrible."

I knew nothing of a headache.

Bit by bit I got the truth out of her. It should have come as no surprise. I had to keep a neutral face, though Mama lay staring at the ceiling, as if she were a psychoanalytic patient, bringing forth deep childhood memories from a thick haze of recall. After dinner, when she had felt funny, she definitely felt funny. I had known her as well as a mother knows a child. We had flipped our roles a long time ago. Mama had two children, though, and that day her plan was to please her other child. Ronald wanted her to be all right, so she was all right. Never mind that after she felt funny, she got an excruciating headache. "Excruciating!" she said, a little too much saliva in the third syllable, but otherwise clear as a bell. Inside, my mother was all there. Word origins were all there. Excruciating: *cruciare*. Ronald would have been pleased. She had told no one about the telltale headache. Not even when we walked in the park. Right up until she fell.

So the stroke had happened hours ago. Her window might have closed before we got to the hospital. Before we got to the park, really.

I HAD TO EXPLAIN TO the doctor why she wasn't improving, and he had to explain to me that I was right.

Over the coming days I had nothing to do but think while my mother dozed, and I waited. Unlike Ronald, who could pray away wrong thoughts, I could not help what went on in my mind. I thought about me. I didn't know what to do about Los Angeles. I needed to take my mother to wherever home was going to be for the unforeseeable future. I sat up most of each night in her room at Baptist, alone with only my mother for support, but I couldn't ask her.

She would say that Ronald and Elizabeth could look after her while I was gone, and I would have to say back that I was afraid she would be better off with a sleeping bag on the neutral ground. Out in the open the chances were better that no one would do her harm. Criminals didn't have salt shakers and pushy prayers.

There also was the matter of Nozie. The first evening, my mother was under sedation and kept mumbling what sounded like, "Nose, nose, nose," and I would rub her nose, though she had a free hand, and finally she said, "Cat." Her cat. Named Spinoza, reduced to Nozie, a hat-tip to Ronald's dear Baruch. He went to my house the first night, but the second night he moved to Ronald's house, litter box and all, despite Elizabeth's fear of toxoplasmosis. Ronald acted like Nozie was a second-chance of some kind when he took him. I hadn't seen that kind of affection in a long time.

Hospitals were ruled by insurance regulations. No amount of pleading for clemency would win her two more days. Money determined everything. I said I would pay a thousand dollars a day. "This is not a kennel," the nurse said.

I was going to have to cancel the PBS interview. When my mother was sleeping, I took out my cell phone and called Mr. Souriante's direct number. I felt like crying, because he was such an important man, and this was such an important validation of my work, and I had planned to fly out there and figure out everything I knew about how I expressed myself during the trip while my mother did the crossword. Just as he answered, Ronald walked into the room, and I turned my back on him so I wouldn't be interrupted.

By the time the conversation was over, I was sobbing. Mr. Souriante understood. He understood family, he understood strokes, he understood priorities, and he loved this part of the country. He was born in this part of the country. Since we were going to tape, this was an excuse to come to New Orleans, to see how things were since his feature on Katrina, to see my studio, to go see a cousin in Mississippi. I tried to speak, but I kept on crying. I was going to make a wonderful interview subject, I told him. I wanted to tell him I loved him when I hung up.

"What was that all about?" Ronald said, with no particular menace.

"I canceled my interview in L.A."

He hesitated before speaking. Perhaps something about the hush of a hospital room soothed Ronald. "It isn't such a big deal," he said. He honestly said it as if he was consoling me.

I wanted to tell him I worshipped PBS. The thought made me smile. So Ronald smiled, too. "He's flying in from Los Angeles to talk to me in my studio instead," I said.

Ronald's smile faded. "Really? For Channel 12?" he said.

"They were going to pay for Mama and me to fly out there," I said. "This is a serious interview."

My mother was waking up, smelling acrimony in the room. Her eyes were closed, but I saw a crooked smile. "Never...changes," she said.

Ronald went over to her and told her he'd come to talk to her about making arrangements for when she left the hospital. That was news to me.

"Cesca has...power...of...attorney."

Ronald knew that. Ronald had pitched an unholy fit when he learned that. Of course an unholy fit by Ronald had involved no raised voice, no four-letter words, no expressions of negative feelings. Ronald quietly assassinated me by dredging up anything he could find that would sound bad in a job interview, though he did it very matter-of-factly, as if he were listing courses I had taken in school. Cesca was divorced and flighty and artistic. Cesca had no money sense; money flowed into and out of the bank, and Cesca never kept a balance. (How did he know this?) Cesca had no morals and would make evil decisions. (Having a moral code was something to get around, as far as I could see from the news.) Mama had told him that sometimes decisions had to be made on instinct, and giving power of attorney was one of those decisions. My mother didn't believe in instinct. But she did believe in making statements that had no comebacks.

Ronald didn't get angry on the outside.

"Well, there's no need for power of attorney right now," Ronald said to her. "You have all your faculties. You have to make some choices. That's why I'm here, to help you make those choices."

"I guess I'm not going to Los Angeles with you," she said to me.

"She canceled her trip," Ronald said. *She.*

Mama tried to sit up, but couldn't. "Cesca!" Cesca is a difficult name to say when half of one's mouth is compromised. But I understood.

"He's going to come down here to interview me," I said. "Ronald should have told you that first."

My mother grinned. "So...I'll...still...meet...him?"

I told her that he knew all about her. Out of the corner of my eye I could see that Ronald was perplexed, as if he could see going to California to see someone he'd heard of, but not someone named Tevor Souriante.

"You could stay at my house," he said to my mother.

"Mama needs a special diet," I said instead of what I wanted to say.

Ronald started to laugh. "It's a good thing I'm here," he said to my mother. "Cesca wants to starve you to death."

What?

"There's not one ounce of fat on this woman," he said, waving his hand over my mother as if she were a cadaver in a freshman medical school class. "You would take her to your house and feed her stems and twigs, and she'd be dead inside of a week." He turned toward my mother's head. "Sorry, I'm just trying to make a point."

I tried to explain to him, right there in a hospital room, standing over a hospital bed, everything he needed to know about nutrition and should have learned over the years, starting in about fourth grade. But he shared all of Elizabeth's buzz words—fiber, nutrients, protein—all of which were valid when taken out of context. They were the building blocks of a balanced diet, but not when they were the vessels of toxins and poisons. To Ronald sodium was about as abstract as faith was to me. Only when he was sure it transcended reason would he believe in it.

Ronald's style since he started school was to select what truly interested him and to learn it perfectly. If it was boring—as were English literature, European history, biology, and classical music, to name just a few of the big ones—he shoved it off to the side with contempt. As a child in a secular, rational home, he pulled that stunt off in some measure. But now he took a lot on faith. I'd have thought believing about what goes on at the cellular level would be easy now.

I asked him if he would believe a doctor.

"Do you know what the word 'believe' means?" Ronald said.

I remembered what I'd learned in college. Like my mother, I did not come to what I knew without making sure of what I believed. I refused to transcend reason. Doctors spent years steeped in reason. I believed doctors. When they told me something based on research, I chose to know it.

"Okay, would you know it if a doctor told you?"

"Will...you...two...cut...it...out?"

That is when it came down to my mother making the decision. We argued in front of her as if she were a court judge, and I had no fears, because I knew the judge preferred my line of reasoning. This wasn't a time for fairness, not when her life was on the line. She probably would have liked eating preservative-loaded meats on white bread with mayonnaise at Ronald's, even though she never ate that way at home. And she probably would have enjoyed getting through the day on extra cups of coffee at his house, too, but that's all it had taken to half kill her in one afternoon. In my talking points I promised I'd go to Whole Foods and buy chicken and fish and make meals that tasted good, and she'd have a zillion books to read, and I'd watch out for stroke triggers because I believed what doctors told me. In fact I knew what they said was true.

"I...want...to...go...to...my...own...house," she said.

From behind me Ronald made a move toward her. She couldn't see his hands moving up, ready to be lifted in supplication. But she knew him well enough. "No," she said.

"How did you know what I was going to do?" he said.

Mama gave him a half smile, which was all she had.

"Matthew 7:7. Ask and it shall be given unto you," he said.

I wanted to say that if Mama asked me, she could have what she wanted, but it wasn't true.

CHAPTER FOUR

RONALD AND I REACHED an agreement without input from my mother or Elizabeth, which seemed unfair all around, but it worked for me, so I didn't complain. Elizabeth would take off work to help me set up my house. I was taking off work, too, but Ronald didn't consider what I did to be work, so letting Elizabeth out of the office was the only sacrifice in the deal. I thought about breaking down what I earned by the hour and letting Ronald compare it to what he probably paid his wife, but I didn't want to know my own numbers, so I let it go.

Because my mother was moving in with me, for Ronald's purposes I had to be careful that any changes made were not for the better. He made that clear. If he saw my house looking improved at my mother's expense, I would have to pay him. That was easy. Whoever designed medical paraphernalia had no aesthetic sense. "She's renting, she's renting," I made sure to tell Elizabeth that morning, each time a delivery came. My office space next to the kitchen was to become the rehab room. It had been shiny clean before it had to be dismantled. I might not have kept my checkbook balanced, but I kept that room under complete control. I knew I had years of files that were going to come out in a few months so I could read them and sound articulate for Mr. Souriante. But they were neatly stored. I could not have one slip of paper visible, or I could not allow myself to go into my studio. So it looked as if I never went in there.

"Thank goodness you never use your office," Elizabeth said, looking around as we dismantled it.

I told her my website left a very small carbon footprint, but I expected that to mean nothing. Carbon footprints sounded as if they were related to dinosaurs, and I hadn't gotten up my nerve to ask her or Ronald about Darwin yet. As a child, Ronald could identify every dinosaur in his book of a hundred before he was seven. He would have had to erase that entire compartment of his brain. I supposed he had made sure Elizabeth washed her brain, so she could teach foolishness to their children, too. Even though they went to a fine private school where the science department surely would have refused to put up with students who opened their mouths and spewed creationism. This was why my mother wondered about the enormous disconnects in Ronald's way of living. He hungered to be an uptown man of substance, she said, but sometimes he talked like he was in the advance guard of the governor, who was giving government money to tiny private schools that taught the Bible to the few who had learned to read. "Maybe Ronald isn't such a conundrum," she said with laughter in her voice. "Maybe he's just like the governor. A governor has to make sense to someone, doesn't he?"

"We don't believe much in ecology," Elizabeth said.

"What do you believe in?" I said.

"That's an awfully big question." She was looking so far to her left that her irises almost disappeared.

It was the first time I'd ever crossed the line with either of them, and I was nervous. I wanted evidence to bring to my mother. "Well, how about, do you believe in what he believes in?"

"Sure."

I shrugged.

Together we moved my desktop computer into my bedroom. It would be my new office. For the time being. I could go back and forth, up and down the stairs, to keep my portfolio current. For the time being.

I didn't want the process to take too long because I needed to go back to the hospital and learn as much as I could about what lay ahead for me. I'd won the tug-of-war among the three of us as to where my mother would go from the hospital, and the win was a loss. As a woman who felt she had won something the day she found herself alone in a house where she could walk around in her underwear and eat without utensils, I wasn't triumphant over getting a staff. A staff of strangers. Ronald loved the word "staff." He loved talking about his staff. Staff. Staph. Made no difference to me.

We had to wait for the delivery of a small piece of equipment that would monitor my mother in the night. I was interviewing sitters that afternoon for the overnight shift, but I didn't want the person I hired to doze off and let my mother die. *I'm sorry; I work two jobs*, would not cut it if my mother stroked out under plain human supervision. Ronald weighed in on that reasoning when we set up the plan. He thought the machine and a baby monitor at night should have been enough, as long as Mama was going to be in my house. That or a sitter. Not both, surely. "Overkill is a very good idea under these circumstances," I said.

"When she gets better, I'm going to tell Mother you're throwing her money around like Monopoly cash," Ronald said. I told him she was well enough; he could tell her now. We were in the visitors' lounge at the hospital. He got up and left the room, was back in three minutes. "Are you in collusion?" he said. "Her exact words were, 'Overkill can't do any harm right now.'"

While Elizabeth and I waited for the monitor, I asked her if she wanted lunch, and before she could look at me as if I were offering her dog food I said she could order a pizza, my treat. "You can even bring pepperoni into my house," I said. "I'm a purist, but I don't impose my wishes on other people."

She looked at me to see if I was implying anything, but I genuinely wasn't, much to both her surprise and my own, and she smiled.

"YOU DON'T REALLY NEED help, but I'm happy to keep playing hooky," Elizabeth said. She picked up a big slice of mushroom pizza and took a large bite from the drooping end. She didn't like pepperoni, she'd told me. Besides, she'd have felt funny, eating meat in my house. Cheese didn't feel so bad because she thought my philosophy was all about pain, but she would respect meat no matter what. I chose not to tell her about the suffering caused by the dairy industry. She was trying so hard.

I couldn't believe it. This was something like the Tizzy I'd introduced to my brother almost twenty years ago. I couldn't remember the last time we'd been alone. I mean, we'd been alone in her kitchen for a minute or two the week before, and I'd talked to her on the phone a couple of times to make arrangements when she answered instead of Ronald, but this was our first honest visit. I had to be careful.

"What would you be doing right now if you were at your office?" I said.

"Definitely not eating pizza, that's for sure."

That surprised me. Pizza seemed like the kind of fast and lazy food Ronald would have around simply because it tasted good. He had no idea what in particular was in it, unlike the sodium-powered recipes he watched come together for Thanksgiving. Ronald was a skinny man except in the middle, the kind of man doctors on television warned was fat only around his organs. Elizabeth had peaked at plump, and the children still burned off everything. I imagined their arteries coated in cheese, their livers and pancreases swimming in animal fat.

"We run on caffeine and sugar," Elizabeth said. "Ronald picks up Krispy Kremes every morning on the way in. I never have to worry about him straying." I looked at her funny, because Ronald and sex, even in the hypothetical, wasn't anything I wanted to think about. "I mean, it's three rooms filled with fat women." She looked at me to see if my expression would change. She was daring me to think she was fat. I didn't have any reaction. She really wasn't fat. "I'm talking obese!" she said happily. "They love Ronald, but not like that."

I'd only been to their business once in the twelve years since they'd turned it into JesusCleanup and gone viral. Given the Internet, I once said to Ronald that I thought it was strange that his teams so far covered just the southern region. I guessed it was mostly where people needed their homes to be right with God after someone had died at the hands of someone who was clearly wrong with God. I couldn't see much use for JesusCleanup in, say, Idaho. Ronald told me I was wrong, just to look at how strong the good Christians' voices were in politics in that part of the country, and I never spoke of it again. I wondered if he was going to franchise or just be satisfied sending out his teams of wide-eyed believers, who also could scrub, hundreds of miles in every direction.

"You have no idea of the logistics," Elizabeth said. "You know it's the family's responsibility to clean up their property. That's why we get no business in New Orleans."

I had to think about that for a moment. New Orleans was the murder capital of the country, with more killings per capita than any other city. But murders were by poor people, poor black people, on poor people, poor black people. Ronald charged $600 just to come out and hose down the sidewalk. A grandma whose twenty-year-old grandson was shot in a drive-by had enough trouble burying him; she was going to wash down that sidewalk herself and let people in the neighborhood set up a cross and put flowers and Mylar balloons and stuffed teddy bears next to the remaining stain. Ronald had to go to the suburbs and the rest of the state and neighboring region to get his customers. No business in Orleans Parish. And Ronald did nothing pro bono. Salvation comes from faith in Jesus and not as a result of one's good works, according to Ephesians, Ronald had told me many times.

"You sit at a desk all day?" I said. Some people could do that. I could fight with software for no more than twenty minutes before I ran out of a room.

Elizabeth nodded, her cheeks happy and full.

"I do a lot on the phone," she said eventually. "You have no idea how nice I am for hours on end."

I remembered Tizzy, who was a naughty voyeur with me, back when she was starting college, and I was doing graduate studies, and age didn't matter because New Orleans was the place to range free and break icons, not worship them. I often regretted giving her to my brother. Opposites had snapped together, and then gradually she had lost her strength and had become polarized to his way. I'd been thrilled when they started doing crime-scene clean-up because I thought Tizzy would see nightmares and take me along, or at least tell me about them, but before I knew it, Ronald's daddy died, and he discovered the glory of cleaning for Jesus, and Tizzy began using her given name, and she began quoting her husband who quickly turned into a good Christian out of whole cloth, and she began flipping through the New Testament. Cleaning for Jesus had looked a lot like a stroke of keen, desperate, get-rich-quick business acumen to my then-husband William. If you asked Ronald, it had been a divine revelation. I never asked Elizabeth. Nor my mother. No need.

"You don't see dead people?" I said. She knew what I meant.

"Not since we found Jesus." She gave me a sad little smile.

I was having a salad loaded with tofu and spinach, and I stuffed a big forkful into my mouth. Clearly I had become a woman who ate alone a lot. The fork was for show. I had to do a lot of chewing and discreet tongue-searching for spinach on my teeth.

"Did you know that bodily fluids are biohazards?" Elizabeth said. "I think that's mean."

"Mean?" That's a word that's possible to say with a full mouth.

"The human body is sacred. I mean, every molecule. Did you know Jews have to bury every part with the dead person? Though we don't get any Jews as customers."

Big surprise.

"No loss," I said. "Nobody murders Jews."

"Jesus was a Jew."

We smiled at each other. There had been a time when each of us knew what the other was thinking, and we recaptured that time just then. Calvary: a JesusCleanup scene.

"Ronald always has had an irrational weak spot for Jewish people," I said. "As long as he doesn't know them personally."

We had the spirit of Ronald in the room. That's an odd thing for me to say, I know. All I mean is that two people were thinking about him, and even when I was by myself in my house I tried never to have thoughts of him. But I had to admit I was wishing for evidence of his truly holy life. I wouldn't like him for it, but I would win the debate with my mother.

"Ronald's sure different from the person I grew up with," I said.

"Not really," she said.

I didn't expect that. *What?*

Elizabeth giggled. "What he is and what he does are two different things," she said.

What?

"He's always the same person. He just knows more."

What?

"Cut it out," she said.

There was going to be a lot of defining to do when I reported that one back to my mother.

"SO!" I SAID AFTER a while, "Tell me about what you do."

No one ever had asked her that before. Possibly because a desk job was a desk job. Even if it meant she was sending teams out to mop floors where crime-scene investigators had gone through with Q-tips picking up microscopic bits of brain matter. "We ordain them as ministers," she said. "They pray as they clean. I talk to the police before I assign a team. I send the right people out. If it's nothing but arson and accelerants, I don't need to be as careful as if a child has been shot accidentally in the attempted murder of her father."

"That happened?" I said. This was like old times. Often when she was starting out, then-Tizzy would see a complete crime scene and get the whole story. No story was ever happy or funny, but we were dark and angry young women, and we wanted bad dreams and gratitude that our lives weren't as rotten as other people's.

"It happens all the time," Elizabeth said. "One will fascinate you in a macabre way if you're young and stupid, but none of this is anything but tragic after a while."

"Oh, come on," I said. "Not dead children, and not innocent victims, but everybody drives slowly past a mystery."

Elizabeth shrugged. "I guess I chose the wrong slot in the business. Ronald runs all over the place, ministering to the grieving families, and the crews go out and get to play detective while they scrub and pray, and I just run the operation."

"You're the boss," I said.

"Oh, you don't read the Bible."

I gave her a look that said, *You really do?* I knew her as an undergraduate. I knew the kinds of courses she took. Tizzy took Logic. Logic was reason in its purest form. A person did not use faith to figure out logic. If she dealt with religion, she waited until she didn't get graded on it. The Bible was a very big book to read as an extracurricular activity.

"First Corinthians tells you that Genesis is right, that the head of the woman is man," she said, as if I might not know that a person could get that kind of homily from Sunday-morning television. Or a husband who needed to make a point. "I complement my husband. Ronald's my leader."

I opened my eyes wide. As wide as they would go. I zoomed in on Elizabeth's eyes, which weren't open very wide. I came within about nine inches of her face, so close I could smell pizza. "Damn," I said.

She opened her eyes wide. "Our life is good and right." She kept her eyes focused on mine. "We're doing what we were born to do."

I blinked, pulled back. I knew better than to argue with—or even talk to—an irrational person. She wasn't lock-up irrational, but she wasn't one to do a lot of tracking. "Okay," I said.

"I'm not casting aspersions," she said.

That meant William.

She hadn't liked my husband in great measure because he came right out and mocked Ronald for his piety. William was an agnostic, which made him confusing to talk to, but for my purposes, his mockery of Ronald kept him married to me a lot longer than was good. William had huge doubts, and he was far, far past organized religion, so he saw the Bible the way my mother did, as a compelling historic relic and nothing more. I would have divorced him sooner if he'd quit telling Ronald he was an idiot sooner.

All Elizabeth saw, naturally, was that I had failed to stay married, and that made her better than I was. It also made Ronald better than William was, but she'd had to feel that all along. Not necessarily because of what the two men believed, but because Ronald was more complex and interesting. William worked for Merrill Lynch. His possibilities were limited, Elizabeth said, by the sins of men. Ronald had no such limits. I wondered where attempted murder of his own mother fit into the picture, but I didn't ask.

She wasn't wearing any makeup except a little blush, and her face was showing lines and fading. She looked older than I did, if only because I used dark streaks on my eyes and mouth for distraction. Elizabeth was going to go right past me and die, and I didn't want that. "We used to have so much fun together," I said.

"That was a long time ago." She wasn't arguing. She was a little wistful, I thought.

"We could do this again?"

She leaned back, folded her arms across her chest. "I'm playing hooky today. And only because Ronald has to go to Beaumont."

The idea of having Ronald sit and wait with me instead wasn't pleasant. Ronald didn't like to waste time, and that was just for starters.

"I'm not in his hierarchy," I said. "I'm sure there's nothing in the Bible that says a brother can tell his sister what to do."

Elizabeth had to think about that, sort of as if she were going through a mental inventory of quotes and finding nothing. She grinned. "You know what's interesting? I can't think of any relationship in the Bible between a brother and sister that's not incestuous."

I shuddered. I hadn't even wanted to hold Ronald's hand on Thanksgiving. "Thanks a lot," I said.

She leaned over and hugged me.

She was gone before the first woman came for the sitter interview. I was glad. The woman was carrying a Jehovah's Witness brochure.

CHAPTER FIVE

SCIENCE CAME TO SAVE me in the most peculiar way.

My mother had been in my house for two weeks, and I had learned the labyrinth of no freedom. One stranger and one damaged person I loved were there at all times, and I was in charge. If the two a.m. sitter thought my mother was breathing funny, she didn't phone Ronald. She didn't phone the doctor's answering service. She walked into my room and said, "Ms. Price?" I wanted to ask the night sitters if they thought I was lactating, producing the only life-sustaining force, but they were too weary. I napped. I etched and decorated a "do not disturb" sign for my door. But I wasn't a person.

Then I took my mother to see Dr. Michael Rosenthal. He genuinely surprised me. He'd seen me at the hospital, when I'd been the daughter full of frightened questions and he'd been the doctor full of gentle answers. Possibly he'd noticed I was the sister tormented by the brother broadcasting piety, or so I liked to think at the time. When I was the age when boys I grew up with went to medical school if that was their choice, I assumed they looked at human organs and whispered to themselves, "Evolution," and blew off their childhoods of Sunday school. Of course that didn't explain the number of friends I'd had growing up whose fathers had been doctors, but I'd figured religion was a social thing. With a Jewish name, Dr. Rosenthal surely didn't take Ronald seriously.

"You're Cesca Price!" he said when he walked into the examining room.

My mother was on the examining table in a thin gown, already compromised by the stroke's limitations, and I hoped he wasn't going to ignore her. Even though I was flattered. He turned right to her. "Please forgive me, Mrs. Price. I like to draw, and I admire your daughter's work." Mama gave him a lopsided little smile. It helped that he hadn't called her Trisha.

And there is where it started. I offered to look at his work. He gave me honest hope that Mama was making slow progress, and in return I gave him honest hope that he was quite good with pencil and paper. Patients were in the waiting room, but for a few minutes he let me and my mother into his office, no small feat when she was in a wheelchair. He was astonishingly good. He drew from imagination. Mythical beasts. He drew from life. Fully realized portraits without a wasted stroke. I said I would come back another day. He said he had some paintings. I said he might have a real career one day. He liked that. "Were you flirting?" my mother said in the car. She was talking better now.

"Good God, no," I said. Dr. Rosenthal wore a wedding ring. He was my kind of attractive man, with dark hair and olive skin and green eyes, but I had my own rules. No pain. My only thought had been of emotional bartering. I would make him feel good about himself, and my mother would become his special patient. I'd seen the wall of patient files. There must have been thousands of patients in his practice. He was a kind doctor, but how far could he spread that kindness? Even I was having a hard time feeling kind when I was woken up at two in the morning for my only patient.

"He'll like you," I said.

"I don't need him to like me. I need him to be clear-minded about me," she said.

"You want him to be motivated to keep you alive."

I glanced over at my mother. I was on her left, her good side, and her mouth was turned upward a little. "I'm not going to try to get out the name of that oath," she said.

"Well, if I had as many patients as he does, I'd be happy to see a few die off."

That wall of files was disturbing. Looking at it was like looking at the cityscape of Chicago from an airplane. Chicago more than New York for some reason. It stretched out forever from the lake, tall, crowded buildings, and I could not imagine breaking out of anonymity. The airports I flew into in New York brought me over Queens neighborhoods that weren't hopeless. It seemed possible to have a reputation in New York.

"Dr. R. acts like you're his only patient when you're with him," Mama said. "Rosenthal" was as hard to say as "Hippocratic."

"He's not acting."

"Ah, Chess," she said. She only called me Chess when she thought she saw through me.

He was a very decent man. But I had no use for a man. Even a married man. I already had a staff in my house. And Klea was coming at Christmas. Temporary people never seemed temporary in the moment. I wondered if that was the way it was for doctors.

HE MADE A HOUSE CALL, and Mama said nothing when she heard he was coming. She knew house calls were an anachronism, though of course anachronism was a word she couldn't have dredged up, let alone enunciated. "I'll tell you the truth," he told her. "I want to see Cesca's studio."

"How refreshing," my mother said. "A man who tells the truth."

"He's a man of science," I said.

"The best kind," she said.

My mother was making me nervous. With anyone else, I could claim her lack of self-censorship was a symptom. He knew better. I checked him out of the corner of my eye, and he looked amused.

The sitter on duty stared. Her name was Shellonde, and she had been my mother's housekeeper after Ronald and I moved out, but when she got too tired for physical labor, she became a sitter. It made great sense to hire her for my mother's day shifts whenever possible. They knew each other, or at least Shellonde knew my mother. I couldn't imagine Shellonde ever had seen a doctor come out to a patient, unless that doctor had lived next door, and it had been a dire emergency.

He had two paintings with him. They were oils on canvas, two by three, and he carried them correctly, back to back, wrapped in an old comforter. When he unwrapped them and lay them down on the work table in the center of the studio, I was relieved. They were very fine. Nothing like what I did. Landscapes. They had an impressionistic quality to them, but he had his own style. And a palette of reds and ochres that was truly original. They weren't attractive because of the color, but my immediate sense was that he'd spent too much time looking at bodies. So who cared? They were visually smart.

"Have you exhibited?" I said.

He shook his head, no, not at all like a doctor.

"Because?"

He was blushing and shy, which made him even better looking. "It never occurred to me. I just paint in a room in my house. It has a wall of windows, you know." He looked up at my skylight.

"I can tell you haven't had classes," I said.

"Pretty obvious."

I meant it as a compliment. Natural talent often was destroyed by classes. Teachers inhibited raw artists. I figured I'd spent half of my working life getting over the hand-holding of my early instructors. Though I could have been grateful if I'd wanted a career as a portrait artist who charged rich women uptown tens of thousands for paintings of their small children sitting in white frills with purebred puppies.

"Never take classes," I said.

"Oh!"

I asked him if he wanted to get into a gallery. It seemed logical to me. Why would a person paint? For pleasure, yes. For escape; I could see that. Dr. Rosenthal already had a definition of himself. But he surely knew that the day he died all those files on his wall were going to be distributed to other doctors, and a few weeks later he was going to be forgotten. For most doctors, that was enough. The power of playing God with human bodies would have sufficed. That had been their choice. That and the money that had been promised back before doctors couldn't get rich unless they were surgeons. But a doctor who painted expected to leave something behind. And he surely didn't want to leave a room filled with canvasses that his wife and children didn't appreciate. They would give them away. Or throw them away.

I had already imagined the future of his work. Without knowing anything.

I ran through the local galleries in my mind. My blessing meant a lot around town. And I never used it. I hadn't shown in a gallery in over ten years because I now sold through auction houses and often wound up in museums or overseas collections.

I told Dr. Rosenthal I could get him a show if he had a lot more work of this caliber.

He wasn't wearing a lab coat, but he did have a stethoscope around his neck. He was a doctor, but he wasn't a doctor. He had power, but he had none. "I can't believe it," he said.

I offered to come look at his studio.

"No," he said. Not at his house.

TWICE A WEEK MICHAEL Rosenthal came to the house to check on my mother and leave a painting or two. He came more often than Ronald. His visits were at the end of the day, just before nightfall, and he compressed a few worlds into each.

To anyone who might have paid attention, his visits were house calls with by-the-ways at the end. My mother was his reason for coming. Once he suspected a TIA in her, explained what that was, promised there was no need for alarm. "Do you want something to be wrong?" he said to her when she asked him if he was sure.

"Do I look like that kind of woman?" my mother said, and I was going to dare her afterwards ever to accuse me of flirting.

"Oh, I thought you might like a little paid vacation at Baptist," he said.

"I just love data, that's all," she said.

"Trust me," he said, "numbers aren't always your little friends."

"Get out of here with your pure rationality," she said happily, clear as a bell, no vestiges of a stroke to be heard in that sentence.

Her diet had as little sodium and fat as mine did. I never told her or the doctor that. I wanted to accuse Ronald of attempted murder, but it would hurt her feelings.

On each visit, when Dr. Rosenthal walked to the studio he was transformed into a nervous schoolboy, frightened of my judgment, and we talked, even for only ten minutes, of what he saw on a painted horizon. I learned pieces of his life story, of what happened to a Jewish boy in New Orleans who rode the streetcar and saw the sisters making the sign of the cross in front of Jesus at Loyola, then celebrated an antiseptic Christmas. Skepticism came fast, and he wanted me to see it in his paintings.

Ronald, on the other hand, came and sat in my mother's room in great patches of silence for ten minutes until he felt he could leave. "This doesn't do me much good," Mama said to him one afternoon.

"I pray for you."

"While you sit there?"

"I'm trying to respect Cesca's rules," Ronald said.

I was standing in the doorway for this. "I appreciate it," I said. "But I don't have rules."

"Not having rules is a form of having rules," Ronald said.

I was tempted to tell him that I bet I obeyed more of the Ten Commandments than he did, but he would want to sit down with a sheet of paper and go down the list, item by item, make a comparison, prove me wrong. I felt I had him at honoring parents, but honoring was a pretty ambiguous word. So was unsuccessful killing. And coveting was an interesting matter, which depended on whether anyone could see inside his heart. On the other hand, he definitely had me when it came to loving the Lord and keeping a Sabbath and a few others. I'd have to take him to the mat on graven images. Ronald was the type to keep points. By the time I was fifteen, I'd quit playing Monopoly with him.

Ronald didn't get up. He didn't look as if he was praying, though I wasn't sure what a person looked like when he was praying. Maybe his eyes would scan back and forth, or he'd blink a lot, or he wouldn't blink at all. Right then he looked like a man who was thinking. Not thinking logically, of course, because Ronald had trained himself not to.

"Dr. Rosenthal comes to the house," he said.

"Isn't that wonderful?" my mother said.

"That's suspect," Ronald said.

"I'm happy to explain," I said. "I wouldn't tell Dr. Rosenthal this, but it started out as a sort of barter. I figured if I helped him with his art, he'd be sure Mama got the best medical care. Thank goodness his art is really good."

"You're sleeping with him," Ronald said. He suppressed a smile.

"Fuck, no," I said. Ronald opened his mouth to object. "My house, my non-rules," I said.

"Men and women can't be friends," Ronald said.

I folded my arms in front of myself and glared at him. I had a little residue of bad feeling because he had cornered my friend Tizzy and made her into a paving stone.

"It's not what you're thinking," he said. "All else aside, there is always going to be one or the other with sexual feelings."

"What if one is married?" my mother said.

"Does that person have faith?" Ronald said.

"Isn't this a hypothetical discussion?" I said.

"Actually no," Ronald said.

"Make it hypothetical," I said. "Give me an answer if the people have faith and if they don't."

"I'm leaving," Ronald said. "This is about you and someone like you, so I rest my case."

"Can't we ever have a pleasant conversation?" I said.

Ronald didn't answer.

ON THE PHONE DR. ROSENTHAL said, "This is Mike," and that meant he expected me to call him that, but there's something about calling doctors by their first names that is impossible. Unless I went to school with a doctor, and I wasn't his patient, he was going to get the title. So I called him nothing. I would mention him by the full "Dr. Michael Rosenthal" if I saw a gallery owner. I had a few promised appointments.

We were in my studio talking about expressing ourselves. Tevor Souriante wasn't coming for almost two months, but I needed to have a lot to say, and discussing art with Dr. Michael would stir up my thoughts. Gracie's belief that I was like Kandinsky gave me a nice talking point—the utterances of thirteen-year-olds were always interesting. But Kandinsky was a rotten son of a bitch, and I wanted to be able to say that with a smile. Dr. Michael thought that was amusing but it didn't get me very far. "What about his spirituality?" he said.

He knew that right then my brother was elsewhere in my house with my mother. We had talked about Ronald. It had been important for some reason for me to let him know that I was ungodly. Or at least not a Jesus fanatic. I didn't know a lot about being Jewish; what I knew came mostly from my Jewish school friends, and their overriding religious structure had been built on healthy cynicism and full knowledge that they had to live for today because nothing else was coming.

"That's a good point," I said. "If I'm trying to distinguish myself from Kandinsky. I refuse to be spiritual. I guess all I'm doing is having a one-sided argument with a thirteen-year-old kid, huh."

"A pretty savvy thirteen-year-old kid," he said, looking around my studio. My paintings did seem to have the pure abstraction of Kandinsky's, to exhibit his refusal to show any hint of natural form. But I knew where the natural forms were. I loved natural form. I spoke through natural form. Since my father died, and I had learned how to move myself from natural form to abstraction, I felt I was able to honor my love of both. In the weeks after his funeral, I had saved myself only by drawing him less and less recognizably until finally only I would have known he was my subject. Both my spirit and my art survived the loss.

"But she just sees pretty pictures," I said to Mike.

"I know your messages," he said, and started rubbing my shoulder.

What?

I looked at him funny.

He pulled his hand back. "I just meant your paintings are like mine. You believe what you can see, but you're not coming out and admitting it."

It was my turn to be shy. "How did you figure that out?" I said. The message of my work was that I was a certain kind of person. I had no spirituality; I accepted nothing if it wasn't proven to me. When I painted, I started with concrete mental images, then obscured them until no one except me could see them, so my work was purely abstract. But his?

"I'm a scientist, don't forget," he said. "You have to stand far away from my work. But then you can't see what's real."

"Up close, too," I said.

He smiled, and I had to look away.

CHAPTER SIX

I WAS NOT GOING TO escape Christmas. With my mother, Klea, and Klea's boyfriend Seth in the house, it was going to be a four-to-four score against Ronald's household. Or that was the way Ronald saw it when he said I was long overdue to host a holiday meal. I reminded him that my menu was different from his, and he reminded me right back that Elizabeth had told him that I had been flexible on her pizza. I knew she had told him I'd been open-minded. I told him I would cook a fish. With the head and tail cut off, a fish seemed less like it had been a living thing than any other animal except even lower forms of seafood. Klea would help me. She didn't know it yet, but she would help me. I didn't like touching flesh.

Fish was not the first subject brought up at the airport. Neither were sleeping accommodations. I let it all be humdrum, about checked bags and short-term parking, wanting Seth to think I was easy wallpaper. Maybe he had heard of me, outside of Klea. They both went to Hampshire College, where knowing the arts and maybe being in the arts were the reasons for going there and feeling no pressure. I had been a guest speaker there once when Klea was in elementary school, and she had worked that fact into her admissions essay, but I had promised her that my existence had had nothing to do with her acceptance. She needed to know that. I wanted Seth to ignore me so I could know all about him.

"You would not believe what stress Seth has been under," Klea said when we got into the car.

"I thought the purpose of going there was that they leave you the hell alone," I said.

In the backseat, Seth laughed out loud. I liked him instantly. Mostly because I knew he liked me instantly, too.

"Of all people, I'd think you would know that the worst pressure is when you're trying to get something out," Klea said.

I thought about making anatomical references, but that would be the straight route to annoying Klea, and we hadn't gotten to the pay booth yet. I told her I never gave myself deadlines.

"Never?"

It was a good question. I thought of Tevor Souriante, who was getting closer every day. And of course there were shows where I wanted to finish a painting in time. "Okay, I hate deadlines," I said. "Is that better?"

"People think you go to Hampshire, you're totally free, but, really, maybe it'd be easier taking exams all the time, you know? I mean, the exam comes, and then it's gone. Seth had to write an entire composition for violin. What if it hadn't happened?"

"It happened," he said from the back seat.

"Damn," I said, "I didn't see a violin case in your luggage."

"Right, like we're gonna check something worth a few thousand dollars," Klea said.

I told her I was joking, that I just wanted to show off Seth to her uncle. Klea fell silent. She was won over. Outshining her suffering little cousins wasn't anything she ever wanted to do, but she knew coming in that Ronald was going to fault Seth for anything he did. An original violin piece would have been a good start. Though for all I knew, there might have been a musical equivalent of Thomas Kinkade.

At the house I didn't make them guess. "As far as I'm concerned, where you sleep has only to do with how many beds I have to make up," I said. "I put sheets on Klea's bed, but if you two want more than one bed, then go find one and make it up yourselves."

Klea dropped her duffel and reached out to hug me. She didn't say anything because she didn't have to.

I wondered whether Ronald was going to claim he needed an aspirin and reconnoiter on Christmas. No, I decided, that wasn't my brother's style. He was going to come right out and prowl.

DR. MICHAEL PHONED ON Christmas Eve from his office. I was surprised that he didn't have the day off, but he said he was not in a business that closed shop, though he would take off early. "People do hold on for Christmas," he said, and I thought, *Oh, good, Mama will live through tomorrow*. She was doing well, as far as I could tell, but for all I knew, some mechanism in her mind was wearing down and would shut off as soon as she saw her children and grandchildren all in the same room.

Dr. Michael wanted to know if he could drop by my studio. That wasn't the best day. In fact, it was probably the worst day. He promised it was just about a drive-by, and I thought that was odd, because going out of his way was not a practical move for a man who did important things for a living.

No one was paying attention when I slipped through the door into my studio to meet him. He walked in through the outside door in his coat, and I saw he was carrying a small gift. Wrapped in gold paper with a red ribbon. Were we that kind of friends? My Christmas list had almost no friends on it. Mostly family and people who delivered to me and didn't earn enough to live as well as I wanted them to. The only friends left were the ones I'd have chosen as family. Dr. Michael hadn't crossed my mind when I made the list, though maybe he should have.

"Oh, no," I said.

"Oh, yes."

It was jewelry. It was that kind of box. Jewelry was personal. Even comical jewelry was personal. I opened it carefully. I honored wrapping paper; I especially treated ribbons with care. I might throw them away eventually, but I never ripped.

In the box lay a silver chain with a medallion, square with rounded corners, silver, too, with a tiny replica of a painting in the center, glazed and perfect. I recognized it immediately. One of Kandinsky's landscapes. It took me a moment to remember the Italian name he gave them. Paesaggios. No one ever had given me a gift that was more for me.

I didn't want to look him in the eye, but I had to. He was standing right in front of me. Dr. Michael, who now was Mike no matter what, was a beautiful man. That dark hair and olive skin and green eyes were what I always liked in film stars. I'd married a man with blond hair and blue eyes and sun-damaged skin and soon realized the attraction was never there to override character. I was terrified of attraction. I looked Mike in the eye, tried to think of something else, but couldn't.

He leaned down and kissed me.

"No," I said. He leaned over and kissed me again, longer.

"I thought I was reading you the right way," he said. "I apologize."

"I wanted to be your friend," I said. I wasn't going to tell him how I'd started out.

"I'm sorry," he said.

I was holding a gift from someone who had listened to me.

"I don't know what I've been thinking," I said.

I DIDN'T SHOVE MIKE to the back of my mind. I let the sense of him float around, protecting me from caring too much about the rest.

I wasn't sure if it annoyed Ronald, but I told the family that Shellonde was going to sit down with us for dinner. It was her shift, and if she didn't come to the table, she would have to sit in my mother's room and eat a sandwich from home. Possibly Shellonde would have preferred that, but I gave her the option. I even gave her the option of a plate after dinner, but she said, "Ooh, I'm not gonna miss this for nothing."

I felt a little drunk, and I hadn't had even a sip of wine.

Getting down to eating was going to be awkward, even if it was Christmas, which technically was a Christian holiday celebrating a highly improbable event. Though that was the point of it, that too long ago to be documented, a miraculously born woman had a miraculous birth and got miraculous gifts from miraculous visitors. The baby was a big deal, too, of course, but there were no sonograms, no photos from the delivery room, no snapshots from his childhood. Only a lot of beliefs transcending reason. At my table was a Jesus-loving family of four. Plus Shellonde, who seemed to be one of them if I could go by her occasional "bless me, Jesus" and ignore Ronald's wish to disenfranchise her. But the Prices on the distaff side ran close to numbering four: my mother, Klea, and I, all women of pure reason, could count Seth among us. He was a Jew from outside New Haven, Connecticut, which pretty much demanded that he be steeped in only what his senses could perceive. So what kind of ritual should we have?

The guests were all standing behind their chairs. I was in the doorway to the kitchen, watching to see what everyone would do, knowing it was the worst course of action for a hostess, but feeling like a spectator. To my surprise, Klea was the only person who scrambled into a seat. Seth remained behind his chair. It wasn't religion, I guessed—it was upbringing. He was waiting for his elders to be seated. Ronald's family were all standing, waiting for orders. Shellonde slid my mother onto a chair, then stood behind the chair next to hers. "Oops," Klea said, looking around, but she didn't get up. "You may all be seated," Ronald said, sounding like a preacher man. Maybe he was going to let it slide.

"Let us all take one another's hands and bow our heads for a moment of prayer," Ronald said when everyone but me was in a chair.

"Hey, Ronald," I said, holding up my index finger.

Elizabeth gave me a pleading look.

"I'm not going to beat him up," I said. Very good-naturedly.

Klea giggled. Seth was trying not to laugh.

"This isn't your house," I said.

"We're eating your crazy fish," Ronald said. "Fish is for Lent, not Christmas. I would think you could compromise."

"Not when I don't know what's coming out of your mouth until it's over," I said. "For one, Seth is Jewish."

"And you know nobody likes Jews more than I do," Ronald said.

Klea shot straight up from her seat. Her chair fell behind her, and the table didn't move. "That's so fucking Christian of you."

"Elizabeth, take the children out of the room," Ronald said.

"Hell, no," Levi said.

"You see what you're doing?" Ronald said to me. "Levi, you'll answer to me later."

Suddenly all I could think of was my food. Hot fish was good. Cold fish was terrible. Any fish that died for nothing was a waste. "Think about my dinner!"

"To heck with your dinner," Ronald said.

"Ooh," Klea said.

"Listen, Klea," Ronald said. "No matter what you and your mother and your grandmother walk around saying, you're born a certain way. You were born Christian, just like Seth was born Jewish. You just need to be reborn in Christ. And Seth needs to learn about the Lord Jesus Christ, or there's no future for the two of you. He's sleeping in your room, I noticed."

"Mom!" Klea screamed.

"How can you believe what you're saying and think Jews are so excellent?" I said to Ronald.

It took Ronald a moment to answer. He looked as if he was working to find patience. "I think that's a very rude question to ask on Christmas Day," he said.

"Compared to snooping in my room?" Klea said.

"I don't think we need to stay here," Ronald said.

Despite a doctor's presence in the whorls of my brain, I could feel a headache coming on, and I never got headaches. To me that meant all the blood vessels in my head were constricting to protect themselves, and constricted blood vessels were dangerous in someone like my mother, who might be reacting this way, too. Or so I imagined. I looked at her. Shellonde was looking at her, too, almost as if she were a gauge of how dangerous this meal was getting. Ronald was red in the face, but right then I didn't care if he blew an aneurysm.

Elizabeth stood up. "Look, everybody calm down. I'll say a prayer, and then we can eat, and nobody will be any the worse for wear."

I think she said "God" maybe once. She never mentioned Christmas. But she gave a lot of thanks. For my mother, for Seth, even for the poor fish.

CHAPTER SEVEN

I WAS WEARING THE NECKLACE, a secret with myself. My dress had a scoop neck, and it wasn't hidden, just lying there nicely for anyone to see, but I wasn't a person in that mashed-together family who ever wore anything of note. Every now and then I would acquire a piece of jewelry with meaning, not of aesthetic or monetary value. Especially after Katrina. Artisans around the city would go to craft markets and sell "ain't there no more" jewelry and refrigerator magnets and lamps, and I bought a bracelet with little lozenges remembering bakeries and furniture stores that were antediluvian. What I hung around my neck or wrist meant something to me, and no one ever cared.

But Gracie spotted the Kandinsky all the way across the dining room table. "Is that one of your paintings?" she said. She was squinting, as if the medallion were the tiniest television set she'd ever tried to watch. I told her it was a Kandinsky. "See!" she said. "I can get you totally mixed up."

Shellonde turned to my mother. "You owe me five dollars."

"Shh," my mother said, clearly in cahoots over something. She was all right. No one had blown her arteries to bursting this time.

Ronald reached into his back pocket for his wallet. My mother asked what he was doing.

"I don't want you in arrears," he said. "Especially on Christmas day."

"Your mama done lost a bet," Shellonde said. She was a woman who flicked away pity if it came her way, and it almost never did.

"Hush," my mother said, not particularly meaning it. She cast a quick glance in my direction. I couldn't read my own face, but I figured she liked what she saw. Not only was I riding endorphins and pheromones and whatever else I couldn't see but knew existed, but after Mike wore off I had put away three glasses of Chardonnay in the kitchen. I had decided not to bring wine to the table. My mother couldn't drink, I couldn't offer any wine to Klea and Seth because they were underage, and I didn't want to struggle with Ronald over it. I thought it might have been legal to serve alcohol to minors in one's home, but I wasn't sure, and it didn't matter to me. My law was that they could have it in the kitchen where no one would quibble with me. Klea and Seth already had put away a few glasses. I'd come right out and told them they'd need fortification to get through dinner.

"Where you got that necklace?" Shellonde said.

"I got it around my neck!" I said.

That was the sorriest New Orleans joke. Little boys who tap-danced with bottle caps on their sneakers in the French Quarter would say to an unsuspecting tourist, "I bet you five dollars I can tell you where you got your shoes," and the tourist would always take the bet, and the little boy would say, "You got your shoes on your feet!"

"She got you," my mother said to Shellonde. Mama was enjoying companionship. I wondered if she was going to want to stay bedridden so she could have a paid constant friend for the rest of her life. But she was only sixty-seven. That was the best age for craving solitude, for enjoying freedom from responsibility after rearing children and tending a strong-minded husband. Though I thought being forty-three was pretty excellent, too. Even if the husband never had been strong-minded or well-tended. In my case, solitude also meant no one had rights that could supersede my works.

"How did you ack-quire that necklace?" Shellonde said to me.

I looked around the table. This was the only conversation. Everyone was silent, even though the subject should have been boring to almost half of the people there.

"It was a gift," I said. "From someone who likes my work."

"What I told you!" Shellonde said, leaning into my mother.

"What?" I said. I would treat them like schoolgirls. They would enjoy themselves.

"I told you not to flirt," my mother said to me.

"Whatever you're thinking, you're wrong."

"Your mother has a boyfriend," Mama said to Klea.

"No, I don't."

"All right!" Klea said. She motioned to high-five me, but I was holding onto the edge of the table. I thought of going into the kitchen for a few sips of wine, but I was an easy drunk, and might start staggering. I closed my eyes without closing them and thought of Mike kissing me.

"What do you two think you know?" I said.

Shellonde was in some kind of cups. I wondered if she had sneaked in a bottle, but she was too protective of my mother and her job. Perhaps she was inebriated from knowing something no one else knew. "I see that man car when he come here. Your mama room got a window big enough to walk through, you know."

"You're in a court of law here," I said.

"Shellonde watches TV, too," my mother said. "You're not playing with an amateur."

I laughed, but Shellonde was the only other person who did. Klea had her hand over her mouth, and Seth had his lips pressed tightly together.

"Dr. R. don't come here and not see your mama," Shellonde said. "Excepting this morning he drive right up, don't come to the house, no. He go to your studio, carrying a present, no bigger than a jewelry box, and what we see? Jewelry. That good enough for a court of law?"

Ronald was looking at Shellonde incredulously. I couldn't tell whether he was stunned that a person who was staff would be so presumptuous or whether he was absorbing the possibility that I was fooling around without the benefit of a marriage blessed by God. The

Ronald I grew up with wouldn't have registered a reaction to either. He had been too focused on quantitative measures.

Ronald flung his napkin on the table. "This is awful!"

"Why?" I said.

"Because I'm right."

I laughed, and my dear Klea laughed with me. I hoped Gracie and Levi were learning something.

"Look," he went on, "we'll set aside right away the fact that there's never a good reason to have the hired help at the table. I don't eat with my staff. I bring them doughnuts every day, and they think I'm a real prince, but each of us has our place. What bothers me is that we're sitting here joking around about committing adultery right in front of my kids, and all of you think it's funny."

"I am not committing adultery," I said. "The man gave me a fucking present."

"No man gives a woman a gift unless he's getting sex," Ronald said.

I looked at Elizabeth. "Is that some Christian doctrine?" I said.

"Cut it out, Cesca," Ronald said.

"No."

"Why else would he give you something so personal?" he said.

I explained to him that I was helping him with his artistic aspirations, and this was his way of thanking me. Which wasn't exactly commensurate with what I'd put out, given that this kind of jewelry usually cost about forty dollars on the internet. Of course, I added, Dr. Rosenthal came to check on our mother. I didn't say anything about bartering, because that wouldn't have been fair to my possible feelings about Mike.

"You ever think of writing fiction instead of painting?" Ronald said. "You're one great storyteller. That's such a big fat lie. No one with any sense would believe you. I'm a good Christian man who'd never cheat on his wife, but I know how weak most men are, and he's not going to come here making house calls unless he gets to go into more than just one bedroom."

"You have a filthy mind," I said. I wished I weren't so lightheaded. I didn't sound as if I meant it.

"Oh, you can tell the truth," Klea said to me. "I think it makes you way cool."

"Trust me," I said, "if I could have Dr. Rosenthal at this table right now, making lascivious noises and driving your uncle insane, I'd be a happy woman. But he's probably with his wife and kids, eating Chinese. Right, Seth?"

"Talk about stereotyping," Seth said. "We have a Christmas tree and exchange gifts."

"Wife?" Ronald said.

"I'm not sleeping with him," I said.

"Committing adultery is one of the worst sins," Ronald said.

"I bet you don't even know technically what adultery is," I said. "Not that I'm committing what you think it is. But even if I were having sex with this man, I wouldn't be so-called sinning. So please eat your fish, which to me is a crummy thing to do. This fish had to die for you, and on top of that, you're wasting food."

Ronald was pursing his lips. "Are you going to tell me that it's worse to kill brainless animals to keep from starving than it is to have sex outside of marriage? What are you thinking?"

"Did you hear what you just said? Of course it's worse. If for no other reason than that sex outside marriage is usually a victimless good thing." I heard several forks drop. I looked around. "He's not starving," I said.

"Not to mention," I went on, "that adultery is not all about sex outside of marriage. That's the trouble with you Bible-thumpers." I tried to sound reverent. "You don't know what the book actually says."

My mother was looking a little pale. So was everybody else, including Shellonde.

"Like premarital sex is okay?" Levi said.

I started to open my mouth to give Levi a good explanation of why a fourteen-year-old boy should not be having sex because it wasn't good for him. Morals had nothing to do with it. But Ronald was so sure he was right that he barely could repress a smile. One of the best parts of his life was being holier-than-Cesca. He had a tone especially for such occasions, mostly distinguished by his enunciation of every syllable.

"You step into it every time," he said slowly to me. "Your ignorance isn't saving you at all. You're damned to hell, Cesca, damned to hell. And don't start telling me this is your own house, or I swear I'll come over there and beat the living daylights out of you." He hadn't raised his voice.

I kept an even tone, too. It always had driven Ronald crazy. "Adultery is only about a married person having sex outside of marriage. I have *never* committed adultery. But that doesn't matter anyway. I've never had sex with Dr. Rosenthal."

"Mom!" Klea said.

Ronald stood up to come around the table. He hadn't laid a hand on me since we were children. He'd balled up his fists many times, but I'd always repressed a smile. I bet he didn't weight much over 160, but angry little men were like Chihuahuas and always wanted to bite hard. I stood up. I was only a couple of inches shorter than he was, and I was wearing heels in case anyone got ideas about walking in the park. He'd have to come at me eye to eye. He bumped my mother's chair as he rounded the table.

Wrath, Ronald, wrath.

"Will you two stop it!" Mama said.

"Hit him first," Klea said.

"I mean it," my mother said.

"Y'all making your mama upsetted," Shellonde said.

At that I put my hands up in front of my face, palms forward, a gesture of peace. "Calm down," I said to Ronald. "This is stupid."

He kept coming at me.

"I mean it," I said, and reached forward to take his shoulder. "This isn't good for Mama."

He looked in our mother's direction. "You really buy into everything she says, don't you," he said.

I saw a mask of horror come over Mama's face. She looked as if she was pretending to grimace in fear and pain to frighten us into easing up on each other. I told Ronald he had to stop.

"I don't get it," he said, stopping in his tracks. "You say you have no God-given moral code, but you think you're so good."

"Which one of us are you talking to?" I said, looking to my mother conspiratorially.

Her eyes didn't catch mine. They got wide. Then wider. Her head jerked.

"No!" I screamed. I reached for her. Shellonde reached for her. And then my mother fell over onto the table, her face hitting her plate, bits of fish spattering onto the tablecloth.

CHAPTER EIGHT

I DID CPR UNTIL THE EMTs came. Ronald stood stock-still over us, shoulders back, hands open in front of himself, almost as if my mother and I were barroom brawlers who would hurt him if he got too close. I didn't have time to think, but later I would be so angry that I would wonder if Ronald was having a moral dilemma, watching us, trying to decide if I was interfering with God's will, or if it was ordained to prolong life at all costs.

I wouldn't think he was wishing her dead. I *would* begin to think this was the time when I was going to have to answer my mother's "if anything happens to me" question. Nothing made me doubt Ronald's faith. But I owed it to my mother to question it—and to question it completely.

Of course Mike was on call on Christmas Day. There was always an article in the paper about B'nai B'rith members volunteering at soup kitchens on Christmas because Jews didn't have a holiday, and the article would invariably mention Jewish doctors who covered for their Christian friends. Soup kitchens and hospitals: those were the two places that had to keep going no matter what. Even groceries and pharmacies weren't so urgently needed. Katrina had taught us basics.

Mike met us at Baptist. "Us" was me, Shellonde, and my mother, Shellonde following in her car. Ronald and Elizabeth had said they would stay behind and clean up. They couldn't handle it. I believed their terror. I *knew* their terror. Accepting it was something else.

Klea later told me she had been furious. "You better not charge my mother," she had said to Ronald, looking at the bits of fish and candied carrots on the floor behind the chair where my mother had been sitting.

I had watched enough television shows about emergency rooms to know Mike was giving us as much special treatment as we could have. But the truth was that my mother was in critical condition, and I wasn't supposed to see many things. Shellonde's credentials consisted of nothing more than age and patience. She stayed right with me—on the clock, I told her. "Shoot," she said.

Mike was not an ER doctor. He did not need to be there. But he stayed around, oversaw each procedure, reported back. He wasn't wearing a lab coat, but he did have a stethoscope around his neck, and that made him strong.

Mike took me and Shellonde into an empty examining room where he could talk to us privately. He'd known Shellonde long enough to treat her like family. They had my mother on life support. She was intubated, which was all right for now, but they would want to get her breathing on her own eventually. He wasn't sure what went wrong. He'd had her on blood thinners, and he trusted I'd fed her right and kept her activities to a minimum. He looked apologetic, as if he'd failed me personally. Most doctors weren't like that; most doctors were arrogant and fearful of lawsuits. No doubt Shellonde was thinking this was because we were having an affair, but I knew it was because he was this way with everyone. He painted like a man who broke easily. "Sometimes we just don't know how these things happen," Mike said.

"I know how it happen," Shellonde said. "You know how people say, 'you gonna make me bust a blood vessel'? That's what Mr. Ronald done did. He get all up in Cesca face, her mama have a stroke right there at the table. That man screaming like he five years old."

Mike looked at me. I nodded my head slowly. "My brother got a little out of control at the dinner table," I said. "But I don't think--"

"You probably don't want to go assigning blame," he said.

"Just you watch," Shellonde said.

I PHONED MY HOUSE, and after almost enough rings for the machine to pick up, Klea answered. "Hey, they didn't know who should answer the phone," she said. I asked her if they could see on Caller ID who was on the line, and she said, "But what if Gammy was dead?"

"So they picked you?"

"Pretty much."

I told her to put her uncle on the phone, and when she said, "Uh, oh," I said that Gammy wasn't dead. Her "oh, good" gave Ronald a split second in which he could become fearless. I could picture them all standing around the phone.

"So what's going on?" he said.

Shellonde was standing next to me making umpire gestures with her hands and motherly shakes with her head. She knew I was fighting my anger.

"We really don't know what triggered the stroke," I said.

"It was probably a coincidence that it happened just then," he said.

"Probably," I said with no conviction.

"We were both getting out of control."

"The doctor just walked in," I said. It wasn't true.

"Doctor? No comment," he said and hung up.

It took until nightfall to move my mother into an ICU bed. I sent Shellonde home and got the night sitter in. I would go home. I had learned my lesson when my father died. He had had a spouse, of course, so I wasn't the caretaker, but I had been a serious griever, and I needed to sleep and paint. But I did neither, and grieving wasn't natural, and it never stopped, and I never slept, and I never painted. Then one day my mother said, "Go to your studio." I'd sat in there for two solid hours. It was at the time when I was most determined not to paint forms that resembled anything recognizable. I wanted a world of my own imagining so that I might treasure the shapes and dimensions in my real one. I didn't need hallucinogens. I needed intense quiet. My mind couldn't silence itself. I had seen my father the day before he died—he and I both knew he was going to die—and no matter what I did, I could not forget his face. I could not stop going back to that true image. I wanted to walk out of my studio, but I had promised my mother. So I drew my father's face, free-form, from memory. Pencil. Tore the sheet off. Drew it again, less accurately, more abstractly. And then again, and again, until I was ready to make a painting only I would recognize. So I went one step further, and I put up a canvas and did a painting in which even I saw only form. I swore then never to stop.

I WAS AT THE HOSPITAL for morning rounds, hoping to see Mike. It was a free-floating want. I let the sitter go for a breakfast break and sat by my mother, who was breathing steadily on her respirator. I wanted to talk to her because she would hear me, but I didn't know what to say. I knew she didn't want to hear how Ronald and I were getting along. That was the last subject she'd had to deal with when she was conscious. And if she had any awareness, she didn't need me to tell her Ronald hadn't come to the hospital after the stroke. I wondered if she'd be amused to know that my entire house had reeked of fish and broccoli when I got home. He had scraped all the uneaten food into my garbage can. No leftovers, no disposal. Elizabeth had taken the children home, and for the first time in his married life he had done kitchen patrol. Wait, my mother definitely would like that. It wasn't contentious, and it wouldn't make her feel too ignored. "Fish and broccoli," I was stage-whispering to her. "Do you know how bad that smells?"

"I guess if she retched it would be a good neurological sign," a voice behind me said, and I stood up straight from my chair, as if caught out.

"Good to see you," Mike said. "Though not here."

"I've been thinking," I said without thinking.

He nodded. "Plenty of time. Really, all the time in the world."

I hoped that meant my mother was going to be his patient for many years, but I didn't think so. It meant the opposite. I asked him if he knew anything, and he said that at that point he couldn't know much more than I did. It would take time. Something in the way he said "time" led me to believe that this was not all there was in the world, in fact, just the opposite.

"You need to wake up, Mama," I said.

"She gets a little more time than that." He had a pretty terrific smile, teeth straight but not bleached white, slightly comical because he grinned all the way back to his molars. I liked his mouth. I didn't care if he saw me noticing it.

"You need to get ready for Tevor Souriante," I said to her. I told him about my interview, and of course he knew who Tevor Souriante was. PBS meant something to a doctor who painted. I made sure he understood that my mother was the one I wanted to excite.

"Maybe we can have coffee sometime while you're here," he said.

I told him that I planned to have sitters around the clock, then I pulled him away from my mother who could have been listening and said that I had learned when my father died that if I didn't go back to my studio I would never stop grieving, that I knew I shouldn't already be grieving over my mother, but I surely was losing part of her, that already I had lost part of her before this stroke, and probably speech wasn't coming back, though I still spoke to her, and comprehension would remain, or she might die, and then I started to cry.

He put his arms around me. I was careful not to let my face rest on his lab coat because it would be so easy to get eye makeup on the clean white of it. I could feel his body for the first time. I felt its warmth more than even its solidity. I patted his back, whispered, "Thank you," and pulled away, precisely because I wanted to stay like that for a very long time. And there was no reason not to. Anyone could have walked in, and my face was streaked with tears. It seemed to me that whenever he held me the next time, and a next time would come, he would take away sadness, too. No matter what.

MY PAINT WAS HEAVY on the canvas, thickeners added to the acrylics. I was using a palette knife, doing impasto technique, making the canvas look as if I'd done underpainting and overpainting. I had layered before but never for a reason. Obvious thickness never had been my style. To me now it was a representation of time, heavy time, existential time, minutes telescoped as if they were hours. At times in my life when I'd been in physical pain, I'd thought, *So this is what the French philosophers had meant; if I wanted to feel as if my life was long, I needed only to suffer, and I would feel that I had a greater allotment of life.*

I stayed in the studio and sent extra-sensory messages to my mother. She and I always thought—not believed, thought—that it was possible there existed a dimension beyond our senses that might not yet be fully developed or understood by science. It wasn't supernatural foolishness; it was natural. ESP messages never had worked when she was conscious, of course, but it didn't hurt to try when she had no outside distractions. I told her I was going to watch Ronald for her. I would get her an answer.

When the phone rang, it startled me. It was Andy Campagna. I'd had shows in Andy's gallery when I was starting out. He wasn't my first, my launcher, which meant he hadn't taken a real risk on me. Andy felt he owed me a favor, because he could claim me but not own me, and from time to time I would give him a few paintings to put into a local retrospective. "I like his stuff," he said.

"You're not just bullshitting me."

"Okay, I love his stuff."

I was starting to tremble. It had been a long time since acceptance had meant anything to me. "Are you calling to tell me something good?" I said.

"Does he have enough for a show?" Andy said.

"I wouldn't have shown you those pieces if he didn't." I was cool, like an agent.

Andy was quiet for a moment. "So how do we go about this?" he said.

"Sweetie, you've been in this business since I first picked up a brush." It was true. Andy was so old that he'd settled down with a partner before he could get AIDS. Half of his friends were dead, and I'd watched him lose competition by attrition when he didn't want to.

"Okay, I guess I don't know how to ask whether you have an interest in the work," he said.

Oh. I forgot about greed.

I told him this was my mother's doctor, and right now my mother was on a respirator, and my only interest was having a happy doctor, but not a doctor who was too distracted to make rounds. "So, see, it's probably not in my interest for him to have a show, but I want him to have it anyway."

"I know what you're up to, Cesca," he said, almost chanting.

"You do not."

"Uncle Andy is glad to help you out."

"Oh, shut up." I said it with great affection.

I called Mike on his cell. He'd given his number to me because he wanted me to have it. He hadn't said anything more than that. I'd learned it by heart using a mnemonic. I didn't know how to program phones, so I used mnemonics. It was the final glob of left-brain matter I used unless money was involved. I sometimes wondered if Kandinsky used music the same way.

"You won't believe what just happened," I said when he picked up.

"Your mother woke up."

"No." I told him it was about something unrelated.

He thought for a few seconds. "Clearly this is sudden," he said.

He was daring to be amused.

"And good." He didn't say anything. "You're a doctor, you can be brave."

"My paintings?"

"Yes."

"Someone liked my paintings?"

"A gallery owner liked your paintings."

"Oh, good God."

"Yes."

"I wish you'd told me in person," he said.

I told him I'd be happy to tell him again.

THE NEXT TIME I saw him was not going to be remembered for excited talk about paintings. He asked me to come to the hospital, and he left it to my judgment whether I wanted to bring Ronald. There was only one reason for such a call. I saw no reason in the world to bring Ronald.

Mike met me in my mother's room, held out his arms, and thanked me for the Andy connection, then said we had to talk. My mother was not going to get any better. He didn't tell me this like a doctor. He didn't sit on the front of a chair and lean forward, elbows on knees. He told me while he was holding me, and then he held me some more. I thought of my mother, right there in the room, and of imagining her sitting up and grinning sheepishly, and then I thought of her taking tentative steps, and then I thought of wheeling her out to the curb, and then I thought that none of that was going to happen, and I started to cry. Softly at first, and then harder, thinking of her never joking with me again, my never making her laugh again. I wanted to disappear into Mike and not have to open my eyes and move forward. He held me for a long time, until I needed to let go.

"I guess you know why I said maybe Ronald should come with you," Mike said.

Oh, God, my brother and I were going to have to fight. I had medical power of attorney, and I knew my mother's wishes, but Ronald, who said life was valuable unless it was a pig or a fish, was going to obstruct me; I knew it. "Can I just take her off the respirator and tell him she died?" I said.

Then I thought about it. I was saying this in front of my mother. What if she could hear me? And what if Mike was wrong? I didn't want to kill her when she wasn't going to die. And maybe Ronald would do the opposite of what I expected. Maybe he would press me to let her go. Maybe he wanted her dead and would find a biblical citation that made that possible. Mama had millions. Easier millions than Jesus. But millions that Jesus would say were Ronald's. I couldn't remember what good Christians said about interfering with nature when Terry Schiavo was on life support. It had seemed to me then that wrongheaded arguments could be made for both sides.

"I take that back," I said. Mike gave me a gentle smile, a smile that was genuine and nothing he'd learned in school. "I need to know she's not there. Can you do an EEG or something? I mean, that's all the proof I need."

"For you, of course," he said. "Or is this for your brother?"

"Medical science doesn't work with Ronald. Right now I'm not sure how much it's going to work with me." Someone who knew a lot was going to roll my mother into a futuristic room or roll a futuristic machine into her room and send back a file, on paper, on a screen, that would give a keen prediction of my mother's future.

"I'll give you something you can see," he said, and with the care he might give a premature baby he pulled back the sheet covering my mother, revealing her left foot. He told me to watch closely. I got up close, and he pinched the back of her naked foot, just above the heel, firmly, no nonsense. It would have made anyone with any nerve endings flinch, but my mother had no response. "It's a way to know," he said. "An old way, but a pretty reliable one. Still, your brother wouldn't believe it." He placed the sheet back.

I told Mike I'd wait for the results before I phoned Ronald. He didn't ask before he kissed me goodbye. It was a soft, chaste kiss, a promise of expedited results in that kiss, but also of long familiarity to come.

CHAPTER NINE

I WAS SORRY I'D ASKED for the EEG. She wasn't brain dead. She had brain stem activity, which meant Mike and I hadn't looked at her foot closely enough, I supposed. A fish is a brain stem with instincts and possibly more cognition than we know. My mother probably had no instincts, which she didn't believe existed anyway, but the EEG showed some cortical brain activity. With or without it, Mike's point was that after so much time, the prognosis was wretched. That was too ambiguous. I didn't need to argue with Ronald. I needed to argue with myself. Mike was bargaining with the neurologist to give my mother a few days; as distraction I would bargain with Andy for a spring show. But Andy knew my mother was going to die, and no one conducts business when death is coming. That was a rule in art circles, at least in New Orleans. As soon as death arrived, of course, it was a free-for-all.

To talk to myself, I called Klea.

Klea had been ambivalent about leaving to go back to school. It was simple, Gammy or Seth. School had nothing to do with it. Her teachers would have understood and let her stay in New Orleans and worry or grieve or whatever she needed to do, working long distance. But she'd had four days at Christmas with Seth, and she'd learned that she needed him. I wasn't sure exactly what he did, though I liked him. He might have been as little as a presence that protected her from her uncle's family. He might have been a good talker or laugher or listener. I didn't want to think about the distinct possibility that he was just a lover who distracted the hell out of her. In the end, she opted for Seth.

When I thought about it, any girl who chose to stay home because of her grandmother would have gone back to school and heard nothing but, "What, your grandmother, are you for real?" Even at an anything-goes school.

"She's really not there," I said.

Klea took a little time trying to find the right thing to say. "No," she said finally.

That actually was a helpful answer. She was talking to herself as much as she was talking to me.

I told her I had to make a decision.

"What do you mean by really not there?"

I had to explain the terms, the medical tests, the definitions of what science determined constituted being a viable life form. I said Gammy had told me long ago what she considered a worthwhile life for herself, which was considerably higher than that of anything Uncle Ronald would eat.

Klea started to cry. "You and Gammy are so funny," she said.

"I whisper jokes in her ear all day," I said. "Hearing might be there a little bit. But she doesn't process it."

Klea grew quiet for a second, snuffling. "Don't you wish you were Uncle Ronald?" she said. "You watch. He'll come in and talk to her spirit hovering over the bed."

We both started to giggle. I surely wasn't going to replace my mother, but already I had a new appreciation for my daughter.

"Oh," she said. "You know the right thing to do. She's probably in some kind of pain, and you're not hurting her for someone else's happiness. She's not going to be a pork chop."

"She could donate her organs," I said.

"People want sixty-seven-year-old organs?"

"I'd rather have her corneas than be blind," I said.

"Well, don't tell Uncle Ronald."

I told her I was thinking of not telling him anything except that she died. "Too bad you don't believe in lying," she said.

I'D CHOSEN MY OPENING statement for Ronald. *It's time to take Mama off life support.* A declaration. I could go over to his house, be outnumbered, two to one or even four to one, and with that pronouncement, he would have a hard time arguing with me.

Though now I'd decided I was going to have to take on Mama's role as skeptic. Especially while she was still alive. If I could whisper to her that *maybe* she was right, that *maybe* he was a phony, I could feel a little better about saying goodbye.

We sat in his living room, Elizabeth, Ronald, and I. I hadn't been there since my mother had her first stroke, right there, feeling funny, having to pass it off as nothing because it was Thanksgiving at Ronald's house and he wanted her to get over it. Nozie chose to jump onto Ronald's lap, I noticed. He scratched her head.

"So you didn't come here to tell me I won the lottery," Ronald said. "I just want you to know in advance that Elizabeth and I apologize for not taking as much responsibility as you with Mother, but we both work full-time, and you don't, and I'm very sorry. So if you've come to try to spread the chores around, maybe you can give us something to do that we can handle from our office. Maybe her bills or something."

"We have to take Mama off life support," I said. It was the saddest my voice ever had sounded without crying.

"Are you sure?" Ronald said. "You know if it's about insurance, we'd pay cash." He didn't sound as if he meant it. But maybe I was slipping into Mama's mindset.

"Did you hear me?" I said.

"Sure, but listen to me," he said. "I've read all about hospitals and budgetary constraints. I know what pressures doctors are under. I just need to be certain."

He was taking his chance to go after Mike. "I don't want blame for making this decision," he said. "You may think that doctor is in love with you, but I guarantee you he's more in love with the bottom line."

I stood up and grabbed my purse.

Elizabeth reached out and took my arm.

"Let her go," Ronald said. "I'll call Alan at Baptist. Administrators override doctors any time. I'll make sure everything is in order."

"I have power of attorney," I said. "I don't have to get your permission to keep her or let her go." I pulled away from Elizabeth.

Ronald stood up slowly enough not to surprise the cat, then grabbed my shoulder. But not in a mean way. Possibly this was a first. "Let's talk," he said. That was good. I gave him a small smile.

We sat at the edges of our seats, hands folded on our knees. "We need to start with straight facts," I said.

Ronald raised his eyebrows but didn't interrupt.

For that I was grateful. I told him about the EEG. "I overrode straight facts myself," I said. "Technically she's not brain dead, so deciding to take her off life support is not going with the facts."

"So--" Elizabeth said.

"So it's tempting when I see her, but we can't just keep this breathing brain stem lying around. That's too Norman Bates."

"You're sick," Ronald said. Ordinarily I would have sworn he meant it, but now I wasn't going to be sure. If he was pretending, it was nice evidence for my mother.

I told him he was right. I was punchy with nerves.

"Look, if I read you right, Mother is alive," he said. "Then somebody turns off a machine, and Mother is dead. Right? It's that simple, right?"

I nodded. "It might be seconds. It might be days."

"But there's a direct cause and effect," he said. "Well, I am not going to commit murder. That's worse than abortion. A lot worse than abortion. I value life. All life."

Oh, God, now everything he said sounded fake.

"All human life," I said.

"You eat broccoli," he said.

We were both being horrible.

Against all I would have expected of myself, I said, "I don't want her to die."

"Then what's your problem?"

"She would want to die," I said. "She had a living will."

"No one living in Christ would have a living will."

What? My mind was terribly tired. I wanted to go off and work on what he'd just said. It was so beautifully nonsensical. To a real Christian it made complete sense. To a fake Christian it passed the responsibility to the heathens. And to anyone with wit, it made perfect poetry. My mother would have loved it, would have said it over and over.

"Mama wasn't 'living in Christ' when she executed that will," I said. "She talked it all through before she did it. She even joked about being a big useless problem in your living room instead of dying and decided against it." It was true. She'd described herself as a giant bowl of protoplasm, sitting between Ronald and his television set, needing stirring every hour around the clock.

"She's living in Christ now," Ronald said.

I looked at Elizabeth, and she nodded in agreement.

Neither looked me in the eye.

Ronald had gone to the hospital when I wasn't there and had had the chaplain christen my mother as a Methodist, which was the best he could come up with. It was good enough for Ronald's purposes. It was then that I knew my mother wasn't a sentient human being. Being christened didn't count if she hadn't made a conscious choice. And she wasn't conscious. Of that I was now sure. I was less sure what I knew about Ronald.

"Think what you want," I said. I corrected myself. "Believe what you want."

MY CELL PHONE RANG when I was still in the car on my way to the hospital. In New Orleans it was possible to get from any one point to any other point in twenty minutes, and the distance from Ronald's house was nowhere near the distance from parish line to parish line; more like a tenth of that, so I knew he'd had under three minutes to think about it.

"Elizabeth and I have talked it through," he said. "Go ahead and do it."

Just like that. As if he were telling me to buy my mother a purse.

I told him, "All right." The time would come later when I would ask him, or more probably Elizabeth, exactly what had transpired in those three minutes. I imagined she had said one magical thing, and I needed to know what it was. I'd have liked to think it was for my own comfort, but I wasn't that kind. I wondered if it had anything to do with salt.

Shellonde was on duty when I reached the hospital. She didn't know what was going on, but she had had her share of plug-pulling in her day. "I been expecting this news a little while now," she said. "Hospitals don't let you lie here when you not gonna walk out." I wondered if hospitals took black people off life support faster than white people. I hoped they didn't, but I had my doubts—and I had the feeling it had nothing to do with insurance.

"It's not as bad as you think," she said, though she didn't look as if she was finding solace anywhere. "I don't know why, but to me it's kind of peaceful. Don't get me wrong. I know your mama not no Christian, even if Mr. Ronald come up in here with the preacher and say he make her one."

So Shellonde had witnessed the christening. I hoped she hadn't signed anything. That would have been unfair.

"And I know you not no Christian, neither. But it's peaceful. They don't hurt her, no. She just relax, like she tired of breathing, and they let her stop."

I looked over at my mother, whose chest was moving up and

down with precision, and would do so as long as the hospital had electricity. If I didn't know it was artificial, I would think she was struggling, moving that air so she could pump that blood so she could make those organs filter and channel and process. If that body wasn't working much more than a brain stem, it was all right to break the cycle. No need for me to have small clues about Ronald. Finding the truth about him was for her posthumous life, where she wouldn't be around. I just would tell her I loved her, because love might be all the cortex could take at the end.

Mike would be the one to do it. And he would do it on my schedule, not on his. Ronald said he had to work, and when I said we could do it after work, he said he had to be out of town. I told him if he didn't want to be present, he just had to say so, and he said so. "It's really murder," Ronald said, "and I don't want to be an accessory." *And what about soup cans?* I wanted to say. I reminded him I had his permission, and even though I didn't have evidence that would hold up in a court of law, I was sure God witnessed it. "See, you do believe," he said. *Or maybe you don't*, I almost said.

All I had to consider in choosing the time were numbers and Shellonde. Did I want Shellonde with me? If I did, it only would be fair to schedule on her shift, but she quickly disabused me of that notion. This was going to be her last responsibility to Mrs. Price, and she would stay as late as she needed to. Oh, God, I needed to cancel the next sitter. Shellonde knew her from the daily changeover; she would call her and spare me the need to make the call. So all I had left to consider were numbers. My mother was crazy about numbers. We'd talked a lot about them, and about whether our interest in numbers meant she and I were secretly spiritual, or maybe simply obsessive-compulsive. We eventually decided we were aesthetes. I was an artist and she was my greatest fan. We loved symmetry in numbers, especially repeating digits, and we took great delight in choosing computer passwords and PINs and in remembering phone numbers by mnemonics. It would be a gift to my mother to give her a perfect time of death. The date was January 22. Tomorrow was January 23. One-two-three. I asked Mike if he would come tomorrow for a time of death of 4:56. He figured it out right away.

My mother wasn't brain dead, he had to remind me. I didn't want to think about that. Mike told me I had made the right decision. I had put my mother first. Her quality of life counted. Moreover, he said, she couldn't donate organs. Transplant teams wanted young, healthy hearts and lungs and kidneys, and no matter how pure my mother's world view might have been, her major organs would not have served any purpose. "Like what they put in the paper sack in the turkey?" I said, and he laughed.

I stayed at the hospital the rest of the day and all of the night and the next day, feeling free to go home and shower and change clothes, telling my mother out loud where I was going, why I was going, when I was coming back. Just as if she were her old, independent self. Otherwise, I sat close to her, just in case she and I had been right, that there were dimensions we didn't know about yet, that people with near-death experiences had been right, that they had hovered over their beds. I wanted to be in her picture. I went out to get food and brought it back. Whole Foods was close by, and I could make myself a salad. I could eat it under her ceiling screen. Four o'clock arrived, and I began to feel nauseated, shaky. Four-fifteen came, and I started to cry. At 4:30 Shellonde walked in, and I was shaking and sobbing. My big worry was that Mike would be late. My mother would be late for her death.

Each minute was long. Those were my final minutes with my mother, and I wanted them to end. Shellonde stood by, not on my mother's screen, and I stayed next to my mother, checking my watch, telling her it would all be fine, that I would miss her. Mike walked in at 4:40. He put his hand on my shoulder. Shellonde didn't care. I saw her expression, and it was one of gratitude, that I had him. This was why my mother had a till-death-us-do-part bond with Shellonde. Her wisdom of no rules that could not be broken. I hoped I wasn't going to have to miss her.

My mother looked young and more peaceful than she had in a long time. Nurses had removed all but one of the lines going into her body. Lying on her back took away so much of the damage of time. Her face was smooth; her hair flowed back. She wasn't grimacing the way she did so often in the days just before. I knew Mike would remember her as a person. He would see beyond the respirator.

Mike told me he was early, wanting me to know that it would happen on time. A nurse slipped in, and she fiddled with Mama's IV line once Mike had given her a whispered directive. I focused on my mother, I stroked her head. She wasn't particularly clean, but this was a private moment, and no one was there to judge her. I tried not to watch what Mike was doing. The only line into my mother's arm led to a small vial of clear liquid, and I didn't want to know what was in it, but I saw that now it was Mike himself who was focused on being precise in calibrating it. That didn't concern me. It would do whatever it did in silence. It was the panel of vital signs and the machine powering the respirator that I didn't want to watch because they were visible and noisy. I focused back on my mother. I watched her breathe. Maybe she would keep breathing. Maybe she would keep breathing for hours. Days. Weeks. Maybe she would recover. Mike began to move around busily. I checked the wall clock. 4:55. Mike opened the IV, quietly touched a switch. 4:56. My mother stopped breathing. The line went flat on the monitor. He whispered, "Four fifty-six," to the nurse, gave me a little hug, whispered that he would phone in a little while, then slipped out of the room.

CHAPTER TEN

I *NEEDED* TO TELL KLEA. I *had* to tell Ronald.

It was dark when I got home, and the news wasn't urgent. I was alone, and I was entitled to anything. So I dialed.

Klea saw me on Caller ID. "You don't have to say anything," she said instead of hello. She was crying.

I gave her time. Silence was fine for both of us. "Can you tell me?" she said finally.

"It was just the way Shellonde told me it'd be," I said. "Like she was tired of breathing, so she stopped."

"Shellonde, oh, God, Shellonde." Klea adored Shellonde. I couldn't think about Shellonde. I couldn't lose her, too. "How'd they do it?" Klea whispered.

"I have no idea," I said. "Well, I read about Jackie Kennedy once, and she had morphine, but I don't know. I just know it was very much all right."

"Amazing. You're the one who left the room when they put poor little Vincent to sleep."

I was in a darkened room, but I squeezed my eyes shut. There was something I couldn't deal with in saying goodbye to a dog. Maybe that I had no way of shutting down as I did with my mother.

"Today's January 23," I said, forcing a calendar onto my mind's eye. "The time of death was 4:56."

It took her a moment to track me. "Oh, one, two, three, four, five, six. Gammy would have been happy. I love you both so much."

"I love you, too." Pain and joy were now completely indistinguishable.

"I'm so glad Seth met her," Klea said.

SHE WAS GOING TO find Seth right away, spend the night distracting herself in an enviable way. I would spend every minute filled with dread and nothing else until I talked to Ronald and put him behind me. I didn't have my mother to protect me. She hadn't been an arbiter for many years, but I still had had a mother, and that had counted for quite a lot. Maybe losing her would turn Ronald into a magical new brother. Maybe he would come clean. Or be a true believer. One who honestly knew nothing about nutrition facts on food labels. I wanted a close relative, but I wasn't a fool.

I phoned his house, and Levi answered on the fourth ring. "Hey, we're at dinner; can he call you back?" he said. No hello. That was the world of Caller ID and young people for whom no telephone rules had been created yet. Though I'd have thought that Ronald would find some, possibly in the liturgy. I told him I had something important. Levi halfway covered the phone, and I could hear him calling to his father that I said I had something important, and then I heard something to the effect that he was sure I could wait. "Tell him he knows exactly why I'm calling," I said and hung up.

I waited for the phone to ring right back, but it didn't.

Anger would have been a good gift, but it didn't come. Maybe I had used it up. Maybe I didn't want it. Maybe I wanted calm. Calm was the prize of solitude. No responsibility for anyone else. No behaving in a civilized way, wearing clothes, staying clean. With solitude I could strip naked and lie on the carpet and dribble chocolate into my mouth, eyes closed. If I wanted to. But I also had the freedom not to want to. Solitude.

I went into the kitchen and opened the refrigerator and looked at everything and realized that, even though I hadn't eaten much all day,

I wasn't hungry. Hot tea seemed right. I made hot tea. I could break the solitude. Talking to Mike would be good. Seeing Mike would be better, but that wasn't possible. I knew he would phone. I sat on the sofa with scalding tea, one lamp the only illumination in the house, and tried to think of anything besides my mother slipping into peace, her skin smoothed, her hair lying softly around her face, a good image but too full of loss, so I closed it off, but then my thoughts went to saying goodbye to Vincent, and that was just as sweetly unbearable, so I closed my eyes, able to drink tea without seeing, and I made myself imagine the painting I was working on, thinking I might sleep well that night, and the phone rang. I had forgotten about Ronald.

"You don't do that to a person," he said. He'd had twenty minutes to come up with that line, and twenty minutes to build up a good head of fury. I'd given him a gift.

"I told Levi it was important. When your mother is going to be taken off life support, you have to consider the possibility that I'm not calling about nothing. I didn't specify why I was calling."

"Levi said you said Mother was dead," he said. "We were just trying to have a little normalcy around here. You know, trying not to think about Mother. That was so wrong."

"You ask Levi," I said. "All I told him was that you'd know why I was calling."

"Your word against his," he said. "Listen, you know very well we eat at the same time every day because it gives the kids stability, and I knew upheaval was coming. You did it on purpose."

All else aside, the subtext of that was that Klea was unstable. We'd been over that before.

"Did you ever think that when I've just watched my mother die I might not be looking at my watch?"

"I bet you know exactly what time she died," he said.

"Well, sure," I said. "It's just like knowing when a person is born. It goes on a certificate."

"I rest my case."

"Your fucking mother just died," I practically screamed. "Are you going to get all litigious with me?"

"Mother, do you hear that?" His voice was soft, but I was sure he was looking up at the ceiling.

I could hear Elizabeth in the background, making calming motherly sounds. "I don't need to calm down," Ronald said.

"Let me talk," Elizabeth said, close to the phone. Next thing I knew, she was on the line instead of Ronald. They were not the type to talk on separate extensions.

"I'm sure you've made arrangements," she said.

"Actually not," I said. It was good to hear her voice. "Though you have to have someone in charge, so I told them Lake Lawn. I guess they'll come after the autopsy."

"How long's that take?"

I could hear Ronald in the background saying, "How long's what take?" and Elizabeth saying, "They're doing an autopsy." Next thing I knew, Ronald was on the phone again.

"Who gave you permission to desecrate Mother's body like that?"

"What?" I'd heard of orthodox Jews getting upset about autopsies, but even they gave in if it was forensically necessary. I thought that was fascinating, the way they wanted all the parts, right down to bits of skin, to be put in place before a body could go into the ground. They had rules about getting bodies into the ground within twenty-four hours, too. Jews were interesting because I didn't think any of their laws transcended reason. All the faith stuff started after Jesus started doing miracles. Well, really, it started when he disappeared from that cave, and everybody started writing about his life and seeing all kinds of miracles in it. Jews were the next closest people to pragmatists, so I figured they had some logic in their laws. I'd taken a lot of time trying to figure out why they ate some animals and not others. When I realized it had to do too much with sanitary conditions and not enough with compassion, I blew them off as arbiters of what I'd eat. After all, most Jews had origins closer to the equator than mine, and they had rules about dairy most likely because of lactose intolerance. I didn't use milk products because I didn't think cows should be crammed into sheds and pulled at all day.

"Technically Dr. Rosenthal gave permission for the autopsy," I said. "But as for family permission, I'm the only one who needed to decide."

"You can't do that."

"It's possibly happening right now," I said. I doubted that was true. Few doctors worked regularly at night, and I was sure that pathologists chose their specialization precisely so they could go home for dinner and go back to work at nine in the morning. Dead people never had emergencies. Almost.

"You need to call it off," Ronald said. "Her body needs to be buried as an entity that can be resurrected on Judgment Day. They're going to throw stuff away."

Where did he get these ideas? And why did he make life difficult with them? He could be a true Christian if he needed to be without adding new curlicues every day. On the other hand he could have announced he was a Christian, and his business would have thrived without his even making his wife and kids do all that praying at home.

"What if I'd donated her organs?" I said.

"That would have been all right," Ronald said, completely self-assured. "The people who got them would be buried with them, so Mother would get them back."

I was tempted to ask him what would happen if Judgment Day came while the recipients were still alive, but my mother was dead, and fighting with Ronald was no fun at all.

"I'll tell them to put everything back," I said. "I'm sure they're used to Jews."

"As usual, I don't have a clue what you're talking about," Ronald said, "but you better not tell them she's Jewish."

A FUNERAL IS POSSIBLY THE most complex public event known to civilization.

I was sure the people at Lake Lawn had been trained to handle families in all permutations of grief. And families with schisms and realignments. I'd lived in New Orleans long enough to know that they'd put a lot of deeply unloved dead people into the ground, not to mention a handful whose passing was tragic enough to draw endless lines of genuinely sad strangers. But I found it hard to believe that they'd had to arbitrate so extremely over what constituted a proper send-off. At worst, they might have had a minister who had to negotiate the hymns or the readers, or maybe they had a family fighting over having a service drone on and on for an hour because the son wanted to have a Mass. But Ronald was ordained, and I was free, and we were about as polarized as it was possible to be, and Mrs. Hirsch at Lake Lawn was Jewish and sat somewhere on the continuum between us but wasn't going to be of any use because she was trained just to be gentle.

Ronald let me speak first. "Look, I'll put it in the simplest terms possible," I said. "He wants to pray 'til he can pray no more, and I know my mother would not want one word about God, not to mention Jesus. She had nothing against prayer, but not as a bludgeon. My brother would tell everybody my friends and I are going to hell."

"Do you believe in hell?" Mrs. Hirsch said. Being Jewish in New Orleans, she surely had been told where she was headed more than once.

I could feel Ronald was about to open his mouth to say something. I knew him too well.

"Oh, come on," I said to him. "You know very well that being told you're going to hell is a proper way of saying to go fuck yourself." Ronald shifted in his seat. He was outnumbered. Though that usually didn't stop him.

To her credit, she didn't blink. "Can you compromise?" she said.

Her tone was so sweet that I wanted to shout at her. Ronald and I had known each other for almost forty years and had compromised on almost nothing. Why did she think we were going to resolve the world's most ancient dilemma, not to mention our own, because she spoke in such a nice voice?

"Would you like to tell me what a service would look like when one person wants to praise Jesus to the high heavens, and the other person knows the right thing is to eulogize her mother and leave religiosity out of it?" I said. "Not religion, religiosity."

"I know you're very angry right now," Mrs. Hirsch said. "It's perfectly natural to have such feelings at this time."

I stared hard at her, probably proving her right. She was a puffy little woman wearing a navy blue suit. She had too much abdominal fat, and she had those nice plump arms that were as big as my thighs. She looked like the type who went to the beauty salon every week and had her hair washed and curled for her. It occurred to me that she might have been no older than I was, but she was much closer to death. Or she might as well have been. Nothing ever was going to change for her.

"Has anyone ever had two funerals?" I said. "You know, like some people have two weddings?"

Mrs. Hirsch brightened. She must have been on commission.

"You mean like a bride who has two dresses? Two different services with two different caskets? I can see you might have vastly different tastes. We have some lovely Christian-themed ones and then there are simpler styles, though for burial--"

"Hold it right there," Ronald said. "This surely is not Rent-a-Coffin."

I giggled.

"Oh, no," she said. "We could never sell a unit after we'd had your mother in it, even if it's just for a couple of hours. You'd have to pay for it."

It was tempting to ask what she expected, that we'd exhume her every six months and transfer her, but Lake Lawn didn't seem like the kind of place for levity. At least in public places. "For Chrissakes," I said, "All I'm talking about are two separate services. Same room. Same coffin. Same flowers. Maybe a different guest book. No big whoop."

Mrs. Hirsch's expression didn't change. Good saleswoman or good poker player. She thought about it for a moment. She had checklists in her head. I could see her eyes start to gleam. "Let's see," she said. "There are visitations and wakes and all sorts of different parts of a funeral, you know. Some people even have one service at church and another graveside. Or a memorial at a later date. Or something public and something private."

"I'm an ordained minister," Ronald told her. "I think a separate service at a church would be good. Now if I had my own church--"

"But you don't," I said.

"But I will."

Mrs. Hirsch ignored us. "Would you like to contact a congregation where you preach?"

And what nice clean murder scene would that be?

"One venue," I said. "Right here. No limos leaving the premises."

Mrs. Hirsch was not liking this bare-bones approach.

"If you have services at two different times, you'll have to book the chapel twice," she said in a tone that meant she had won something, and she could move on.

"Well, there you go," I said to Ronald. "Separate but equal. You can flap all around Mama, and she'll never know. Then I'll have the funeral she wanted. If you pay enough, the *Times-Picayune* will run an announcement explaining everything."

"Mother certainly will know everything, or what's the point?" Ronald said.

For his benefit, I looked up at the ceiling.

I looked at Mrs. Hirsch. I told her I'd handle the details.

Ronald said, “But I have veto power.”

“No, he doesn’t,” I said in my older sister voice.

Mrs. Hirsch looked slightly wild-eyed, as if she’d just personally negotiated a tricky détente between Israel and the Palestinians, and now it might come undone.

“He’s lucky I let him come today,” I said. “He’s even luckier there’s going to be even one prayer uttered in the presence of my poor, dead mother. Good thing words don’t do any harm. Especially after you’re dead.”

A NOT PARTICULARLY DIGNIFIED memorial took place two mornings later. Ronald and I didn’t have to do a coin toss; my going first made sense for both of us, though neither of us could have said why. Throughout the chapel were friends of my mother, indistinguishable at a distance from my art friends because most of them were idiosyncratic the way she was. White, black, brown: they all colored their hair and wore bright hues on any occasion, and though it wasn’t obvious in the crowd, these were outrageously quotable people. My mother had entertained me with anecdotes about seventy-year-old women who called themselves GILFs, which, she said with pure joy, meant they were “grandmothers I’d like to fuck.”

But most of the heavy crowd was from the art world. The guest book was filled with signatures of painters that, found at the bottoms of canvases, were worth tens of thousands. I would have been flattered, but local artists and critics always turned out for our own, in some measure to see one another, probably also in some measure to reassure ourselves that we wouldn’t die alone the way we worked alone. Collectors came as if to reconnect with me; students did, too. My ex-husband William was there, but he chose to stay to himself, not approach me, talk to the occasional person who recognized him from the past. He caught my eye, and the message sent was, *I’m here, but I won’t bother you.* I never felt more like holding him than I did right then. But I honored his honoring me. It was the way a funeral should be, people coming through and hugging me and being instantly forgotten because I was exhausted. Half an hour after starting time, whoever was there sat down while I spoke of what kind of person my mother was. I had prepared a few notes, but I could have come unprepared, having only to look at her friends and remember.

"My mother made me what I am today," I said. "Now before you start thinking I'm going to brag like a bar mitzvah boy--" I paused for the laugh I got. "I only mean that she made me into a woman who could believe I was her best friend. We saw eye to eye. She and Daddy fell in love at Woodstock, and it was ironic: they made their money buying radio stations. Which was funny because she was a secular humanist, and the science of radio waves confounded her. We talked about it sometimes. She reared me believing what she believed, or, rather, knowing what she knew, and forever after we had a prism of truth that we looked through together. Right before she had the strokes that led to her death, she would come out and say that she knew coffee was bad for her. And then she'd say, 'Oh, I'll have just one more cup.' She wanted to have the truth. What she did with it was another story." I smiled and got back a roomful of grins.

Everyone there loved her, and I went on to tell them about the time Mama and her friend Vijay called the chairman of their Neighborhood Watch a fascist pig because he only put notices in the white people's mailboxes on the uptown-downtown streets and not in the black people's mailboxes on the lake-river streets. Vijay was in the room, her uptown-downtown-brown skin pinking up. "My mother had a lot of money, but she didn't live like it," I said. "She supported maybe a half dozen artists in this city for as long as a year, but only they knew it." I saw several in the room, and they got pale, even though all were surviving now.

Suddenly I wasn't just speaking in front of an audience. I was saying goodbye to my mother. She wasn't there. She never was going to be there. "I can't believe I'll never see her again," I said, and I walked down into the crowd before I began to cry too hard to say anything more.

Instrumentals of John Lennon music had been playing, and the sound became more audible without my voice. I'd chosen my mother's favorites, no matter whether the rhythms sounded out of place there. "Starting Over" came on just then, and I went from wanting to cry to wanting to laugh. I wished so much for an afterlife at that moment, so my mother and I could share what just had happened. "Oh, God," I said to whoever could hear me, "of all songs to play now. Mama always said that worship of John Lennon was as close as she got to belief in a transcendent being." A ripple of laughter encircled me.

And then I stayed to protect my mother from whatever Ronald might do a few hours later, after the air had cleared of iconoclasm. Ronald hadn't been at my service, and I'd been grateful. I'd felt free.

I'd promised I wouldn't speak or move, so I could be there. My presence had to count for something. Lake Lawn gave us a small reception parlor in addition to use of the chapel, and Ronald had arranged for food and beverages. I saw nothing on the table that I would eat. The drinks were non-alcoholic, but they all were carbonated and sugar-sweet. Big two-liter bottles next to bowls of ice with tongs. Those tongs were a classy touch. But Mountain Dew was not. Large platters of sandwiches were arrayed at strategic spots on the table in case there was a big crowd, and all I could think was that each was made from the kind of bread and sandwich meat that would kill my mother, except that she wasn't going to be eating here. Or dying here, either. This was homicidal food, but party food always was. No crudités, which usually were my mainstay at such spreads; I could fill up on carrots and feel full until I could get to more food. Cheese. Crackers. But Swiss and Triscuits. Ronald's favorites. If no one ate them, he was going to take them home. He was sparing no expenses because it was Mama's money.

I could not believe the turnout for the Ronald funeral. We had had an unusually long write-up in the paper in keeping with the need to make it clear that there would be two separate services. So anyone who knew either of us couldn't miss the obituary if he or she was a regular scanner of the death notices. But that didn't account for what must have been over two hundred people crammed into the modest chapel. I'd had a lot of people, but not this many. It was more than standing room only. People were spilling out into the corridor. And unlike at my memorial, no one came, paid respects, and scurried away, having done the proper thing. They looked as if they were all there for a Sunday service. I didn't understand. Unless Ronald truly was expecting to have a church, as he'd mentioned to Mrs. Hirsch.

Ronald was the dry-eyed preacher.

"Thank you for being here today. We have come to celebrate the homecoming of Patricia Price. Yes, the homecoming. Patricia was my mother, and she was a good mother. And a good grandmother. And in her time she was a good wife and a good daughter. But we are not here to celebrate her life. We are here to celebrate her passing unto our Lord Jesus Christ."

I was glad my mother wasn't there. That was cold thanks for never taking sides.

Ronald held forth as if he had been doing this for quite a while, as if he meant it. He didn't quite look like my brother.

"We are here together to rejoice in our Lord Jesus Christ. Yes, rejoice, even on a day of sadness. We all know that this life is just a temporary one, filled with sin and sinners. Sin and sinning. It can't be helped. But we can pray for forgiveness. In ourselves, in our fellow man. And some of us will be saved. You know who we are. We have found Jesus, and our day will come when we will join him for all eternity because we have been saved. I look around this sanctuary, and I see nothing but salvation. Am I right? Is there anyone here who has not chosen salvation? Stand up and I will bring you to the Lord."

The room was silent. I certainly didn't move.

"I am sure you recall that in the past I spoke of my mother not having been saved. Yes, my mother Trisha Price. And yet I am telling you that she is with our Lord Jesus Christ. Have no fear. I told you. This is a sanctuary of salvation. Yes, while she was still here among us, she was baptized in the Lord's name, and now she is with him. Praise Jesus. Can I hear a 'Praise Jesus'?"

"Praise Jesus!"

Baptized?

I hadn't seen such goings on since I'd been to a black Baptist church. Ronald, my scrawny little brother, was pulling all this call and response out of these people dressed in black. Who dressed in black for a funeral anymore? I heard a lot of salvation and praise. I did not hear a lot of my mother.

Then Ronald pointed at me and said, "Should I help my poor sister save herself, she who has not found Jesus?"

"Yes, Lord!" a woman shouted from the second row of chairs.

Right up to that moment I'd been trying to squeeze some respect out of myself for Ronald's sake. I respected my ex-husband for being a financial genius, even though I thought manipulating money wasn't terribly honorable. I needed to be Ronald's friend now that we were the older generation.

But not when he traded on my sinfulness. Not matter what he was, I was show biz.

I waved my hand, palm forward, as if to say, *No, thanks, I'll pass on the cake*, and there was a chorus of, "Yes, Lord!"

Ronald raised his arms to get the attention of his flock, conducting them like a choir, pulled back his elbows to signal quiet.

"She knows what awaits her, and she has seen her mother's close call, and I am working with her," he said softly. "Do not worry about this woman. Let's make today a day of salvation!"

I had no idea what happened next. I escaped into Parlor E to wait out Ronald's finest moment. I thought I might ask the mortuary personnel for a cup of tea because I certainly wasn't going to have anything Ronald had ordered. I found Gracie sitting in one of the chairs along the wall. "When'd you come in here?" I said. I was thrilled to see her, and she knew it.

"About thirty seconds before you did," she said. "I know you're supposed to be going to hell, if that's what you're wondering."

"Are you afraid of me?" I said.

"Hell, no," she said and started giggling. I made a mental note that I should start thinking back on Gracie.

I had walked out of the Ronald Show with eye-rolling indignation, but I wondered how Gracie had managed to sneak out. Her father wouldn't miss one of his minions, but he would have noticed his own daughter slipping out of the room. I commended her on her sneakiness.

"I hid in the back when it started," she said. "That's one good thing about having so many people. Not even my mother knew where I was."

"Where did all these people come from?" I said. I hadn't recognized any of them. Which was strange. In New Orleans, no one ever had more than two degrees of separation from any other person. But this crowd looked as if they had been bussed in from another decade and another state, maybe Oklahoma or Missouri. I knew nothing about those states except they were nowhere. I was not a snob. But I didn't like synthetic fabrics, and I didn't like sanctimonious hair. It wasn't as bad as the hair on the polygamists in the throwback, child-molesting compounds, but it was close. This was an Elmer Gantry crowd, hand-delivered to the twenty-first century, ordered up special for Ronald.

"Daddy's been building up his following," Gracie said. "He's got a website and everything. He does ads on TV late at night for JesusCleanup. I think he put the funeral in an ad last night. He's just been waiting until he gets rich."

"Oh?" It seemed to me that Ronald was pretty well off. There was gold in those pools of human detritus.

"Yeah, you need a lot of money to open a church," Gracie said. "He's got his eye on this one out near Kenner. It's empty, but the thing is, you need maybe like a million dollars to actually buy it."

I didn't say a word. Gracie was in just the right mood. Evidently her father had never announced my surefire damnation to hell before, and it set her off.

Her voice got low and confidential. "From what I see, if you have a church, you get all rich and famous, and everybody thinks you talk straight to *God.*" She said "God" the way she might say "Santa Claus." Gracie was looking me straight in the eye, expectantly.

I looked right back at her. "People do think that," I said.

Gracie looked disappointed, it seemed to me. I forgot she was only thirteen.

"Honey, they only think that. You hear me? Some people get famous, and some get rich, but as for the rest? I'm the wrong person to talk to."

She gave me a tremulous little smile. "Daddy's going to use a lot of his fortune, but don't tell anybody I told you that."

I heard the word "fortune."

NO MATTER WHAT Mrs. Hirsch might have tried to figure out, an interment was an interment, and it couldn't have been done twice. In the end, we handled it the way attorneys did in criminal trials. We broke the day into three parts, and the burial was part three. I didn't want to see myself as the prosecutor and Ronald as the defense, but I did want to get the final word. We agreed that only he and I would go to the grave. He could speak first, then walk away, and I would speak second, then walk away. He argued that if I believed what I believed, I'd be talking to the air, but I told him I'd be talking to myself, and I'd remember what I'd said, and that was good enough. He was happy with that, because I would have to hear both of us. I was sure he expected me to change my plan, to beg him to hear me out, but I didn't.

And why couldn't Elizabeth and his two children come? Ronald wanted to know. I asked why it couldn't be just the two of us. "You're just saying that because Klea couldn't be bothered to come to her own grandmother's funeral," he said.

I was too insulted to cry. Klea wanted to do right by her grandmother, but Klea also believed that dead was dead and knew her Gammy thought that, too. She was off in rural Massachusetts and would have to travel long and hard to get home, and when I told her to stay and do her school work, she felt she had her grandmother's permission. Besides, if she'd come she wouldn't have had Seth to protect her from her uncle.

"Mama would have told her not to waste money coming down here," I said.

"I would think Mother would want to see all her family standing graveside," Ronald said.

I told him that's where he and Mama differed, that I was doing things the way I figured she would want them, and what she would want, cast forward, would be her two children together, nothing extra.

"So you believe she'll be there," he said.

"I believe I'll be there," I said.

"I don't get it," he said.

"Oh, yes, you do."

And that is how it went. Ronald had no audience, except me, my mother, and God, or so he would say, so he prayed for about two minutes before slinking away. I stood over the grave and said, "Mama, I will miss you for the rest of my life. And to the best of my ability, I will try not to let Ronald ruin everything you tried to do." Then I, too, walked away, but my head was high. I knew my audience heard me.

MIKE CALLED A FEW DAYS later to give me the highlights of the autopsy results. The rest would come in the mail if I asked for them. He read me one passage: "The neuropathological findings in the present case provide a link between a clinical situation that could cause a sudden perturbation of cerebral hemodynamics and a specific cerebral vessel lesion, namely, fibrinoid necrosis." I asked him to translate. "We took into account that everyone was going crazy at the table, so the pathologist finds your brother's behavior sent your mother's BP sky-high, and she stroked out. That's why you wanted the autopsy, isn't it?"

I didn't tell him that I hadn't been exactly passive when Ronald attacked me. But I didn't feel guilty. I was sure my mother's last thoughts were that one fine day her children were going to be the best of friends.

CHAPTER ELEVEN

I HAD HOPED MIKE MIGHT show up for one of my mother's funerals. I hadn't cared which one. If he'd come for Ronald's, he'd have been no more out of place than he probably was at most of his patients' funerals, justified in his silence when others prayed. Afterward he could have said to me, *What was that all about?* knowing he wasn't going to offend, especially when I was damned to hell and strode out with my head held high. He could have come to the memorial service I'd held for my mother and seen the world of art. He even could have been introduced to Andy. But it was a work day. It was also something of an admission of guilt, it seemed to me, to show up. He probably went to very few funerals of patients. He'd been practicing for a long time, and if he was good, his patients got older. He was getting a reputation as being effective with old people, and his attrition rate was slow as more came flooding in, aiming for eighty-five, then ninety, then ninety-five. He couldn't care about them all, though he probably did. They were all mothers and fathers. Or sweet aunts and uncles.

He phoned. It was late in the afternoon after the burial. Walking away from the grave and getting into my car and going home to an empty house had not been a healthful ritual. There was a reason why people invited everyone over to the house after a funeral. It wasn't just to unload all the heavy food that had been piling up all week and threatening to rot in the refrigerator if it wasn't eaten that very day. It was to talk and smile to the point of exhaustion. Of course someone else would clean up the kitchen and return all the platters, stripping away that output of energy, and at the end, the mourner would be left alone in a neat, empty house, but her head would be replaying all the gaffes and hurts of the afternoon, and the actual sadness would find no place. When Mike called, I was at home with the purest sadness.

"I thought you might want to sit shiva for about an hour," he said.

I had no idea what he was talking about.

He explained that Jews had as many rituals as you would expect surrounding death, and he wasn't sure how much spirituality was involved, but they seemed to soothe the survivors. And he had a feeling I had no way to soothe myself because reality wasn't a lot of fun along about now.

"I could get drunk," I said. I didn't mention the blunt in my glove compartment. The older it got, the more I thought of it as a talisman.

He laughed. "Sitting there getting drunk by yourself would be just as bad as sitting there being sober by yourself." He was inviting himself over. I asked him how he was going to manage to explain an hour away from his actual life. He was on call, he said. When he was on call, he could be anywhere.

When a man is on call, you don't bother with word games. We began making love for the first time the moment he walked through my door. I was a patient, and he had to travel to see me, and no doctor needs to tend a patient for more than half an hour, even if she has no heartbeat, especially if she has no heartbeat, and I definitely had a heartbeat, so we went quickly, and yet we went slowly, as if we'd been waiting for this for quite a long time. Which we had. I wanted to kiss and kiss him. We kissed and kissed, and out there our bodies moved as if they'd done this so often. I'd never let myself think of making love with him before, though maybe I had.

"This is different," he said before he left.

I hadn't thought of my mother while he was with me. Once he was gone, I thought of her with a sweeter unhappiness, knowing she had predicted what happened tonight in her own way, seeing that I was flirting when I had no clue, betting on my Christmas gift, when I hadn't expected it. She was gone, and I knew she was finished, over with, but when she lived she'd expected tonight, so I didn't have to miss her tonight. After all, the one reason people grieved was that the person who died wouldn't get the future. That was even something Ronald would say. Maybe he would say Mama was going to rise up and commune with the angels, but he couldn't say she was going to see fireworks on the Fourth of July. Or ever meet Tevor Souriante. Mike was going to be my mother's gift for the future. She had enjoyed moments with him while she was still alive. It was better than anything she could have put into her will. And I wouldn't have to split him with Ronald. His wife was another story, but I wasn't going to think about that.

IN THE PRACTICAL WORLD, a person like me was left with nothing but wishes and bets. I had no powers outside of myself that might fulfill my hopes unless I counted the government or people with money. Laughable books about secrets of self-empowerment came and went. I almost envied people who talked like Ronald: they could look at the ceiling with faith that dreams might come true. I was sure I'd heard someone besides just Ronald say, "Ask and it shall be given to you," and it was a quote from the Bible, definitely not anything a normal person would say to another normal person. Even most preachers had had to do some explaining about why God didn't answer prayers.

Part of me expected Ronald to call right away. That was the cynical part, the new detective part. The other part hoped my old self was right, that Ronald was a good Christian, that he wasn't a vulture, ready to swoop down. But I had become cynical for a reason. I was cynical because I'd been watching people for a long time, and I had to face it: most were about two steps away from doing something that could land them in jail for life. Ronald was possibly one of them. In fact, Ronald of childhood possibly had been my earliest lesson.

I made a bet with myself. I gave him until noon. I would give myself no penalty if I lost. I would reward myself by telling Klea if I won. Either way, I thought I'd know only about greed. Which wouldn't answer Mama's question, really.

He didn't disappoint.

I was in my studio the morning after the funeral, keeping my promise to myself of trying to paint no matter how I felt. I would switch brain sides in the afternoon and start making phone calls. I had a lot of business to take care of, and I planned to handle it all myself.

The phone rang. "What are you doing?" Ronald said.

I told him I was working in my studio.

"What's wrong with you?" he said. "Have you talked to the lawyer?"

There were many questions he could have asked. Had I done anything about securing the house? Had I been to the post office? Had I called the bank? There were a few tasks that needed handling right away. The lawyer could wait. Days and weeks and even months.

I said no, the lawyer could wait. So could the financial advisor, who was my ex-husband William. And the real estate agent. "Mama just died, you know."

He was silent for a moment, and I was surprised. I would have thought he'd call with an answer to that one. "Mother was a very efficient woman," he said finally. "I don't think she'd want you to be so cavalier about taking care of business."

"I don't think she'd want you to be so obviously greedy," I said.

"Is that what you're thinking? Is that what you're thinking? For all I know, she cut me out of her will completely. She's always favored you."

Well, she should have after you freaked out in the lawyer's office after Daddy died, I wanted to say.

I was aching to get back to a pencil sketch I'd started; the interruption was ruining my momentum. "Mama went out of her way to treat us as equals," I said.

"So you admit she liked you better," he said. He was a small boy. Poor Ronald.

"I'm working," I said softly. "I'm going to hang up now."

The phone rang three seconds after I hung up. He had me on speed dial. "So when are you calling her lawyer?" he said. "You want me to call him?"

"I have power of attorney," I told him. He was breaking my work spirit now. Pesky little brother. "I promise we'll see the will, but on my schedule. Now calm down, or I'll think you're waiting for a big bonanza."

I wanted to say that I knew he was waiting for his *fortune* to buy a church, but then Gracie would be promised hellfire or something more temporal. Unless Ronald thought Elizabeth was the one who talked, in which case he'd threaten something Elizabeth would consider suffering, but I would consider liberating, like divorce.

"I'm a man of God," he said. "I'm only living in the material world until the day I'm resurrected with my Lord. Money means nothing to me."

Aw, Ronald, come clean.

"You have a really nice house," I said.

"It's an all right house."

"If your friend Jesus dropped in and saw four bedrooms and three bathrooms and an in-ground pool and a Mercedes and an Infiniti—wait, scratch the cars; they're not part of the house—okay, granite countertops, and a cathedral ceiling in a 150-year-old house, well, even Jesus would flip your money-lenders' tables."

"Cesca, I don't make fun of what you believe in."

I apologized, without pointing out that I believed in nothing and now wondered if he did, too. "If you don't like money, why do you and Elizabeth traffic in death?" I said.

"We bring God to families."

Ronald had a hard time with arguments because I stored his history in my brain and one day would lay it out on the table in front of him. "You were doing it with no God whatsoever and not making money," I said. "You only started making money when you brought God into it."

"See?" he said.

"No," I said.

I HONESTLY HAD NOT known what was in the will. Mr. Alverson told Ronald that was the truth as far as he knew. Ronald was pacing all over the conference room in the law office, toeing chairs out of his way, and it was terribly embarrassing. Even though the walls were waist-high cherry wood wainscoting, then frosted glass almost to the ceiling, we were on a main walkway in the labyrinth of offices, and we were audible to anyone nearby. "I don't care what you think went on," Ronald was saying, "my mother probably showed her copy to Cesca. Or at the very least she told her exactly what she was planning to do.

"You want to tell me why on earth a woman would put this kind of responsibility in the hands of someone who doesn't even draw a straight line, much less add up a column of numbers? I'm the successful businessman. At the very least, she could have divided up the estate and sent us on our separate ways."

He looked at me with what could have been rage if he wasn't full of principles. "As it is now, you're going to be tied up with me for the rest of your natural life. You figure Mother thought of that?"

I gave him a gentle smile. "With one wobbly stroke of a pen, I can cut all ties," I said.

Ronald stopped and looked at me expectantly. "You would do that?" he said.

"I'm sure I'll do it one day," I told Ronald. I turned to Mr. Alverson. "You think Mama had a special reason for her decision?" Mr. Alverson looked at me with a "go on" expression. He knew who his client was, on top of being the executor of the estate.

If Ronald could behave for spirits he said he couldn't see, I wondered how he'd handle his older sister.

My mother had placed him in trust into perpetuity. And I was the trustee.

The estate, not including the house and its contents and her car, was valued at $5.6 million. The will didn't spell that out, of course. I had enough business sense, much to Ronald's surprise, to have contacted William, who was still our mother's financial advisor, and gained access to her account online so I could see what was in it at her time of death. His half was enough to buy a mighty fine church. I had a feeling my mother knew that. I also had a feeling that my mother had not lived a reasonable life only to see half of her money go into a building where she thought Ronald would dupe innocent people and especially dupe his not-so-innocent self.

Damn, I missed her.

Ronald was actually doing arithmetic on his fingers. "My God, with the house that's way over three million apiece," he said.

"Before estate taxes," I said. "And if you liquidate, don't forget capital gains."

"Who told you all that?" Ronald said.

I looked at him. He was serious. This was a man with a fine income, but he clearly had no investments. Any child who puts a thousand dollars into the stock market learns about capital gains the first time he changes his mind. As for estate taxes, all he needed to do was watch television. I restrained myself. I was closer to feeling sorry for him than I was to making him feel like a fool. "I can't remember not knowing that," I said. "And it has nothing to do with my marriage. If anything, William preferred to think of me as purely artistic."

"You really think I believe you?" Ronald said. He turned to the lawyer, who was willing to put up with it because of a phenomenon called billable hours, also a term I'd known for far too long. "This is another example of Mother favoring Cesca over me. I'm sure she gave

Cesca stocks all her life before she got married and taught her all about investing. No wonder she's so rich. I really should file suit."

"If your mother left you one dollar and the rest of her estate to your sister, you'd still have no grounds," Mr. Alverson said. "That's some free legal advice."

"That's beside the point," I said. "Every nickel I've ever invested came from my earnings." I turned to Ronald. "Why are you so angry at Mama? You know, she wasn't dumb. She could tell."

Ronald ignored me, spoke only to Mr. Alverson. It was like a divorce proceeding. "Do you know what quote-unquote 'work' Cesca does for her *living*?" He made air quotes. "It looks the same as it did when she was ten. She's just playing around and tricking people into thinking it's worth money. Believe me, I've tried to understand it, but what she does is not work."

As compared to walking ten steps behind murderers?

Mr. Alverson nodded. He owned two of my paintings. That's how I knew he liked my art. A person who bought one was currying favor. A person who bought two was sincere. "She's something of a genius," he said.

Ronald fell silent. If he ever was going to hear celestial voices, that was the time. His angels needed to tell him that his on-high mother had made Cesca his new deity, and he at least needed to pretend to worship her or he never was going to have the earthly goods his heart desired, no matter what prayers he might offer up, no matter how much he said he didn't care for money, because surely Cesca was as canny as her mother, and even if he prayed for her instant demise, she surely would have made provisions to have someone equally cold to take her place.

"I'm keeping the cat, you know," Ronald said.

"That's a good start," I said.

"All I'm saying is, I want to keep the cat," he said.

When it was time to leave, I told Mr. Alverson that it was time to rewrite my will. He didn't have much time, so I hand-wrote a codicil. I spelled out everything I hoped Ronald's angels would have told him if they were shifty little fellows.

CHAPTER TWELVE

I BELIEVED SHELLONDE. "IT'S NOT about the money, no," she said when she phoned. She was coming over to get her final check, but she also was coming to pay her respects. That's the way she put it, but, really, she was coming to grieve with me. And to be my friend. To say that we would know each other after we no longer had a reason to. I needed her. It was the price I was going to pay, of not having a mother, of long ago having declared autonomy, that women would have to have a little power in my life. The intrusion of men was frightening, but women would come in and out and do no harm.

Shellonde brought a fat bouquet of yellow lilies and yellow roses and full greens. "I figured fresh flowers would be good along about now," she said. Actually they would be the only flowers in my house. I had let Elizabeth take all the spoils from the funeral home. Ronald wanted them. I figured he needed them as evidence of something.

I made coffee with hot soy milk and a few drops of almond extract for both of us. Shellonde had grown to like my concoction when she'd worked at my house. She took a sip, and her eyes filled up with tears. "Good thing I'm not gonna drink this nowhere else," she said. "Make me think of your mama."

"It makes me think of me," I said, and she smiled.

I'd learned enough about Shellonde's life over the past few months to be able to ask the right questions. I didn't know all of her children's and grandchildren's names, but I knew several of their stories, open-ended stories, with a man or two running off to Texas and little girls who made honor roll. "I bought a book once called *Why Males Exist*," I told her. "I didn't read it. I just wanted it on my shelf because it was so skinny."

"Girl!" she said. "You too much. But you right. I can't think of one worth shit." Her eyes twinkled with joy over her cup as she took a gulp of coffee. "Wait," she said. "What happen with that doctor? You gonna tell me he useless as teats on a boar hog?"

I told her I didn't know, which was the truth. The thought of him filled me up, but that meant nothing.

"I know he let your mama die," Shellonde said. "But that's about him being a doctor. You can love a man even if he a failure."

What?

"Your brother tell him, Don't be coming around my sister if you kill my mama. Else you be wind up in hell. Bad enough you already a Jew."

"Is he insane?"

Shellonde looked at me with an expression that said she was sorry she'd ever opened her mouth.

"Sweetie," I said, reaching out and patting her arm, "Dr. Rosenthal kept my mother alive a lot longer than she had any hope of being. He's a great doctor. My brother, on the other hand, is a little out of control."

Shellonde started to cry. "You don't know how relieve that make me," she said. "I want it to be that way. I don't want your mama to die because of a bad doctor. And I sure don't want you running off with a man who can't take care of you."

I told her I wasn't running off with anybody. Didn't she remember that I had a hard time understanding why men existed?

"Doctors something else," she said.

"And married doctors are something else again."

"Why you doing that?"

"What."

"I'm not here to tell you what to do, no."

I glared at her, but with amusement. My expression said, *I'm sure you've noticed that nobody tells me what to do.*

"Oh, baby, I hope you not thinking I'm judging you because you messing with a married man. Shoot, that's his problem. Everybody know that a single person can't commit no adultery. Only a married person can break that ten commandment." Not Ronald, I thought. "I'm just thinking you deserve way better than half a man. A whole man barely enough; what a half man gonna get you?"

"Freedom?" I said.

Shellonde thought about that for a moment. "Freedom nice if you got the money for it."

I apologized. I knew Shellonde had washed parts of my mother that in another century I would have had to clean, and she had done it because she had no choice. I would never know, of course, whether privilege had made it possible for me to earn hundreds of thousands of dollars for my talent. Born into poverty, would I have been a scribbler on the side, laboring for a small wage, daydreaming of a rich man, knowing absolutely that no doctor ever would look at me? Or maybe becoming a nurse, or even a sitter like Shellonde, hoping to catch the eye of an MD, because I would gladly give up my freedom for such a man, no matter how homely or nasty?

"You don't need to say you sorry," Shellonde said. "I got no man in my house, and I know just what you talking about. A man is trifling. A man want your paycheck, and then he think you gonna cook and clean. Freedom worth every cent you make."

I flung myself back on the sofa, kicking my feet with pleasure.

"So I should let his wife have him?" I said.

"You getting the good parts?" she said.

I had a feeling she meant anatomically. To me the good parts were something else. "We have the same interests," I said. "And he's smart. And he's a doctor. He can write prescriptions."

Her eyes flew wide open.

"No, I'm not selling drugs."

"You like him," she said. "I see it on your face. That go a long way."

It was pretty much all that mattered.

I WAS AT MIKE'S OFFICE when the call came. We had figured out that the easiest way to meet was for me to go there on Sunday when he didn't see patients, and the building was empty, and he was supposed to be doing rounds across the street. We could go into an examining room and use one of the tables. I didn't know if it excited him, using that little room where old people whined about their compressed discs and shingles. But for me, it was more of a chance to play voyeur than if I were touring the back rooms of a celebrity home. Patients never were let loose in doctors' offices. Patients never were allowed to manipulate examining tables or move the stepstools, or turn the lights on and off. Or look in the cabinet. It was definitely the narrowest bed on which I'd ever made love, but I never noticed. I pretended there were patients in the waiting room, that nurses were moving briskly in the hallway, that the pager would go off any second, and I was lost in the fast, frenetic lovemaking until he yelled out so loud I was sure his receptionist would hear him, though of course she was at home in front of her television set.

That day my cell phone went off just seconds after I'd pulled my clothes on. I was trying to run my fingers through my hair casually, as if I didn't care how I looked. Mike was cleaning up, knowing the maintenance crew had already been there on Friday night. No one would look for damp tissues in the trash can, but still he pushed them all the way down.

It was Elizabeth on the phone.

I told her I would have to call her back. I must have been breathless because she said, "Did I catch you in the middle of something?" and innuendo was in her voice. It seemed to me that the innuendo connoted no lovemaking in her life for quite a long time.

Sex, maybe.

"Actually, yes."

"Can you get away? Like right now?" She said it with understanding, as if she would accept it if I said no, but she hoped desperately that I would say yes.

I was going to leave in a few minutes anyway. Mike and I never had more than a few minutes. So far the limited time made me very happy. "Probably. Why?"

"I have to talk to you. He's going to kill you."

Mike was behind me, leaning against me, his head next to mine, hearing what came through the phone, even though I wasn't on speaker. He took my shoulders and turned me around. I could read his expression better than I could figure out what he was saying. I told Elizabeth to hold on. I gave him a questioning look.

"She's speaking literally," he whispered. I frowned. "I mean it."

"That's just an expression," I said to Elizabeth. "Right?"

"No, he really says he wants to kill you."

"Oh, come on," I said. "Even I know that's one of his ten commandments. For Chrissakes, there was even a big billboard saying, 'Thou shalt not kill. God.'" For a long time, a billboard at Martin Luther King Boulevard and Claiborne Avenue had those five words in black on white, so huge it was impossible to miss, screaming out to Central City and everyone heading past to the east. Ronald didn't need a billboard. He really didn't even need religion. He'd grown up in a moral, humanistic household. His sister didn't kill animals for food.

"I don't think that's on his mind right now," Elizabeth said.

Mike was whispering, "Go, go," and I told Elizabeth to name a place where we could meet. I was amused more than anything. Ronald refused to say "fuck," so I couldn't imagine that eternal damnation for committing murder wouldn't scare the bejeezus out of him. Killing me straight out was different from ordering a brine-bloated turkey. He'd wind up in a burning pit with Jews and people like me. Unless, of course, he didn't believe himself.

I CHOSE THE COFFEE SHOP at The Rink. It was close to where I left Mike, but it was nowhere near Ronald's house or office. If Elizabeth was sneaking around behind her husband's back, she surely didn't want to get caught by him. It would be just her luck that he would accuse her of meeting another man and committing adultery, when in fact she was just trying to head off a simple murder. And a simple murder that would point at him as the only logical suspect. I wasn't a person who made people angry. Some artists had enemies, but I wasn't one of them. No, the only person who had damned me to hell recently in a public forum was my brother.

I got a soy latte and a bagel with jam. I could trust bagels. Elizabeth had no worries. She had a mocha latte and a blueberry muffin.

"So why do you think he wants to kill me?" I said, without lowering my voice.

"I just want you to let him have his money."

I flopped my arms down onto the table. "You're a helluva negotiator," I said.

She smiled, and I decided right then that I was going to get Tizzy back.

"Maybe half a million?" she said.

"You need to start high if you expect a low amount." In the art world, you kept bidding upwards. But I wasn't going to counter with a higher offer.

"Oops," she said and gave me a pleading look.

"If I don't give him money, is he really going to kill me?"

"He's furious."

"Isn't that a deadly sin?" Here I was again, trying to remember the Seven Deadly Sins, using the dwarves as touchstones. Sloth always came up first, but rage was never far behind. Sleepy and Grumpy.

"Not compared to murder," she said. "He's come right out and said if you don't give him his money, he's going to kill you."

I hadn't outweighed Ronald for many years, but I'd always considered him puny and unathletic, not to mention unhandy—he'd always had to pay carpenters and landscapers and electricians and plumbers. Definitely not the type to stab or strangle or beat me. I knew in a fistfight I could take him.

"Did he put you up to this?"

"God, no," she said. She looked surprised by the possibility. And unaware of having used her Lord's name, possibly in vain.

Tizzy hadn't touched her muffin. She'd hardly touched her coffee. She looked a little nauseated. She might have been living as what my mother called a "leapin' screamin' Christian," but I suddenly had a feeling her old self was still in there somewhere. It was buried deep, but it seemed to me that murder was getting on at least one remaining raw nerve.

This matter of killing people was going to make things easy for me—as long as I wasn't killed. It all came down to thou-shalt-not-kill. Oh, and a smattering of thou-shalt-not-covet. Ronald said he bought the entire list. Tizzy might not have picked up on the coveting part, but murder was hard to ignore. Maybe not murder by salt and screaming, but definitely murder with a deadly weapon.

Since my mother's death I'd been looking for a new closest person, and for one moment even had considered Ronald. Now Tizzy seemed a good candidate. But I had to proceed gingerly. She was still Ronald's. He and I long ago had learned to draw a line through the entire universe and tried never to step over to the other's side. It would take a while for Tizzy to get her sense of humor back. "What are you suggesting I do?" I said. Test.

"Give him the money."

That could mean anything. She could be on his side; she could be on my side.

"Why?"

Tizzy didn't answer right away. *Why* was the right question.

"Because he wants it?"

"Try again," I said.

She scanned the shop. Still Perkin' was not a hangout for right-wing religious fanatics. It might have had its share of die-hard Republicans, but they all went to the Episcopal Church. No one was going to rat her out to Ronald. And Ronald himself wasn't going to walk in. We were in the dead center of the Garden District. Generally, sloppy crime scenes didn't happen there. And if they did, people had paid help who didn't pray while they cleaned up. At least not out loud.

"He really wants to kill you," she said. "I mean, he has a gun."

"He bought a goddamn gun?"

She didn't flinch at *goddamn*. "He's owned a gun forever. He's got a license to carry a concealed weapon. He says if he's going to a crime scene, it means he's going where people commit crimes. And he says self-defense is surely all right with God."

She studied my face. There was a tiny smile at the corners of her mouth because she knew what was coming. "How does he make this shit up?" I said.

She shrugged and almost let a smile break out. "I wonder if you've just answered all my questions without my having to ask them," I said. "Though I really would like to know *why*."

The smile didn't break. She shrugged, and to me that meant, *Aw, come on, Cesca.*

Ronald wanted to murder me over money. God or no God.

"You know, I'm not handing over half a million dollars just because a hundred-sixty-pound man waves a gun in the air," I said. "This is why my mother put me in charge. Just to begin with, you can't even buy a terribly big house for that price—what kind of church does he think he's going to get?"

"It'd be a down payment."

I folded my arms and sat back. Let her make this pitch. "And what's the monthly note going to be? I didn't know churches generate revenue. Are you allowed to project income for a church? Sounds a little crass."

"Oh, Ronald says churches make millions. That's what he expects anyway."

I grinned. "So this is an investment."

She shrugged. She wasn't looking at me. "Not completely."

"Come on, Tizzy, you can talk to me."

"No, I can't."

"Okay, you can't talk to me, but you can say a lot."

TIZZY HAD BEEN TREMBLING with fear when we left the coffee shop. She didn't trust me at all. I hadn't asked her one more question about the church. I'd changed the subject, to Gracie's art and Levi's attitude and Klea's boyfriend. But all along Tizzy had been staring at me, waiting for me to hurt her. "You can trust me," I told her when we hugged goodbye. "I know how dangerous he is." She protested that he wasn't dangerous, and I said, "I promise I won't do anything to hurt you, okay?" She probably went home with her head filled with worry anyway.

I waited a day to phone Ronald. "So Tizzy says I need to give you a half million for a church."

"Yes," he said, and I was glad we weren't face to face.

"Well, I think I need to take a look at this property."

"I don't see why that's necessary."

"Don't push your luck, buddy, or I'll hang up this phone so fast you'll be damn sorry."

"I suppose we can make arrangements," he said. I imagined someone he wanted to impress was listening in the background. Though I couldn't imagine who that would be since he was on the landline in his office, and no one there needed impressing. I'd say he was trying to impress God, but I didn't know anything about that little friendship. "However, you should be made aware that this kind of real estate is different from residential and commercial. You can't impose the same rules and regulations when you negotiate."

"Seems commercial to me," I said.

We met the listing agent the next afternoon. I needed to use MapQuest to find the church because it was in a part of Kenner where I never went. Actually, the only place in Kenner that I knew at all was the airport, but that was true of most people born uptown. In my lifetime the city had expanded into places that had been sweet country when I was a child. And here was a church that had been built long ago enough to be ready for its second incarnation, if I could use a life word.

I walked in, and my first question was, "So, do you plan on a television show?"

It wasn't so much a church as an auditorium. There was no pulpit, there was a stage, and surrounding it for about 300 degrees was stadium seating rising a good three stories. A little Superdome. Poor Ronald was expecting to attract hundreds? Thousands? All paying every discretionary nickel to fulfill his dreams. I bet he was going to have a bright blue satin robe.

CHAPTER THIRTEEN

RONALD WAS SURE HE had finally figured out how to frighten me into submission. Send me a message that he would kill me, and he could get anything out of me. No doubt he was wondering why he hadn't thought of that before, though of course he had tried it dozens of times over the early years, with a baseball bat or a Cub Scout knife. He'd been so scrawny that I'd laughed at him, which only had made him angrier.

Feeling triumphant, he called to dictate when we would sit down to talk terms. He wanted a morning meeting.

"Hold on," I said. "I paint in the mornings."

"Well, mornings are best for me."

"Then you're out of luck."

"You are so inflexible, Cesca!"

"This is your church, not mine," I said.

He suggested a Saturday, and I said all right, but not in the morning, and that worked. I would go to his house, because Tizzy would be there, and possibly Gracie and Levi, and I was going to make Ronald angry. At my house or in a public place, Ronald might actually shoot me. He would miss, but he would try.

We sat down in the living room with nothing to eat or drink. Good for Tizzy, doing a little Betty Friedan number. But Ronald called her from the back of the house to join us. Someone needed to take notes and be a witness, he said. "No problem," his good wife said.

"So all you need to do is give me a check for the full amount, no lawyers, and I'll put it in my account, and then I'll have the funds for the act of sale," Ronald said. "Sound good?"

I turned to Tizzy. "Write this down." Then I turned to Ronald. "Are you nuts?"

He was genuinely surprised.

I gave him the most obvious information, that Mama hadn't been dead anywhere near long enough for the will to be probated, so there was no way for the estate to be liquidated in any big way. Any liquid funds right now were being used to handle bills accrued during Mama's final days, and certainly there was no obscene amount like $500,000 lying around for foolishness.

"Oh."

I projected into the future, a future in which that church property would surely still be on the market. I couldn't imagine there were too many charismatic Christian preachers who saw glory in suburban souls—and whose mothers would die and leave enough money to buy that tiny coliseum.

I told him I had talked to William, who was staying on as financial advisor. Ronald looked out of the corner of his eye to see whether Tizzy was writing this down. She was. It was to my benefit. I had a plan.

It was complicated, but even Ronald got the drift. I would not sell any of the investments in the estate. That meant I wouldn't give him any cash. Instead, I would help him secure a loan for the full value of the church, which was a cool two and a half million minus what he could get the agent to chop off. The loan would be guaranteed by the estate.

I laid it out slowly so that Tizzy could get it down. "I don't get it," Ronald said. "I mean, I get it, but I don't get it."

"Basically you'd be borrowing two-thirds of your inheritance, and there'd be no problem as long as you paid the note every month," I said.

"That's ridiculous," Ronald said, turning red in the face. "Are you sure William isn't making money off this so he can give it to Klea?"

"The last thing I want is for William to be happy," I said.

"You don't lose a nickel," Tizzy said to him.

"What do you know?" he said.

"Evidently the same thing I know," I said.

I wondered how he survived in business. His mathematical sense had been terrible in school, and it hadn't improved even with a lot of dollars attached.

"The point is that I wouldn't be risking the estate," I said. "Of course, I'm counting on that huge investment paying off, or you and I wind up with a big empty church that we have to unload. Pretty fucking insane, but I'll make sure it's out of your half."

"Why won't you just give me the down payment?"

"Because it's a bad idea."

"It is not." Ronald stood up and approached. He stood there hovering over me. I knew no martial arts, but I could always jump up and hit his chin with the top of my head and surprise him into a long confusion. He put his hand on his back hip for effect. As if I'd believe he had a gun. I imagined a hypodermic full of some lovely sodium compound, the kind the government used in Texas. Was being a woman who stood between Ronald and money a capital crime, punishable by sodium overload?

I leaned back on the sofa, splayed my arms out at my sides.

He didn't move. I didn't move. Finally Tizzy said, "I've already got two children. I don't need one more."

I stifled a laugh. Completely, the way I had been able to do as a child, when it had been absolutely necessary. It involved not breathing. Ronald was looking me in the eye, but he saw nothing.

He turned toward Tizzy. "Don't act that way with me."

Tizzy didn't move.

"Oh, no," Ronald said to me. "You tried to poison my kids' minds. You need to stay away from my wife."

"Aw, come on," I said. I forgot he wanted to kill me. When Ronald was outnumbered, I sometimes softened up. I was still lying back.

"I have a gun," he said, then stomped out of the room. My little brother.

THE NEXT PERSON I heard from was the real estate agent. She made it clear that from then on she would work with me, and Ronald would be out of the picture. I told her I thought that was a little strange, because I was not what she would call a motivated buyer. "Let's just assume that you want this property with all your heart and soul," she said with more perkiness than I ever allowed.

"Let's just say that I'm willing to allow this transaction to take place if the price is good enough, and I'll handle the paperwork," I said. Then I gave her a lowball offer: $1.8 million. The next day she came back and said the seller accepted it, and I was annoyed as hell with myself. I'd thought that taking off over a quarter of the asking price was playing rough. I would always have to wonder how much lower I could have gone. But then it sounded so good that I'd never have to tell Ronald. He'd think I'd been a wonderful sister. I was saving him a lot of money. He could shave off a hundred or so fools from his mailing list.

I even got him 3.25 percent interest rate. It was based on my mother's excellent credit. Of course this was all on hold until the will was probated. But heaven could wait for Ronald's earthly sure thing. Heaven was going to have to wait.

"This isn't what I wanted," Ronald said when I called to tell him what I thought was excellent news.

"Thank you would be nice," I said.

"Not when you've gone against my expressed wishes."

"The last time I saw you, you walked out of the room like you were the lord, master, and executioner, and the next thing I knew, the real estate agent was calling me," I said. "When an agent of any kind calls me, I take that as a signal that I'm supposed to negotiate on my own terms."

"Not when I told you what to do."

I paused for effect. "You want to tell me when in the past four decades it has ever occurred that I am supposed to listen to one thing you have to tell me?"

"Women listen to me," he said. "All women know they're subordinated to me. The head of woman is man; it says so in First Corinthians. I live in a different world than the microcosm you've made for yourself. So you have to forgive me if I didn't know you were going to be different."

"God, you are so full of it," I said. "I swear, sometimes it's hard to admit we're related."

He was silent for a moment. "You'll never understand," he said finally. "You may think we had the same parents, but we didn't. My parents failed me. Jesus never has failed me."

But Jesus found him at a crime scene.

"Listen," I said, "forget about my signing off on this church. I was trying to let you do your own thing without violating everything Mama stood for. But you couldn't ease up for one second. Oh, no, Ronald has to try to play lord and master over Cesca when he ought to know better."

"You think you can control me with money?" he said. "Money? That's just in this world. I have the power of the Lord. You don't scare me. I'll find a way. To begin with, I'm going to talk to my parishioners and find an attorney who'll make you sorry you were ever born. You already opened up the purchase on the church. You can't just shut it down. You've been damned to hell once, and you'll stay damned to hell until you find your way."

Did he remember to whom he was speaking? This wasn't my language. The power of the Lord and even of his attorneys didn't frighten me.

I spoke in the calmest voice I could muster. "Did it ever occur to you to say something like 'thank you' or 'I apologize'? You don't even have to be a good Christian to say those things. Just a good person."

"I don't need to say those things. You need to say those things."

I reminded him that I got $700,000 taken off the price of the church, more than the amount he'd asked for to begin with. And the interest rate was surely less than half what he was paying on his home mortgage. That was good for a thank-you. As for the apology, since I wasn't his wife or staff, did he honestly think that he could order me around? I hadn't seen him ordering his mother around, and I was all he had left in the respecting department.

"I hate arguing with you," he said. "It's impossible to talk to a crazy person. Here." The next thing I knew, Tizzy was on the phone. I asked her how long she'd been watching his side of the conversation. "Long enough," she said, meaning nothing to me, and surely nothing to him.

"Tell him I have just one question for him," I said.

"G'head."

"Remember the day Mama died?"

"Sure."

"Well, maybe three minutes after I left your house, Ronald changed his mind about taking my mother off life support. That's kind of a big decision to make in three minutes, y'know? I would like very much to know what in God's name you could've possibly said to make him change his mind in three lousy minutes."

"We'll have to get together soon, won't we?" she said.

"He's right there, isn't he?"

"I look forward to it, too."

"Good luck thinking up a question," I said.

"No problem," she said.

"G'night, Tizzy."

THE IMPULSE TO PHONE my mother was strange. I knew she wasn't there. But in my mind I went so far as to imagine the connection. She at her house, I at mine, the call going between us. I realized that was the way I was with all phone calls, sensing a channel of air or thought or words between me and the other person in a particular geographical place. So when I needed right then to talk to my mother, for one split second I sensed that channel, even though it had been gone for a while. Then I realized I had nothing, and nothing to replace it.

I wanted to call Mike. But I had no reason to call him. He wasn't even my doctor. I didn't have his e-mail address. This was a time when I wished I believed in the power of prayer. But even that wish was no good. All I had to rely on was hoping and doing, and hoping wasn't of any particular value. Though my mother often said that hoping might have to do with subliminal knowledge of the possible. I hoped he would call. I would do something. I would call Andy. I didn't like this. With any other man I could do the phoning. I only had a small part of this man, if I had any part of him at all. Sort of the way Ronald had with his money.

I called Andy and told him my mother was extremely dead now. He liked that. Death only bothered Andy if people wanted him to be bothered. "You're such a sweetheart," he said. "I'm terribly sorry. Extremely sorry."

"Dr. Rosenthal can have his show extremely soon," I said.

"This is Andy you're talking to. I'm sure even when you're playing doctor that's not what you call him."

"Feel free to call him Mike," I said.

"Oh, heavens, no, I couldn't do that."

I didn't mention that I'd learned to call him Mike. I told him he could do what I did, which was to call him nothing. Andy was fun to leave guessing. I gave him Mike's cell number.

"People don't call doctors' cell numbers," he said.

"Then why do they have them?"

"Oh, Cesca, talking to you is not like talking to anyone else. I swear, if I were straight—"

"You'd still be too old and ugly for me," I said. "And besides, you don't have an MD."

He laughed.

My phone rang about five minutes after I hung up with Andy. It was an ambiguous amount of time.

I asked him what was new.

"I'm missing you," Mike said.

That was still ambiguous. Andy still might have called in the interim.

"Is anything new?" I said.

His silence had hurt feelings in it, maybe real, maybe not.

"I've missed you, too," I said, just in case.

He said he wanted to come over, and I wasn't coy. I needed him too much to put him off. When could he come? He could come as fast as his car could travel. I ran my fingers through my hair. I'd looked neat with a good kind of asymmetry the last time I'd passed reflective glass. "Please," I said.

As soon as he was off the phone, I dialed Andy. "Did you call him?"

"Don't tell me you're going to be that kind of agent," he said. "You and I just talked ten minutes ago. I've got a life, you know."

"So you didn't call him?"

"No, baby, I didn't call him. You sound glad. What is your problem?"

"If you didn't call him, it means he called on his own. You're the best!"

"Oh, sweet Jesus, I had no idea I was playing yenta when I signed on for this," he said.

"If you haven't figured out by now that I don't do much out of the kindness of my heart, you haven't been paying attention."

Andy snorted. "You can fool some people, but you can't fool old Andy. Cesca Price might walk around town acting like the world's biggest cynic, but I happen to know you've got a heart of pure gold. If this man were a troll under a bridge, you'd be in here with his work, mark my words."

"Shut up, or I'll tell everybody you're a homosexual," I said.

"Oh, please, no, not that, anything but that, Br'er Fox," he said.

I wondered why I didn't do a local exhibit. It was so much more personal. I told him about the Tevor Souriante interview, which was beginning to make me a little nervous. I was curious about what he would say. "Ah, baby girl, you're too big for me," he said.

"That's not what I hoped you'd say."

"You'll get over it," he said.

A COMMITTED DEAL WITH Andy was a gift. I was going to give it to Mike while he was with me, no matter what. But I had to admit I wanted gifts from him, too. That Kandinsky necklace was an enduring one, and it was full of thought, but it had no self in it. Andy looked as if he had no self in him, either, but he required personal risk. Coming over and parking in front of my house was something, I told myself; at least it was to Mike. He didn't know my neighbors. Maybe they all were friends of his. I wasn't sure what I wanted from Mike, but I figured I'd feel good if I got it.

It took him only a few seconds. Mike said he came to sit and talk and see how I was doing. Maybe he was lying, but I believed him. Maybe he had read somewhere that this was the best way to lure a woman into making love, or rather into throwing herself at him for raw, thoughtless sex. But I wasn't going to think. I just wanted to talk to someone who liked me.

"I'd like to be a cheerful orphan," I said. We were seated side by side on my most comfortable sofa, sinking into thick pillows.

"You're entitled to a bad mood."

"You wouldn't go screaming out into the night?"

"You might paint like someone with supernatural powers, but I do think you're human."

I cocked my head.

And he knew what I was asking. "Oh, come on. I mean like in the comic books. I read your mother's obituary."

I forgot he was Jewish. Jews had the Old Testament full of crazy stories about Moses parting the waters and talking snakes and an angel telling Abraham to leave Isaac alone, but the only people who took that stuff literally these days were people like Ronald's followers.

"You weren't at the funeral." I said it matter-of-factly, with no blame.

"But I might as well have been. I bet half the crackpots in the city clipped that write-up. I've never seen anything like it."

Twenty florid lines about my very recently good Christian mother and what she had found in Jesus, then twenty lines in another style about her appreciation of local arts and civic organizations and her love of her grandchildren, then one line about the private burial. Nothing about cause of death, which was what I always looked for in an obituary. *Son goes out of control* was the loose translation of the autopsy, but even I couldn't find a way to put that in the paper. And of course only some kind of confession would point to brine in the veins as a contributing factor. Though by the time Mama died, I imagined her blood to be as clean as spring water.

"I hurt all over, missing her," I said.

He couldn't scooch over on that sofa, so he stood up and sat down again, right next to me, and put his arm around my shoulder. I leaned against him and let myself relax. He was giving me the gift I wanted. This was all about me. Nothing was ever all about me.

I started to cry, but silently, and he didn't see, didn't know. I wasn't sad, more like grateful. He kissed my hair. It was a caring kiss, not a taking kiss. I tried not to tremble. He stroked my hair, held me, did nothing more, until I stopped crying and could pull back. I thought maybe I'd had that kind of solace before, because it seemed remotely familiar, but that was far in the past. "Thank you," I said, with a full voice.

He made no move to make love, or even kiss me on the mouth. He wasn't taking anything. I was almost tempted not to tell him about Andy, to let him do all the giving. But the news was so good. I waited until I led him to the door. "You're going to get a wonderful call on your cell today," I said.

"I hope it's from you," he said, and meant it.

"Indirectly it's from me," I said after he was out the door.

CHAPTER FOURTEEN

RONALD SAID IT WOULD be fair to charge the estate if he sent a team from JesusCleanup over to empty out our mother's house. I told him never mind, that $600 for a mop and a prayer was completely unnecessary when half of that money was mine, and half of that service was for him.

It would be a lot more fun to ask Mama's sitters if they wanted to come join me while I worked, if they didn't have new jobs. They all had new jobs, and they all didn't care. Sitting was different, they said. They'd still come. Besides, I had to work in short shifts. There was a limit to how much of my past I could face in a day. I would work in the afternoon, after my time in the studio. If I wanted to keep going after four hours, I would get Tizzy. I suggested that Ronald not charge me for her time. If he did, I would prorate what I earned for my work and charge him for my time. I told him he wouldn't want to live with the kind of information he'd have to see.

I was going slowly. Based on professional experience, Ronald thought I should gut the house in two days.

"You may be a professional locust, but I'm not," I said. "This house is personal."

He was flummoxed because I said we couldn't sell anything. He wanted to sell everything. The contents of the house were probably worth hundreds of thousands of dollars and should have been divided carefully between us for our houses. *After* being valued by an appraiser. It was all antiques, but Ronald said he preferred cash so he could redecorate with sleek contemporary design pieces like the ones he saw featured in *Inside Out.*

"I can't imagine one of those people at your half of the funeral liking that kind of house," I told him.

"I'm not inviting the people I serve to my house," he said. "Though those people would think Mother's antiques make no sense."

He had nothing to hide. His children were good little Christians even when no one saw them. Jesus was taking care of Ronald because Jesus had saved him, but Ronald was taking care of the children just fine all by himself: in New Orleans, being taken care of was what showed up in the records at the Whitney Bank.

Ronald wanted to live in two worlds. And he wouldn't be the first. It was possible to make the society pages by selling vampires, Mercedes, and fried chicken, so why not godliness? Mindless or true; it made no difference. Of course, his kids never would have the pedigree that came from a parent who practiced law or real estate development, but his great-grandchildren would. In New Orleans money eventually got old.

Gracie loved her Gammy's house. I'd seen her when she was a tiny girl walk through claiming she was a princess in a palace, begging my mother to give her the grandfather clock. I remembered the clock chiming on Cinderella. I'd thought it had eyes.

I worked at all the small things, the papers and the consumables. My mother hadn't expected to die. Whoever was helping me on a particular day took home whatever was in the pantry or in the cabinet or closet we attacked. "I'm giving away linens," I told Ronald. "Are they used?" he said. I told him yes, whether they were or not. It was better that these women take them home and give them away than that Ronald get a few dollars off his tax return. He would never use them himself, because linens were for women. As were canned goods and over-the-counter painkillers and unguents. I did the papers myself. One at a time, struggling when I threw away anything with her handwriting. I wondered if she knew when she wrote on those pages that one day I would have this trouble. I had a feeling that she did, and that she expected I would throw such pages away just as she had in life. I found an unopened packet of file folders, to me evidence that she planned to do what she'd left to me. I made categories. I tried to save as little as possible. Klea was going to have to throw all of this away one day. Mama saved a lot of sentimental stuff, clippings and notes. Not so much business; in fact very little business that ever needed tending to again. She would never need to balance her checkbook.

Each day when I went home, I took away everything that needed to go into recycling or trash. I left the house looking exactly as it had when my mother left it. I would empty out everything that was closed, clear off all surfaces. Sheets and soup were easy. Then one day I made Tizzy come over: I said we were going to figure out what to do about china and silver and paintings. I told her this was the first time I needed her. She told me she'd told Ronald, who'd reminded her that the family always had dinner together. I said I'd give her the number of Five Happiness Chinese Restaurant on Carrollton Avenue. They even had a reserved parking spot for pickup.

"Ronald talks a big game for you," Tizzy said. "He's not a total cave man."

We looked each other in the eye, each knowing the other was picturing poor little Ronald covered in hair and wielding a club, and both filled with unexpected sweet amusement. "Okay," I said.

"What makes you think I have any say in what you do with all her good stuff?" Tizzy said when we had flopped back on Mama's French directoire sofa that was designed more for sitting with one's knees pressed together.

I opened my eyes wide at her. When we were young friends, that was all it took. The message was that this wasn't the reason she was there.

"Oh!"

"Really, I don't want to screw around," I said. "Ronald probably only wants a price tag on everything. Unless I've got the Holy Grail in the kitchen cabinet, he doesn't care what goes where. So no need for dividing up."

Tizzy wasn't even trying to give me a neutral look. She was slipping into a smile.

"So we can get down to real business?" I said.

The only way I can describe what came next is to say that Tizzy's face kind of popped open. "Okay, I'll spill it," she said. "I told you I'd tell you, so we're alone, so I'll tell you."

And then she told me what happened in the three minutes between my leaving their house with Ronald having refused to have my mother taken off life support, and Ronald calling my cell phone to tell me he'd changed his mind.

"I said to him, 'Goddammit,' yeah, I said 'goddammit,' 'goddammit, you know you want your mother dead; you probably made her drop dead, the autopsy said so, and if you want all that money, you might as well get it now. You want to get really rich, you need to start out rich, and you know it.'"

"Holy shit," I said. "You didn't."

I noticed she said nothing about the Thanksgiving recipes. But *she'd* done the cooking.

"Actually I did," she said. "Ronald wasn't that extreme, but close. He was so upset after your father died and didn't leave him a penny directly. So what's it eventually boil down to? He's going to get what his father deprived him of when his mother dies. He's waiting for his mother to die. No, he's waiting for his mother to drop dead."

"Aw, come on," I said. "For starters, he didn't need more damn money."

"I know, I know. Jesus takes care of him," Tizzy said. "But clearly not enough. I'd say he's a little confused. I know I'm a little confused. To say the least. I'm getting kind of sick of all this, if you want to know the truth."

"You know whose side I'm on."

She actually looked up at me to be sure I meant it. The poor woman had been messed around with for so long that she'd grown to believe Ronald when he said he was her only true advocate. He had taken her away from me, and she'd come to believe I respected him for that. Part of his and my divided universe law. If she tried to break from him, she thought, I would say she was wrong, and he was right. But I could never be on his side unless he were running for office against a Nazi or maybe a Republican. Never.

The sofa definitely wasn't a seat for hugging, but I slid over and put my arms around Tizzy and held her for a long time.

We went through all the china and silver and decorative crystal and paintings. I told Tizzy that as executor I was acting on behalf of the grandchildren. I had no clue what was going to become of Klea and Levi, but it seemed to me that Gracie had all the makings of an aesthete who would one day cherish her grandmother's treasures. If her father sold all these carefully collected antiques of the future, just so he could be some kind of little man of Jesus with a lot of cash of New Orleans, he would be robbing his own child.

I didn't know what to think when we came into Mama's television room where she had both of her Rodrigue paintings. They weren't a matter of settling the estate; they were a matter of settling an unresolved bet. I couldn't claim one without knowing if I'd won. Yet one was rightfully mine. I would want the Dolores and Pepper painting because it was two identical blue dogs that Mama had said were the two of us. But the other Rodrigue portrayed Cajun women under an oak tree, and Ronald would not want to own it. "Want to put off splitting these?" I said.

I would rent a climate-controlled storage locker for the grandchildren. I would get one on a high floor so no Katrina could destroy their legacy. I knew Ronald would say the estate would be paying out storage fees instead of collecting interest, and I would counter that that was too bad, that some things didn't have a price tag. And besides, if his children and mine grew up to be craven and chose to sell everything, they would get a lot more money than he would get now, even allowing for inflation, so there.

Tizzy just shimmered with love for me that afternoon. She still loved her old struggling Ronald, and maybe her generous Jesus, and she wasn't going to do anything rash. All of this was unspoken, but I knew her so well, and I was satisfied. I might even tell her my secrets one day soon. Once I figured out exactly what my secrets were.

I CALLED WILLIAM THE next day before I went to Mama's house. We got along fine. He couldn't complain that I had replaced him with nothing. He had been what I'd told myself was a nowhere man, filled as my mother had made me with meaning from the Beatles. A well behaved man, doing his job and coming home and voting. But he could not understand what I did in my studio and took me down to Jackson Square to see what artists on the fence did because that made sense to him. On art he was the opposite of Ronald, and their arguments about my work were so wrongheaded that I always left the room. William gave Klea blonde hair that she enjoyed, and he gave me good financial advice.

The main reason I had stayed married to William as long as I had was that he had no use for Ronald. To me that had meant, for a very long time, that William had to be a man of wisdom and discernment, and all I had to do was wait until I matured into discovering his depth. Of course I finally figured out that anyone with any sense would find Ronald to be somewhat foolish, and that was when I unloaded William, but our shared annoyance with Ronald was still a fun bond.

"We probably have to rethink this whole Ronald plan," I said to him.

"I hear you're dating somebody," he said.

"What?"

"How am I supposed to work with you when you're dating somebody?"

William never had recovered from the divorce. He had

misunderstood me, so I had walked away from him, and all he knew was that he wasn't good enough. He still wanted me back because, it seemed to me, it would prove something.

I told him I wasn't dating anyone. For the world, it was true. So far I knew nothing about Mike's wife, and even if she turned out to be a nasty spoiled woman, she needed not to know. Whatever was going on with Mike wasn't a fact. And it certainly wasn't dating.

"That's not what I hear."

"You're going to have to give me your source," I said. I was afraid of the answer. Whatever liaison William had was going to be an unpleasant surprise. Unless it was Klea. Possibly Klea would tell him to make him feel bad. "Is it Klea?"

"My daughter wouldn't want to hurt me like that," he said. "She likes to upset me sometimes, but she's not *that* bad. I know about her boyfriend, and that's upsetting enough."

"Why?"

"Don't change the subject, Chess."

"So who's going around telling you I'm dating someone? Which, by the way, I have the perfect right to do. And also which has nothing to do with your handling this portfolio."

I hoped he'd think that over. He earned tens of thousands of dollars managing my mother's money. She'd told me so.

"Your brother has seen everything," he said. "He came to me to give me his side of this arrangement. You weren't on the level with me."

"Have you lost your fucking mind?"

"Why did you feel a need to control Ronald's half of the estate? Why won't you just give him his money and let him do what he wants with it? He says your boyfriend is a doctor. I bet the guy is rich and thinks he can give you advice. Well, I'm here to tell you that an MD does not know everything."

"Have you lost your fucking mind?" I said again.

"Did I hit a raw nerve?" he said with the even tone that had helped me throw him out.

"The person who told me to keep Ronald under control was you. You! I don't talk to anybody about my finances except you. At least now that Mama's gone."

"So you admit you have a boyfriend."

"Have you lost your fucking mind?"

"Saying it over and over again does not make it more effective," he said quietly.

"You have lost your fucking mind," I said. "You probably plan to go to Ronald's church."

At that he stopped to think. Even William had his limits. That had been the reason I'd kept him longer than was reasonable. Looking askance at Ronald could go a remarkably long way. But not far enough for me to want William back.

"All right, there are some things I don't want to know," he said.

"For Ronald to come telling you stories that he knows will upset you is not playing fair," I said. I leaned hard on the word stories to calm him. "Ronald is in the business of making people believe whatever he tells them. Remember that."

William laughed. He liked me. That was his problem. Right then, I liked me, too. Even if I was something of a liar.

William's head was now clear of everything but numbers. He had reverted to his natural state. So I told him essentially what I had learned from Tizzy, that Ronald was buying this church as an investment, a moneymaker. He expected to get filthy, Daddy-and-Jesus, stinking rich.

Yes, William knew something to that effect, that Ronald wanted to fill up his church so it would pay for itself and more. That's why he, William, had thought using no cash was such a good idea. Hundreds of ingenuous believers would come each Sunday and tithe in the basket, and every month that cash would more than meet the note owed to Merrill Lynch. Ronald could pay himself a glory-to-God salary.

"And how is that different from cleaning up houses full of the blood and guts from dead people?" I said. "Zero difference. Zero difference!"

William laughed again. Damn. I'd forgotten that he was a good audience. That wasn't enough though. A laughing cyborg who looked down on Ronald? Who wanted to wrap her arms around that?

I had to re-explain Ronald's life story to William. He'd known it, but forgotten. Ronald had been an odd, off-putting boy, all grown up into a man who tried to ride roughshod. All that had kept him from caring about his solitude as a child had been his tenuous belief that he was right. Remember? He was no different as an adult. Except he said that he'd found a buddy who stuck by him. Jesus. He'd quote God because, really, what Jesus said was kind of easygoing and New Testament-y, while God gave him all kinds of Old Testament-y permissions, but he'd call out Jesus's name. And everybody left him the hell alone. Venerated him, as he saw it. He was going to ride that veneration into big money. As I saw it, he'd have cars and trips and a house with east and west wings on dozens of acres. A salary wasn't enough for sad, skinny, chinless Ronald Price.

"You still think he believes everything he says?" William said.

William wasn't the person I wanted to share this question with. A promise to my mother was too personal. I didn't say anything.

"So why *not* just give him the whole half of the estate?" William said eventually.

"Come on, think," I said. "You're the businessman."

"What."

"You want to let loose two million dollars so he can invest in a commodity, right?" I didn't give him time to answer. "Now in case you can't see what that commodity is, I'm going to tell you. It's not that church out there near the airport, which eventually will fall down from all the vibrations from the flyovers.

"He's selling one thing. His own charisma. Now I'm going to ask you a question, and it's a rhetorical question. How much money would you invest in the charisma of Ronald Price?"

William got my point. Sort of. "So why do you care if he blows it?" he said.

"Are you out of your fucking mind?" I said just for fun.

"By now, pretty much," he said.

I lapsed into his language, reminded him of my mother's years of low-risk investments, of her willingness to reinvest income, of her wish to leave a good estate. He'd profited, yes, every time she'd made a transaction to ensure her children's future, but that was beside the point. He needed to think of the plan. And the plan had not been, *Let me be conservative all my life so my son can be senseless for a few months and blow it all.*

"Your mother's dead," William said. "She won't know."

It was true that William and I shared philosophies of life, but while I translated being irreligious into a need for a deep moral code, William translated it into permission not to care much.

"I think she gave me power of attorney for a reason," I said. "I think she wanted her wishes carried out. And even if it wasn't explicit that she didn't want Ronald acting irrational, it was implicit."

"Okay," he said. He respected the hell out of my mother. She could talk finance with him. To William very little else mattered. My art mattered only when it carried a six-digit price tag.

"So here's the bottom line," I said. "Ronald thinks he's going to take Mama's money and buy a church which, by the way, will possibly make him filthy rich. We both know that."

"Not the ideal outcome, if I'm honest," William said. "I know you don't believe it, coming from me, but his doing it on false pretenses makes it something even I hate to see happen. He blows hard in public, but I have a feeling God and Jesus would not be what's rolling around in his head if he sat still."

"What's your proof?" I said. William's mind might be just what I needed.

"Look at it this way," he said. "Do you think my clients bought

BP stock after the spill?"

"No."

"Did they buy Exxon when the Supreme Court lowered punitive damages for the Valdez spill a few years ago?"

"I'm sure they did; it meant it was going to be a good investment again. They forgot principles. Nobody's touching BP yet, but not because of principles, though they pretend otherwise."

"There you go," he said. "That's just what Ronald might be doing. A value system isn't part of his business. Deep, deep down he doesn't believe in this Jesus stuff any more than most investors give a crap about whether Exxon destroyed half of the waters off Alaska. All that matters is making money. Get the picture?"

I didn't know if he was serious. William didn't care a lot about the planet himself. "I think you can be a greedy believer," I said.

He was smiling.

"I'm serious," I said. "You're not telling me anything."

He gave me a look that made us a tiny bit married. "Only Ronald and Jesus know what his truth is," he said. I smiled back enough to say we'd always agreed on Ronald.

"Listen," I said, "all else aside, I just don't think my mother would want her money out there tricking people. And whether Ronald believes he's going to float up into heaven one day or not, the fact of the matter is that he wants to bilk money out of people so he can get insanely rich and prove to all those kids he went to school with that he really was a genius."

That put William in the right place. He could pretend all along that he dismissed Ronald as nothing but a foolish showoff, but in truth he had a strong need to have Ronald fail. Ronald had been very contemptuous of William's business ideas. After my father died, the two men tacitly jockeyed for the position of man of the family, divorce or no divorce, even though my mother didn't need or want a man in any role that wasn't on commission. To William, cleaning up after dead people was failure, no matter if it paid well.

"So you're going to tell him no," William said.

"I can't do that," I said. "He talks about killing me, and he's just the type. Don't laugh. People like Ronald always have guns. They always have lawyers, too."

"I don't have all day," William said.

"You forget whom you're talking to," I said. "The market's closed."

"Maybe I have a life."

Poor man. William had been lucky to catch me. Even though he was nice looking in a television-star sort of way, women saw him as wallpaper. And his line of patter wasn't compelling, even among women who cared about money.

"Explain that I'm an important client," I said. He was silent, feeling my power over him, and I didn't want that. It was enough that Klea preferred me. "I'm just kidding," I said. He was still silent.

"Buying church property is a big mess, you know," he said finally.

I didn't know. I'd have thought that in the United States people of every political stripe would have written laws making it possible for every man, woman, and child to buy a church if the spirit moved them.

"It's not what you'd call a growth industry," William said. "Most commercial properties need a down payment of 20 to 25 percent, but for a church? They want 40 to 50 percent."

"Not even a church with Ronald up in the pulpit guaranteeing eternal life?" I said.

"He's not guaranteeing it to the lender," William said. He loved himself for that line. I could tell. Poor William.

I asked him what would happen if Ronald borrowed through Merrill Lynch. I'd been thinking about letting him have a down payment, a measly five or ten percent, $180,000 or so—enough to feed a few families for a few years in the real world—and let him learn his lesson.

"I'll be happy to turn him down," William said. "To borrow from

Merrill Lynch he'd have to come to me with almost a million dollars to start with, and he'd have to have a guarantor to back up the rest. I can tell you're not volunteering."

"Aw, come on," I said. "He needs to learn about money."

"Tell him to call me. I just got an idea. But don't say you never loved me."

CHAPTER FIFTEEN

THE PERSON I NEEDED to know about most was Avis Rosenthal. Learning her name alone took more than a bit of doing, given that the only Jewish women I knew were the dilettantes who opened galleries for fun and no profit or took lessons to make portraits from candid five by sevens or occasionally bought one of my paintings from my early days when my craft wasn't honed. I resorted to AnyWho and the actual White Pages. Then I googled. I could not find a lot, and that told me a good deal. She gave money but very little time. She took no risks, sending her children to the right private school and belonging to the right synagogue and donating enough money to only Jewish causes, nothing cultural. Safe. Her name appeared only on lists.

I checked under "Images." She was in a group in every photo. A woman who disappeared. She looked like a Republican wife. I'd never forgotten Calista Gingrich. A helmet of blonde hair and a thin face with a nose I would have thought she'd have had fixed. I wasn't being mean. I was giving her a lot of benefit of the doubt. I respected her for that nose.

No, I was trying to believe that she was mean. That she damaged Mike, and he deserved better. He never was in any of the photos with her, and that said something, if only that she was lonely. No, I decided, there was no kindness in being photographed giving away one's husband's hard-earned money to help Jews in Africa or New Orleans when so much money was needed for other people in Africa and New Orleans.

I told my mind to be quiet. I was looking for a fight. This Avis was simple. I had no reason to do her harm. When Mike came over that afternoon, I would tell him I felt too guilty.

When he walked in the door, before I could say anything, he told me he didn't have much time. He had to do the grocery shopping.

"Why?"

Because he always did the grocery shopping.

Why?

Because Avis was too busy.

I waited. He cocked his head, as if to say, *So what?*

"Is she busier than you are?" I said. Honest information-gathering.

"I'm sure she thinks so," he said. "But that's the price I pay for painting. She thinks it's an enormous waste of time."

"That's great," I said, and put my arms around his neck and squeezed tight.

He put his arms around my waist and pulled me to him. "God, there's nothing better than a complicated woman," he said.

I thought one day I might tell him I loved him. Avis wasn't going to get my sympathy. I was open-minded, but I refused to consider the rightness of a person with a medical degree buying groceries. I had my own bible of sorts.

After we made love, I lay in the bed and thought about William. I'd had a moment of confusion after he and I had talked. I thought I was a woman who completely trusted her decisions once she made them because they all were so steeped in facts. But sloughing off another person never could be completely based on facts. William wasn't a cartoon, drawn with a few lines. He could say something funny every now and then. He could take care of business—oh, how he could take care of business. He thought Ronald was a fool. What had made me get rid of him? I lay there and looked at Mike and tried to remember. Oh, right. William bored me. Not in a la-di-da way, but in a soul-wrecking way. Was Mike going to bore me in ten years? No. I wasn't going to let him. I was going to send him home to Avis every day to keep myself guessing.

"You better head to the grocery," I said.

"I don't have to go yet," he said.

"Aw, you probably should."

BEFORE WE WERE COMPLETELY dressed, I heard banging on the front door. I had a very visible doorbell, and no one ever needed to use any other signal to announce his presence. But the pounding started and didn't stop, even when I ran through the living room zipping my jeans and hollering that I was coming. I looked through the beveled glass and saw Ronald.

"I've got company," I said through the glass.

Mike came up behind me. I sensed his presence a little in air and shadow, but mostly in the expression on Ronald's face. It went from anger to all-out rage.

"I don't give a crap," he said.

I still hadn't opened the door. It was a valuable door, thick and old and ornate. Ronald could damage it. I didn't know if he could kick it in. If I ever wondered about how well it would withstand a serious foot, I pictured an EMT's.

"Let me in, I need to talk to you," he said.

Mike whispered behind me, "I don't have to go to the grocery." The back of me felt warmth. The front of me felt ice.

Ronald looked through the glass past me. "You have to get out of there," he said to Mike.

"Go away," I said.

Mike stepped around me. No one ever had stepped around me before. Not even my mother. She had been the type to put her hands on my shoulders and speak over my head when I was a child. I'd always wanted to cower behind someone.

"How about we meet you someplace for coffee?" Mike said

through the glass.

Ronald told him it was none of his business. Mike told him back that was a good reason for him to come along. That flummoxed Ronald. "But you're not objective," he said finally.

"This is beginning to be ridiculous," I said. Even Jehovah's Witnesses never talked this long through the glass.

"You can bring Tizzy," I said.

"I'll bring Elizabeth, thank you very much," he said. He had a win.

I gave Mike an insulated cooler for his groceries so we all could meet at PJ's in an hour. Ronald and I had one thing in common, and that was absolute punctuality. I went by the clock on the cable television, and so did he, and I arrived ten seconds after he did, so I was behind him in line. I saw a bulge under his jacket in the back, and I knew he was carrying a gun. "You're armed," I said, not bothering to lower my voice.

"It's perfectly legal," he said.

"Probably not when you're homicidally angry," I said.

The boy behind the counter heard us. Kids who worked at PJ's were still in school and exuded peace. His expression said that he would complain if he weren't so laid back.

"I've never harmed you," Ronald said.

"Not for lack of wanting to," I said.

I found out Ronald's most recent reason for hating me once all four of us were seated at a two-across-from-two table. I was facing Ronald, on purpose.

Ronald had talked to William. William had made a lot of sense on my behalf. On Ronald's behalf, not at all. The way Ronald put it, "Mother didn't need to die for me to do that."

"Unfortunate choice of words," Tizzy said.

I kept my feelings about mushroom soup to myself. Surely they were aware of the MD who'd seen my mother have two strokes, the second one fatal, the first possibly caused by soup-can recipes.

"You know what I mean," Ronald said, looking smaller than he had in a long time. "All I'm saying is that if I wanted to use my house as collateral, I could have done that ages ago."

That was a brilliant idea. One thing I had to say about William, he was a clever money man.

I leaned forward. "You got William for free. That's a pretty good deal," I said. "If he's willing to set up a purchase, you're in good shape."

"Why should I risk our house?" Ronald said. He looked at Tizzy for support. Tizzy looked as if she agreed with him, but I was sure it wasn't for the same reason.

"Because you have faith in yourself," I said with as much sincerity as I could muster.

"Be quiet," Ronald said.

For longer than I liked, it was silent among us.

"Why don't you two compromise?" Mike said finally.

Something happened at the table that never had happened before. For completely unknown reasons, what he'd said right then made perfect happy sense. We'd heard it at Lake Lawn but then it had been absurd. My mother had rarely broached it because to do so would have been pointless; this was one of the few times anyone had dared. I whooped. When I whooped, Ronald broke into a grin. "Now what on earth would that look like?" he said.

"Goddamned if I know," Mike said.

Ronald looked for a second as if he wanted to chasten Mike and possibly even condemn him and loathe him for talking badly. After all, Mike was an adulterer who was making his sister happy. But Ronald caught himself, because there was a remote possibility that this man might get him what he wanted.

"Excuse the expression," I said, "but if you put up good faith money, I'll put up good faith money." Ronald stared at me, and I interpreted that to mean that his idea of compromise wasn't anywhere close to 50-50. "If you don't want to do anything besides use Mama's inheritance to get rich," I said, "I'll...I'll never speak to you again." I'd started to say that I'd know he was a charlatan. But this wasn't the way I wanted to deal with Mama's suspicion. Ronald would condemn me to hell, and I'd never find out.

Mike put his arm around me. "That's not very helpful," he said.

"You're Jewish, aren't you," Ronald said to Mike.

I felt Mike squeeze my shoulder. "That's my ethnic origin. You want to tell me what that has to do with anything?"

"I just figure you'd understand that religion and business sometimes get mixed together," Ronald said. "I really respect the way Jewish people manage life."

I expected Mike to get up and walk out. Instead he stroked my shoulder a little. I read a lot into that gesture. "I understand," Mike said.

"I thought you might," Ronald said.

"Are you blind?" Tizzy said.

"What," Ronald said.

Tizzy scooted her chair so she was sitting at the end of the table instead of next to her husband. I didn't know what Ronald felt, but to me it was three against one. Unless, of course, he said he had God and Jesus on his side. In that case it was a tie. Providing we all carried equal weight, and Ronald and I would each argue that we didn't.

"This man is trying to be fair, and you don't even know you're insulting him, no matter how much you always say you love Jewish people," Tizzy said. "You're not doing a bang-up job with Cesca, either." She paused. "As for me, well, let me remind you that this is a community property state, and I don't particularly feel like mortgaging our house again when we've got two kids. But it beats going in the hole for almost two million dollars just so you can go on what's beginning to sound to me like a magical mystery tour. And by the way, that casserole tasted like crap."

Oh.

Ronald's eyes got red, not as if he were going to cry, but as if he were going to go berserk. Those were the same eyes of his childhood, with the head grown around them. Now that my mother was dead, no one knew the boy who'd carried forth better than I did, and what I saw was a man with a gun. Being in PJ's mattered only because a small part of Ronald still wanted a lot of money. If he were going to go on a rampage, he couldn't do it surrounded by people who were trafficking in sweets and a little stimulation. They would easily identify such a small man who drove off in his large white Infiniti.

"You're going to be really sorry," Ronald said to me. "Come on, Elizabeth, we're leaving."

Tizzy took a sip of coffee, even though her cup probably was empty.

Ronald glared at her, but she didn't move. "I'm serious," he said.

"We came in separate cars," Tizzy said.

"But we're going home together," Ronald said.

"I want to stay until I'm finished," she said.

Ronald turned to me. "What you're doing is between you and me," he said. "You have no right to mess up my marriage."

"Tell you what," Mike said, "why don't we all leave."

RONALD FOUND WHAT HE thought was a more powerful weapon than a concealed gun: an attorney with greedy eyes. Ronald planned to sue to have me removed as executor of my mother's estate. I was notified that he had sufficient grounds to prove I was "not acting in the best interests of the beneficiaries." At least he wasn't alleging that I was incompetent. I was sure Ronald was itching to get up in front of a judge and say that I couldn't draw a straight line and never had balanced my checkbook. But he knew I'd parade William in as a witness or whatever defendants did in courts. William thought he loved me, though cyborgs weren't capable of love. William loathed Ronald, and I'd make an exception for that one emotion, so William would swear on a Bible that I was the most astute person he'd ever met when it came to making financial decisions.

When I opened the mail and saw the legal notice, I wanted to call my mother. That was my first reaction. She was a good listener. She wasn't always the most compulsive caretaker, but she listened right. I stared at the paper with a feeling of sadness. So often I had wished secretly that my parents had quit with just me, that Ronald never had been born. He was a sleepless baby, a misshapen baby when he needed to be round and burbly so we could tolerate his noise. Not much changed through his childhood. Little boys needed to look goofy and innocent, cartoonish when so many teeth fell out, or they were downright diabolical, and I was ashamed of Ronald, as if people looked at him and imagined I would look that way with my hair cut off. I was too young to know that keeping distance between us in public wasn't fooling anyone. Not even Ronald, who might have become pushy because of me. Shame wasn't the issue now. I was feeling that old desire for him never to have existed. I didn't want Mama's money all to myself. I wanted Ronald's children to get half of it.

I put in a call to Mr. Alverson, now my attorney who was handling the estate. I would pay by the hour to have someone take care of me. And then he would go away.

CHAPTER SIXTEEN

TEVOR SOURIANTE WAS COMING to town to interview me and take advantage of the strong possibility that New Orleans would be comfortable at that time of year. He lived in Los Angeles, so I figured he was a little bit spoiled, at least compared to any family he had remaining in Mississippi, because anyone who lived around here was guaranteed misery five months out of twelve, while southern California was something of a paradise most of the time.

We had talked on the phone, and from all that he promised it was going to be remarkably easy. He would have a rental car, a crew from WYES would meet him at my house, and of course both knew their way around the city, so all I had to do was get dressed and meet them in my studio and be ready to talk. "That's the deceptive part," I'd told him over the phone. "Being ready to talk is one thing; being ready to talk to you is scary." He'd laughed, and I'd tried to tell myself that because he was a good laugher I'd be all right. All I needed to do was sit down and look at my paintings and decide what my philosophy of life was.

I figured I'd do a study of myself. I'd be a graduate student for a few weeks, very dispassionate. I wrote down that I majored in painting and minored in photography because that was worthy of comment. Photography was an odd subject for me to have mastered. "Why should I work in something so representational?" I could say rhetorically. And then I could go on to explain how accuracy of an image always was a starting point in my mind before I moved to pure abstraction. That might take, what, a minute and a half?

I watched a few videos of interviews I had saved of myself and took notes of phrases I liked. "People see spirituality in my work, but I see none in my soul, so whom should I believe?" I said once. "Wait, did I just say soul? How's that for a slip-up." I was pretty provocative. Mostly I was funny, and that was what worked in interviews. It didn't hurt that I was young with a good haircut most of the time.

I went through papers I'd had to write in graduate school. Most twisted my mind up because they were about artists like Kandinsky, who agreed with me on almost nothing in the universe, and yet from a distance could be confused with me. I erased that board in my head. The papers in which I had to explore my own work had some old, fine thoughts. "It is possible to be strictly secular in one's world view and still be an artist." "I will concede that talent might transcend rationality, but I don't like to think so. I prefer to think that it can be explained by neuroscience." I scribbled them down. I liked my young self. I agreed with my young self and was surprised that my old issues were still so important. But my young self had been awfully arrogant.

After a couple of days, I had two pages of legal paper covered with penciled notes. I figured I wouldn't look at them until the day before my interview. Then I went back to my painting, and not thinking. If I were to work on a conscious level, I would destroy myself.

THE COURT DATE WAS set for two days before the interview. I asked Mr. Alverson to get a postponement. Mr. Alverson had been my mother's attorney for decades, and he wouldn't have had the business if he hadn't seen eye to eye with her on pretty much everything, which included the subject of my mother's two offspring when it came to money. He was pushing seventy, but he was in vigorous high spirits over the possibility of shutting Ronald up and down. He saw no conflict of interest. He often had controlled Ronald when my mother hadn't wanted to.

"A delay makes you look weak," Mr. Alverson said.

I decided right then that I would go to court on Monday, study on Tuesday, interview on Wednesday, and eat myself sick on Thursday.

The courthouse was part of that complex attached to City Hall. My mother always had had contempt for all the structures in that part of downtown, remembering them going up when she was in her teens and already sensible. "Here you have a city that has nothing but history going for it, so those idiots thought 'modern' was attractive. Modern. Anything built in the 1950s should be imploded," she said.

Mr.Alverson met me at the entrance to the courthouse. I had parked at a two-hour meter across Loyola Avenue, feeling optimistic, but I didn't tell him that. We had to go through security before we got to the elevators, and when the door closed on the elevator, I told him I had nail scissors in my purse. "The scanner wasn't paying much attention." A woman at the back said, "You not what they looking at."

The courtroom was not what I expected. I thought we would meet in an intimate chamber with just Ronald and me and our two attorneys and maybe someone recording what took place. But this was civil court in New Orleans. The city's largest industry and the city's biggest religion must have been litigation if the daytime television commercials were any indication. There was a seating area filled with eager sloppy people praying to walk out rich. They weren't all black, either, though New Orleans was mostly black. Some wore t-shirts bearing the logos of their attorneys' firms, including a little boy who couldn't have been much past his second birthday. Here was the local creed at its finest. I was sure I would hear "Praise Jesus" going up and walking back, but the gods were the TV lawyers.

Mr. Alverson left me in one of the benches and went up to talk to one of the young satellites surrounding the raised podium where the judge was going to sit. Other attorneys did the same thing, jockeying for position, too, I supposed. I didn't see one that I recognized from television. Those pitchmen probably had staff fresh out of law school who took all their cases and got clients enough for a good fee. Staff. Mr. Alverson definitely was the only attorney in the room over forty. Maybe seniority would count. "We're near the top of the docket," he told me when he came back. I didn't mention the parking meter.

I paid as little attention as possible to the cases before mine. I learned what I needed to know, then took out a small, discreet sketch pad and started some preliminary designs. All I needed to know was what might be in the judge's head. I liked her instinctively. She was one of those women who wore glasses all the time and happened to look good in them but didn't care if she didn't. The lenses were small and frameless, so she seemed shiny and positive. And she had a swingy, short haircut with what looked like very natural highlights. No-nonsense prettiness: I saw a message in that. All else aside, I couldn't imagine in my wildest dreams that any white woman in the City of New Orleans would have an iota of patience with Ronald. Particularly a woman who had gone to law school and worked her way up to a judgeship. Ronald gave off an aroma of intolerance, of inapproachability toward everyone who wasn't a wealthy straight white Christian male, and it didn't matter if he was scrawny and myopic. Ronald was in the courtroom, and I noticed that he had chosen a seat for himself where no one would want to sit next to him, in the middle of an empty row towards the back. No one came near except during occasional visits from his lawyer. I recognized the lawyer. Johnny Grapes, a high-school classmate of Ronald's. He'd been just as insufferable as Ronald, but strangely enough, it had been as a basketball player.

I wondered whether the judge ever scanned the room and did a quick sociogram of the people waiting. She could make decisions without hearing cases just on how everyone was behaving. Of course, she also could have second-guessed herself after passing judgments. I wondered if litigants screamed and danced in courtrooms anywhere besides New Orleans. I couldn't miss her telling a man who wasn't much past twenty that he was in arrears on child support to the tune of forty-three hundred dollars, and though he was wearing bright white sneakers, the rest of his clothing did not imply that he had that much money stockpiled anywhere, legally or otherwise. "That's good for your trifling self," I heard from the hallway before the door shut after his baby mama, followed by an unequivocal, "Fuck your ass to almighty hell."

Ronald's and my coming from uptown wasn't necessarily going to be refreshing to the judge. If she was sharp, she would think that we were wasting her time, fighting over millions. Neither of us was injured; neither of us was looking for compensation that would change our lives. A civil court judge with principles had chosen her work to protect the victim from the villain. Ronald saw himself as something perilously close to a martyr.

All four of us stood before the bench, the way I'd seen people do on television, except we weren't separated into boxes or sides. Johnny Grapes presented his case. He ran on and on about how I wasn't acting in the best interests of the one other beneficiary, namely his client. That I had a conflict of interest, literally, that the more capital I kept in the estate, the more revenue there was for myself. He said I was incompetent, that I never should have been appointed, that I earned my living as a painter and couldn't balance a checkbook. And then he told the judge that his client wanted his portion of the estate to buy a church so he could serve God as he had been called by Jesus.

The courtroom got quiet. I heard one woman whisper, "Yes, Lord."

The judge didn't look at her. That was an outburst she could live with.

"Now the executrix is a heathen who wants to stand in the way of my client's service to the Lord," Johnny said, getting some spirit in him despite his lifelong decorum.

"Praise Jesus," said one woman out loud.

"Praise Jesus," echoed several others.

"I'm not going to be swayed by this, uh, assemblage," the judge said.

"He just trying to serve the Lord," one older man said.

The judge raised her hand instead of the gavel, and the courtroom fell quiet.

I caught the judge's eye. Out of respect for anyone in the room who truly clung to religion, her expression was as neutral as she could make it, but she wasn't really in the business of keeping her opinions to herself. I gave her a tiny smile.

"So why are you the executrix?" she said to me. Now there was a bit of amusement in her eyes.

"I'm older than my brother," I said. "But that's really not the reason. I was very close to my mother, and we talked a great deal. I knew what she wanted, and I knew what she believed in. She was very frugal and left a large estate expecting there would be a lot of money for her grandchildren to inherit. So she put me in charge precisely so my brother wouldn't blow through it.

"Your honor, he wants two million dollars to buy a church. That leaves almost nothing for his children."

At those words, "two million," a buzz went up from the front rows, where everyone could hear what we were saying. There were a lot of dreamers in that room.

"That leaves nearly a million dollars," Ronald said. "That's a lot more money than some kids can expect to inherit. When my father died, I didn't inherit a penny."

There was a collective inrush of breath. "What he said?" came from the second bench.

"That man crazy," came from the third bench.

The judge looked at Ronald the interrupter and put her finger to her lips. I would have preferred the gavel, but I had to admit, the gesture was pretty effective.

She turned to me. "Go on."

"The will hasn't even been probated yet," I said. "He may think I'm artsy—" I stopped myself from saying "fartsy" because of where I was, but the judge was no dummy. She was having fun. "But I know numbers, and I'm here to tell you he's using up his entire inheritance if I'm removed as executor. Executrix. He has threatened me in ways I won't even mention. And all I'm trying to do is handle this estate fairly for my mother's descendants. I happen to like my niece and nephew."

I could feel Ronald catching himself from saying something. I turned to him. "You want me to tell the judge how you threatened me?"

"I didn't say anything," Ronald said.

Mr. Alverson said, "Clearly, Judge, there are no grounds for removing Ms. Price as executrix. She's competent, and she has no conflict of interest. If anything, she's looking out for the plaintiff's family more than he is. I don't think we have to belabor this issue. I request that you dismiss this suit."

The judge didn't need time to think. With a full courtroom, she didn't have the luxury.

"Mr. Price, this is a frivolous lawsuit and a colossal waste of my time and the taxpayers' money," she said to Ronald. "I see no grounds whatsoever for removing your sister as executrix of your mother's estate. In fact, you should consider yourself extremely lucky your mother found a way to protect you from doing something foolish."

Then she turned to me. "That said, I have some advice for you. If I were you, I'd want to sever ties with your brother as much as I could. I'd be sorely tempted to give him his half and send him on his way. Though maybe you can protect your niece and nephew before you do it. Your mother trusted you, but I'm sure she didn't want to leave you a legacy of conflict."

I had to smile. My mother was so rational. And nothing was more codified than the law. Yes, it was malleable, but she knew it had to be taken as right on a given day.

I ALMOST COULD ENVISION the compartments in my head. Personal business went into a closed, locked space when it was time for my work to open and expand into what I perceived as an airy, empty, round-walled chamber. On Tuesday I sat at the kitchen table with my notes about myself on the yellow legal paper and studied what I thought about my art and my world, and everything was abstract and boring and nonsensical. Paint over paint, never thick, but using color and pattern to reflect and absorb light. Who wanted to hear that? Who wanted to say that? I wanted color and pictorial space to seem to move arbitrarily, but I would have many private connections among them. That was too abstract. Wait, Mr. Souriante was coming here to do the interview in my studio. I went in to find paintings that would show evidence of what I was saying. It didn't work. These were notes from fifteen years ago, and I was in a gloomier phase now. My older works were all splashy color, and I could say, *Oh, let me tell you about my sweet niece who confuses me with Kandinsky*, but this interview was supposed to be about me now, not then.

I looked at a canvas I was working on. Hell, my mother just died. Was I going to get personal? That would be more interesting than throwing out phrases from the art studio world. I could talk about my mother's influence, her secularism, my early thoughts about the world we see, but my wish to do nothing spiritual. Oh, I was going to do fine.

When Tevor Souriante walked into my house, all that beautifully decorated space in my cranium, the silks and grosgrains and tassels, disappeared, leaving whatever would float in. He was a brown-skinned man, every hair on his face short and individually trimmed. He was sensuous but not handsome in the usual way, more like a man who had been an adorable little boy with round cheeks, and he was so large he seemed to fill my studio like a football player might. He gave off a certain aura of celebrity, too, that would have made me step back if I'd seen him in a public place. He wore a creamy leather jacket and no tie, as if he had planned to make me feel at ease in my own home. If he wanted me to confess to murder, I would do so in front of a camera, and I would know he would make it all right. "I can't believe you're in my house," I said.

He introduced me to my own studio. He and his crew took over the space, but gently, respectfully, assuring me nothing would be any different when they left than when they came. But they transformed the room into a place where he and I would look as if we were supposed to be on public television. Paintings in the background framed a seating space, as if we were on The Cesca Price Show. Two stools were set behind my work table, an easel with a recent painting was next to the table, and a painting in progress lay on the table.

"You have no idea the state of my mind," I said as we moved around. I had no idea what the cameraman was doing.

"Oh?"

Now we were sitting on the two stools, waiting for the go-ahead, and I tried to keep him entertained.

"God, I spent the whole first part of this week in court," I said. "See, my brother is this religious zealot, well, not really, I mean, I don't know, I think it's some kind of pathology, you know, finding God because he was angry at my parents. So how real can that be, even though he might believe it, because, see, he grew up in the same house as I did, and our mother was a humanist. Which I'll tell you all about when we start talking about my work."

Mr. Souriante was nodding, either like a good listener or like someone who thought I was interesting. Or maybe both.

"Anyway, here's this brother who says he wants a couple million dollars to be some sort of evangelist, but I know he'll be bilking people out of their money so he can get rich. Well, extremely rich, because anyone with any sense would be happy with what our mother left him. I don't see any sincere soul-saving in that."

"This is fascinating," Mr. Souriante said. "Now may I ask you some questions?"

I wriggled around on the stool and smoothed down my hair. I looked out to where the camera was, straightened up, then looked back at him.

"Please do."

"So you feel your work is a reflection of your family dynamic," he said. "Or at least of your family mores."

I smiled, and I understood right then why people who are interviewed on television sometimes smile. They are relieved that the person sitting next to them understands, and for the next few minutes nothing can go wrong. They are fascinating. We were going to tape, and I knew this man would edit anything terrible, but I also knew he would help me do well. He had listened to me when I told him about my childhood, and right there on the spot he had made up his smart question.

"I was reared with no belief system," I said, "so I like to think there's no spirituality in my work. Notice I say 'think.'"

"As compared to what?"

The stools were very close. My knee bumped his, and I almost lost my train of thought.

"'Think' and 'believe' were two words that got knocked around a lot in my house," I said, recovering so fast even he probably didn't notice. "My mother and I always like to know something. We don't like to transcend science and reason, which is what spirituality is all about. You know, faith."

"And how does this relate to your work?"

"Oh! Spirituality is a very big issue in art," I said, so grateful to him. "For instance, my paintings are compared to Kandinsky's, but he was deeply spiritual, and I say I'm not. So there's a problem when people read my work as having some kind of religiosity in it when I'm purely rational."

Was I being too boring? Who cared? It was PBS.

"You seem to be a woman with a certain passion," he said. "Is passion rational? Is it spiritual? Might it be reflected in your work?"

I slipped off the stool to reach over and use the dark, sad painting on the easel to illustrate. He probably wasn't aware that I was pressing myself against him.

I told him how it was started just after my mother's death. "I hope it gives off emotional power," I said. "You can see movement and even light. I've done a lot of thinking about the nature of hope, whether it can be explained as a neurological phenomenon. I think it's natural to wish as long as it has no supernatural underpinnings. Probably the same goes for my humanistic values. I'm a good person. Without benefit of an ethical code. So maybe pure goodness for the sake of goodness comes through. I'm more 'Christian' than most Christians. I hope that doesn't sound wrong."

"And yet you have a brother who's deeply Christian in the traditional sense," he said. "Or rather says he is."

"Yes?" I said.

"He claims to have spirituality in his work, and you claim to have none. Is there something very nuanced going on that you haven't considered before?"

I let myself think for a moment. He could edit me. But the more I thought, the more I forgot where I was. Even though I wasn't frozen in front of an audience. My mind was blanking. Ronald and me. The difference.

"Okay, let's compare art to religious expression. Right there you're doing what he and I have done ever since we were kids. We've drawn a line through the universe, and we've agreed that what's his is his, and what's mine is mine. Zero in common. Okay?"

Mr. Souriante barely nodded.

"So if you take someone like Wassily Kandinsky who expresses spirituality in art visually, you can see it. And if you see the spirit of goodness in my art, it's right there. But with Ronald? You can't see what he's doing. He wants to get up in front of as many wide-eyed people as possible and promise them eternal life in some holy spirit, and then they'll give him lots of money. My brother worships God because there's money in God. I'm not knocking religion, but I am knocking greediness using God's name."

My eyes glistened with sincerity. I'd just made a good case for comparisons to Kandinsky. I was alone in the studio with Tevor Souriante. No one would know I was trying to figure out Ronald for my mother.

The interview took an hour. If he had come all the way to New Orleans, he wanted enough tape to fill half an hour when he got back into the editing booth. I felt I'd been interesting and anecdotal and not too polysyllabic. I remembered to squeeze in minoring in photography and how I had had to wean myself away from naturalistic representation of the world, from anything recognizable. I felt I'd made a smooth segue. I kept trying to find a way to slip in Gracie and her talent and her comparison of me to Kandinsky, but it didn't work. I didn't mention Mike, though I ached to do so.

When he said he thought he had enough, I jumped down from my stool and asked if I could hug him. I loved him so much at that very second. We had had an hour in which he had bored right through me, this grand, brilliant man. He had paid attention to me in a way no one ever had before. It was like falling in love with the doctor for the fifteen minutes I was in the examining room. I wondered if he was married. Not that I would pursue him because I was happy where I was. I just wondered whether his wife lived with such intensity.

CHAPTER SEVENTEEN

I NEVER UNDERSTOOD WHY Amnesty International would work on behalf of men who were punished with twenty-three hours a day of solitary confinement and one hour of release into the general prison population. I thought maybe the one hour of forced interaction with others was their punishment. I had gradually created a schedule in which I could be alone all but an hour a day on most days, and I was comfortable and productive and anxious only when an intrusion threatened. Filling that hour with a chosen connection was another story, but I didn't think hard about it.

I was painting slowly, preparing for a show in New York fifteen months from then. I knew what I wanted to do, and I could get up each morning and watch the work emerge. No one was fighting with me, so my head wasn't full of screamers and gun-toters. Mike had his own compartment, his own actual time slot, so I didn't have to think about him until the clock said so. Days were good. Nights were quiet. Phones had no ringers.

I had listened to the judge. As soon as the will was probated, I had let Ronald have a million dollars for his church on the condition that he put the rest of his half of the estate into trust for his children. I'd made Tizzy the trustee, and she said to Ronald, "Touch your kids' money and I'll see you in court." I'd hoped that meant divorce court on top of civil court, for Tizzy's sake, but I wasn't asking. From what she told me, Ronald was filling those seats. Not in the upper tiers, but at the ground level, courtside, fifty-yard line. "You can't call them pews," she said. "That place is like a stadium. Levi asked if he could have the hot dog concession."

I would phone Tizzy at work every now and then because I took some pleasure in hearing about the church. No longer making any pretense of wishing my brother well didn't worry me. He had lost in court, but he felt he had won, and I wasn't as adult as I wanted to be. I reasoned that the Germans didn't create the word *schadenfreude* for nothing. I enjoyed Ronald's gaffes from the pulpit, his heavy-handed reliance on the Old Testament when I didn't think that was what a Christian did. I egged Tizzy on to tell me what he looked like when viewed from the upper balcony. "Is he a commanding presence?" I would say. But what I most wanted was a house count. A dollar count. I'd done the math. A million down meant $800,000 borrowed some kind of way. He owed several thousand dollars each month on a loan that big. I wasn't going to ask Tizzy how much money was dropped in the collection plate. That would have been crass. It probably wouldn't have leaked back to Ronald, because Tizzy was weary, but I didn't want to annoy her myself. I figured it was better to find out a hundred people had shown up, then to let myself guess that maybe each had given ten dollars, and then to figure, *Well, four weeks in a month, a thousand dollars a week, not gonna make it. But two hundred people a week, well, what if each only gives five dollars?* I couldn't help myself. I had put up with his smugness too long, and I knew that now his smugness was all aimed at me.

I had to stop the arithmetic. It was Mike who was supposed to be using my left-brain circuits. Ronald was for the darkened right side; Mike was serious business. Andy had called to set up a show in three months, and Mike needed someone as a go-between for the two of them. Oddly, this would take more energy from me than my show at the Getty after that. It wasn't that Andy needed to be tricked or lied to; Andy was the type who could be told anything true. *My mother's dying; give me a couple of weeks. He's never painted before; give him a show.* But when Andy was putting the reputation of Galleria

Campagna on the line, along with the cost of promotion, I wasn't going to fall short. It was personal in a way that the big museums were not. Andy was going to get paintings that were top quality and framed right. Each afternoon Mike came to my house, and we moved around the studio talking about his work, moving closer and closer until it was time, and then we went into my house and made love, and he went home to Avis, possibly by way of the supermarket or drugstore.

That afternoon, I had spent quite a bit of time critiquing a painting that I thought needed more consistent brush work. I was getting a sense that Mike was going too fast with his latest in an effort to have enough paintings for the show. This painting was using a different palette from his old reds and ochres, a teal and deep purple and a color I'd describe as tomato soup. He was still doing scapes, but this one was of the city, an impressionist slice of a New Orleans street. The composition was perfect, but his concentration of paint was uneven. "Slow down, slow down," I'd said, sounding more erotic than I intended, and he started tugging me toward the door connected to the house. The routine was getting to me. If I wanted a man who expected sex on a regular basis, I'd have married one. I told him we needed to talk.

I sat him down on my living room sofa. Better than a stool in the studio, which would forever be Tevor Souriante's.

"You're making me nervous," he said.

I didn't know anything could make a doctor nervous.

"I don't like the way things are going," I said. "You've got to admit, we're in something of a rut."

He looked baffled. "I thought you liked an orderly life."

I was willing to consider that, but only for a second. "I know I don't like an orderly sex life."

He was silent.

So I forged ahead. I had nothing to lose. "If I wanted an orderly sex life, I'd be married."

"Trust me, there's nothing orderly about a married sex life," he said.

I knew he didn't mean that he and Avis had a reckless, passionate, unpredictable love life. But I wasn't going to let him know I understood. "If you've got such a wild, wonderful love life at home, what are you doing over here?"

He reached out to touch my face, and I took his hand and held it away from me.

"You misread me," he said. "I haven't laid a hand on my wife since I got to know you."

I let his hand go. "That's nice," I said, then I fell silent. So did he.

Finally he said, "I don't know why I stay with her. I promise it's nothing personal."

I smiled. That was a good line.

"So what can I do to make you happy?" he said.

"Try surprising me."

He leaned back. He looked at me. Not in an appraising way. Not even in a studying way. He wasn't making eye contact.

After a while I said softly, "What are you doing?"

"I'm appreciating you."

A good surprise.

TIZZY CALLED TO INVITE me to church. Ronald was going to do a telecast on the public access cable channel that Sunday. "I'm not inviting you because of the telecast," she said. "Anybody with a camera can do it."

So why? I would see when I got there, she said.

Magic shows came to mind. I could be backstage at a magic show. My mother had allowed me to enjoy birthday parties with magicians, and she had let me have Santa Claus and the Easter Bunny—anything requiring the suspension of disbelief—up until I turned six. And then, when other mothers sat their children down to talk about reproduction, my mother sat me down and told me about truth. She had to take me to a magic shop and let me buy a kit so I could see for myself because she had no way to explain what we saw on television. I accepted her truths. With Ronald she had a harder time. He argued about Santa Claus until his schoolmates pressed him with too much evidence. The Easter Bunny was easier because it was too girlish for him even to mention. But magic? He still said he believed Uri Geller had supernatural powers.

And now he believed in the unlimited powers of Ronald Price Junior and his Sanctuary of Divine Grace. Whether he believed in the Jesus who took care of anyone—including the son of Ronald Price Senior—was another story. Part of me wanted to discover to great surprise that Ronald was a truth-teller, that he was in it for Christian goodness. But the rest of me had promised to find out if he was a fraud of the worst kind, a predatory fraud, out for himself, lying that he found Jesus at death scenes. I'd be able one day to think, *Well, at least he's rational.* He would have gotten that message from Mama, to accept only what he could see. No dead Jesus hovering over him. Of course, he wouldn't have gotten her other message, the humanist half of secular humanism, which was to be good for goodness' sake. She was flexible in that goodness: she ate turkey.

I wouldn't go to her gravesite to give her the answer. I would carry it forth in my mind. I would tell it to Klea. Klea would tell her children. That was the hereafter I'd promised my mother.

Tizzy sounded as if she had some facts for me. Even though I still wasn't sure what I knew about her.

I dressed for church as respectably as I could. I owned one dress that I used for funerals. That was it. I'd had it for about fifteen years, and the only change I'd made to it had been to take out the shoulder pads. It was almost-black navy blue with tiny pale blue flowers on it. I could wear it out to dinner if I ever had a stodgy occasion, but so far I'd only needed it for funerals, including my mother's. No one could fault the dress. I even tied my hair back. For all I knew, Tizzy was going to do something about my presence, and I didn't want Ronald pointing at me and saying that I was what a hell-bound woman looked like. If anything, people could think, *Hmm, poor Reverend Price was the runt of the litter.*

The parking lot was full of American-made late-model cars when I arrived twenty minutes early. So this was where I could find the equivalent of the Midwest without leaving home. I tried to blend into the crowd flowing toward the open front doors, but I felt like a cancer, all darkness in a bouncing mass of healthy pastels. The women wore pinks and pistachios, the men, baby-chick yellows and pale blues. "Can you believe we're gonna be on television?" "You set your DVR?" "You're supposed to set your DVD."

Tizzy wasn't easy to find, but I was. "I knew you'd wear that damn dress," she said, deep inside what was supposed to be God's sanctuary. She covered her mouth, and her eyes popped out above her hand, naughty and twinkly and clearly happy to see me.

"I'm not the type to call my girlfriends the night before and coordinate wardrobes," I said, and she hugged me.

Tizzy grabbed my wrist and tugged me down a corridor I didn't remember exploring when I'd come for what I'd thought was surely going to be my only visit to this place. We were moving into some small inner honeycomb of offices. I started to pull back. If she was taking me to see Ronald, I didn't want to play.

"I have somebody I want you to meet," she said.

Waiting in a hallway, looking nervous because he was out of place, stood a pudgy black man, head shaved shiny, suit the most respectable I'd seen since I arrived, khaki, fine cut, not expensive, but making him more different from the crowd than his color, by far. "Herbert Coston, Cesca Price," Tizzy said.

"What are you doing here?" I said.

He laughed.

"Your brother say he might have me come up to the altar," Herbert said. "I take one look in the parking lot, tell him that's a very bad idea."

"Unless you're Jesus come back to earth, I'd say you're probably right," I said. "Actually, if you *are* Jesus come back to earth, I'd say you better get a fast running head start."

"God, you're awful," Tizzy said, with so much affection that I knew she was mine.

"Herbert's the one who prayed over that first murder scene," Tizzy said.

I looked at Herbert. If he was the Ur JesusCleaner, I didn't want to insult him. But he had not stopped fighting a laugh since we were introduced.

"So, where do you usually go to church on Sundays?" I said. *Feel him out.*

"Shoot, Sunday morning come after Saturday night," he said. "I sleep in on Sunday morning."

I exchanged glances with Tizzy. She had expected this. She was mine.

"But you prayed over the little dead kid," I said.

"You want to tell me you don't get very nervous when somebody dead?" he said. "My mama always praying over the least little thing, you *know* she pray over a dead child. Tell you the truth, she made me a little superstitious. Well, really, a lot superstitious. I don't want no dead kid come in on me while I'm sleep."

I started dancing around. "Good lord," I said, "is this what you're going to tell the people out there?"

"You crazy?" he said. I'd dismissed formalities the moment I asked him what he was doing there. "I told my mama how Mr. Ronald probably think me praying done save his business, make him rich, and she say, 'Son, see? You better pray for all you worth.' So I'm a serious praying man. Long as it not no Sunday morning."

"So!" Tizzy said. "I think this has been a fruitful meeting."

I said nothing. Then neither of them said anything. That meant it was my turn. "I guess I'm supposed to do something here," I said.

"I'm not sure what," Tizzy said.

I gave her one of our old looks. The one that said, *Bullshit.*

RONALD LEARNING HE'D BUILT his empire on an old black woman's superstitions wasn't a good plan for the morning of his first telecast. Even I was not that mean. I told that to Tizzy. I wasn't even sure he needed to know I was present in the church.

"He has to know you're here," Tizzy said.

"He'll try to baptize me."

"Not on live television, he won't."

Good point. Ronald had seen me at our mother's funeral in front of an ephemeral audience, and he hadn't exactly emerged the winner going head to head. He knew the difference between funeral-goers and television watchers, though of course he would say that God was in both places. This God that his mother had told him couldn't be explained scientifically. This God his sister had grown up without, just as he had, despite what he would say to inflate himself. God had a way of filling a person up to look much larger.

Tizzy walked into the office first. Then Herbert, then me. I could see Ronald talking to a man with headphones resting on his neck. "I have a guest you'll want to see," Tizzy said.

"I asked Herbert to wait in the hallway," Ronald said. Then he saw me. "What are you trying to pull?" he said to me, and I was tempted to be mean.

"I came just to see, honestly," I said.

"But you met Herbert," he said.

I nodded.

"This is the man who brought me to God," he said. "He might change your life, too."

"If he talks during the service, every damn redneck is going to walk out of here, and you know it," I said. "What are you thinking?"

I had no worry that Herbert would take that the wrong way. I was doing what he needed.

"This is a good Christian congregation," Ronald said.

"You walk him out on that stage, and you watch everybody's face, and if they look eager to hear him, go for it," I said.

If I'd misread this crowd, Herbert could get up and talk about chanting away ghosts. I was *that* sure I knew what kind of people these were. Ronald needed to know the truth, but it was a falling-down truth, not for now. Letting him parade Herbert up onto the altar wasn't right. Even for me.

Ronald gave me a dismissive look, but I'd seen it before. It was the look I got when he would eventually make my idea his own. He told Tizzy to get me a seat, but not in the front row.

As we walked out, I heard him telling the cameraman, "Okay, I'm going to talk to them about what to do with the DVDs before we go live. Don't start until I finish, got it?"

Tizzy left me in an aisle pew, far off to the left in case I wanted to make a discreet exit. But I had no intention of leaving. I wanted to see what happened with Herbert.

She seated me next to another woman who also seemed to be alone, and who gave off a familiar scent. I'd walked into the Salvation Army and the Volunteers of America many times to make donations, and secondhand clothes had that sad, dignified smell of having been washed and hung up and tagged for new, eager buyers. Her yellow skirt had been washed to the point of pilling, and she wore bright yellow leather pumps a half-size too large. Neither of us spoke.

The organ music became louder, Ronald came onto the stage—it was definitely a stage—and as he positioned himself behind the podium the music faded to silence. He was not wearing the robe I expected, nor even a coat. Just a crisp white shirt and a deep red tie. He didn't look small behind the podium, and I knew it was custom-made. He gestured for quiet, even though it wasn't necessary. My little brother was taking over the room on his own paid-for say-so.

Ronald had to break the holiness of the moment with business. But he stage whispered, as if in collusion. "I trust you all left your DVD recorders running," he said. "You can mail the DVDs on Monday. We are going to be the most important church in Louisiana, you know. Louisiana! And then one day, the nation. Think of it. Your faith, echoing across the land. Yes!" The "yes" held the whispered sibilant an extra two seconds. He gave a barely perceptible nod toward the middle distance. That was where I figured the camera was ready to roll.

I hung on every word, every gesture. Ronald was bigger than the child prodigy I expected him to look like. He commanded the congregation with sweeping hand gestures. They sang, they recited along with him. But what transfixed me were the times he held forth. The program said "Old Testament," and Ronald sounded like a man of God. He knew exactly when to bear down hard on a word.

"Many of you have been here before, but for those of you who are new—" Which to me meant everyone who was going to see this on TV for the first time. "For those of you who are new, I'd like to explain how I came to start this church. You will see how it ties into today's passage that we're going to explore in the Book of Exodus. Yes, Exodus, the second book of the Old Testament." He recited what I considered his dubious personal history, of cleaning up murder sites, followed by Calling Number One, that God wanted him and his minions to sanctify crime scenes. They would learn more soon. "Sanctify!" And then, as he served more and more people deep in grief—"Oh, yes, deep!"—he had Calling Number Two, that there was a congregation waiting for him to preach. All he needed was a church where they all could come together. "Come together!"

I sat perfectly still, waiting to see where in the Old Testament he was going to find that vengeful old Jewish God telling him to buy a church with his dead mother's money and whatever all these polyester people would kick in every week without fail.

He came up with the story of the burning bush.

I turned toward the woman next to me hoping for a puzzled expression, but she was buying whatever he was selling, even if she couldn't afford it.

"We are a called people," he said. "You've all read about Moses back in Sunday school. Now Moses was called to do something he didn't think he could do, just like us. We are called people. God is telling us we will be his people by giving our hearts to Christ. If Moses could lead the Israelites to the land of milk and honey, you know God knows what you can do, too, so you should always say yes to him."

He waved his hands all over the place. "Look at each other, because you are a tribe. A team. A family in Christ."

Now Ronald gestured to his left, and Herbert walked onstage. A peevish murmur went through the congregation. From the back I saw a lot of cupped hands around neighboring ears. Even Ronald could read the crowd. He whispered something to Herbert; Herbert looked resigned and relieved; Herbert pretended to fiddle with the microphone; Herbert walked off stage right.

That pretty much did it.

Through the rest of the service, while I paid close attention, I wracked my brain trying to figure out how a person could go from Ronald's ungodly childhood to this wild land of milk and honey and Jesus Christ. Herbert or no Herbert. When I was growing up, I'd looked at the Bible in our home, opening it arbitrarily, just for fun, very often finding names and even stories that I'd heard of. "No surprise," my mother would say. "It's good stuff for movies."

How had Ronald learned to look like a real preacher without leaving his regular routine? I would have to do some poking around. Tizzy would talk me in circles. Gracie might come right out, if she even knew. Maybe I could do some research. The Yellow Pages? The Tulane Library? Not the Loyola Library. The public library was probably best. And then I started thinking about Mike and his pure science and what he might do. Nothing came to mind until I remembered how I'd studied him. I remembered how I'd learned what I needed to know about Avis. Google. Such peace came over me that I could have sworn Google was a holy word.

The end of the service came fast, even though it was long. The collection still had not taken place, but everyone had seen Ronald signal to the cameraman to stop rolling.

"All right," he said, "you can relax. You did wonderfully. But we have a little more family business to take care of. Please, when you go home remember to send a copy of your DVD to Channel 20 with a letter urging the station to give Reverend Price his own show. I'm sure each of you will be inspired by this morning's sermon to express what was more inspiring about this church than anything now on television. Especially in New Orleans, where the world has branded us all as sinners who deserved the flood and destruction of 2005. You need to remember that, while New Orleans had its share of homosexuals and prostitutes and drunkards, yes, it also had a disproportionate number of people who had been saved through the sacrifice of Jesus Christ their Lord. And here was the Sanctuary of Divine Grace, set on land untouched by flood waters; what more proof does Channel 20 need?"

I sat in Ronald's church and thought, *Well, the French Quarter was on high ground, and the only event right after the storm was a celebration of gay pride, so what does that say?* And I thought it was too bad that there was no God to broadcast my thoughts. I also thought it was too bad I couldn't just stand right up and speak. I was losing every possibility of giving Ronald a chance.

The collection plate was passing, and the woman next to me rummaged in her coin purse and pulled out a roll of dollar bills. "What are you doing?" I said under my breath. I did not want my brother to have power over her.

"The minister likes us to give twenty dollars," she said.

I put my hand over hers. I fetched two twenties from my wallet and turned them over. "My treat."

I hadn't looked her in the face, and I wasn't sure if I should. But she took my hand in a way that seemed personal, so I peeked. She was older than my mother. Or at least seemed to be. "The Lord will bless you," she said.

"Please don't come back to this church," I said.

She dropped my hand, insulted.

"You don't understand," I said. "Reverend Price is my brother, and if he's telling everybody to give twenty dollars, he's probably just trying to get rich. You need a church where you're not giving your good money to a bad man."

I got up and walked out of the church. I didn't want to know her reaction.

WHEN I GOT HOME, I sidetracked myself from Google, but only for a couple of hours. I had a book about reading facial expressions and body movement to determine whether a person was lying. I'd bought it for my mother years earlier, then borrowed it when she finished and never given it back. It was my favorite kind of science, Jane Goodall science. It was waiting for me. There was also a DVD Tizzy had told me to make of the service. I wasn't going to send it to Channel 20, of course; I was going to read Ronald. I hoped the cameraman was going to pan in on him a lot. I was sure he would do so because the congregation looked far too much like a big carton of marshmallow peeps to be interesting.

I wasn't disappointed. The cameraman had done this before. Ronald was not the first preacher who from a distance was too small behind even a custom-made podium. I could play polygrapher. There were a lot of head shots, especially when Ronald was doing what seemed to be his version of emoting. And emoting was the best way to lie.

It took me only twenty minutes into the service, as measured by the bar at the bottom of the screen. It took me a lot longer in actual time, of course, because I kept freeze-framing him. Some clues were easy. He touched his face a lot, and that was the easiest giveaway in the book. Anyone with the tiniest bit of self-consciousness about not being deeply honest would have realized that he needed to fight the urge to scratch his ear, for Chrissakes.

"This is such a happy, proud day," he was saying. "God called you out from sin, and you answered. He knew you by name, and you had faith he would not fail you. God never fails someone when he calls them. Never!" With all that excitement, somehow he felt his ear itch, which wasn't a message from God, but rather a message from his subconscious that he was celebrating his ability to drag more people in.

I had to pause the DVD player when he cast his eyes up. Oh, he looked holy, all right, like Jesus on the cross. I would have to check Jesus out, too. You had to know that it depended on which way a person's eyes rolled upward. This was documented by empirical evidence, but I didn't need clinical proof. Except for my point-keeping system. I had to go slowly, because I was looking at him, so his left was my right. But that was just a formality, really. He rolled his eyes up to the left, and that meant what he said was a fiction, hidden possibly even from him. I knew that! I'd seen Ronald lie deliberately all his life. I'd seen his eyes roll up to the right when he was remembering truths as a child. "Let's not forget that if we are with God in this world, we will achieve his kingdom in the next," he said, and those eyes rolled so far up to the left I saw mostly white.

I was a woman of science, and now I had that empirical evidence that my mother had reared me to cherish. Some small part of me wanted Ronald to believe everything he said. Believe to the point of thinking he knew it. I wouldn't have been proud to have a brother who had lost the truth, but at least he would have been a man of integrity.

On the other hand, if he wasn't a true believer, he was a thinker. He thought the Jesus business had come along and made him—and only him—rich, and now he would bilk as many fools as possible of their discretionary monies. Or maybe of monies they couldn't afford. He was no Bernie Madoff, sick enough to be willing to leave greedy people bankrupt. But he'd contorted his mind enough to prey upon simple people who might just wish on stars for happiness and new cars, or perhaps clouds and harps after it was over.

All I needed to do was get on Google and figure out how he did it.

CHAPTER EIGHTEEN

GOOGLING WAS SADLY too easy. Embarrassingly so. All I had to do was type in "video" and "preach" and "evangelical" and if I wanted to, I could sit in front of my computer and look at holy men talk all day about Jesus Christ and God and church and hearing and seeing and believing. YouTube had dozens of hour-long sermons that only had about 120 hits each, which almost made me sad when I thought about Henri the existentialist cat who deservedly had about six million. After a while I was rocking to their vocal cadences, and I gave them each only about five minutes. I didn't find the burning bush, but I was sure it was up there somewhere. I also was sure that if I went back to Ronald's church often enough, I'd hear one of the sermons I'd seen on Google. I had Ronald's number. He didn't even have to leave his house to know how to be a preacher man.

The possibility of telling no one, not even Ronald and Tizzy, or, rather, especially not Ronald and Tizzy, was on my mind. I had maybe the best piece of information about my brother ever, and I wasn't sure what to do with it. When Klea phoned, I thought I might see how the call went, see if I figured something out in talking to her. She wasn't my new mother. She was my daughter I could use as a reflection of myself.

We were going to talk about her.

Klea was in a predicament to which she was more than entitled. She had chosen her college because she wanted to prove she was more her mother's child than her father's. A girl with a mother who paints and a father who is canny with figures can have all sorts of outcomes, and Klea had been lucky in school. She had been a balanced student, and she had had balanced SATs. She could have pushed for MIT, her advisor said, though the idea horrified Klea. She could have pulled for RISD, but it tilted too far the other way. When the guidance counselor put Hampshire College on her list, she read about it and liked it; never mind what she might have to learn. All she saw was a lot of liberty and a branding as artistic—her father would have to give up any fantasies of her going to Wharton for an MBA.

Now Klea had discovered what she wanted to learn, and it didn't have a great deal to do with all the right-brained focus on imagination and subjective judgment and do-gooding that she had signed on for. Klea had left home in the South, where, her grandmother once had said, "You have to beat the foliage back at the door." In Massachusetts she had learned to treasure the bits of green that came up in spring. She never had seen a crocus at home. Klea wanted to study botany. She wanted to keep riding the 5-College bus over to Smith College and wandering through the greenhouse, and she wanted the power she could have over plant life. It would be the purest of sciences. "I won't get all emotional about your eating my little friends," she said to me.

I told her she had my blessing, and she laughed. So what was the problem? I didn't say anything else.

"You know I can't get what I need here," she said.

"Uh, huh." My silence said, *I'll pay for whatever you want.*

"So I'd have to go somewhere else. Maybe Smith? I wouldn't go there straight out of high school. You know." That was a weighty "you know," but I figured I'd hear the reason eventually. I had a feeling it had nothing to do with Smith being as ridiculous as MIT. "Anyway, I talked to somebody in the botany department over there. I'm not crazy."

"And?" This was taking too long.

"I'm sure I can get in."

I told her if she wanted my permission, she surely knew before she called that she had it. Tuition was tuition, and I assumed airfare to the two schools was the same, and she knew without asking that I would think botany was a terrific subject, so why was she calling?

She had a problem. Seth didn't want her to transfer.

Oh?

"Why else would I call you?"

"Silly me," I said.

That was the last thing I said for ten minutes. Klea held forth with fewer and fewer breaths about how Smith was full of lesbians, and she was going to become a lesbian, and Seth was afraid of losing her, and it wasn't natural anyway to go to an all-girls school, because that practically made you gay, and seeing a boyfriend only when you could get a ride wasn't normal, and wasn't she afraid that he would meet other girls because she was so far away, but, wait, Smith was really only seven miles away, and, really, she could buy a car with her savings, and besides, there was the shuttle that ran every fifteen minutes, and she could sleep over practically every night, and, hey, didn't they love each other?

When she stopped talking, I exhaled long and hard, as if I'd just solved all my own problems. "So Smith it is," I said.

After she hung up I realized that my style with Klea always had been to give her enough rope to hang onto, and eventually she saved herself. Sometimes it took years, but if I waited long enough and looked at her in just the right way, she would learn all the right lessons. I tried to figure out if that was empirically true, that I succeeded because I knew what I was doing. That waiting would get me what I wanted. Of course if that were true, I would have my own church. If that were true, I'd know justice existed. I'd know everyone could be educated to know whatever I thought was true. I'd know that if I waited long enough, Ronald would find out that I wondered if he was lying. I decided that I'd give him some time.

I had seen myself without asking anyone to hold the mirror.

I WAS AN EXTREMELY NON-COMPETITIVE person. Growing up with a brother who could claim the half of the universe that didn't interest me gave me constant peace. I owned everything I wanted in the world, so I never needed to grapple. Some artists resented one another and jockeyed for high price tags and name recognition. I thought my only possible measure was my own work. No one in New Orleans art circles knew I was going to be on Tevor Souriante or showing at the Getty.

So when it came to having to share a man, my sense was that if Avis deserved Mike, she should have him, but if she didn't, he deserved me. The two of us women had no reason ever to need to occupy the same place at the same time. That was one of my mother's favorite laws of physics. Mike's gallery opening was trying to break a great law of physics.

"I think I should stay away," I told Andy that afternoon over the phone. He was supervising the set-up for the opening that night.

"Do you want me to hurt you?" he said.

"Oooh, I'm scared."

"Cesca Price, I have told a lot of people that the famous Cesca Price is going to be here."

"You really know how to motivate a girl who's feeling anti-social, don't you, buddy."

"You want me to pull a Jewish guilt trip on you?" he said. I laughed. Andy Campagna was as far from Jewish as they came. "I've been in this business in this town so long, I'm an honorary Jew," he said.

I knew I had to go. I also knew I could trust Andy. I had had the goods on him for too long on too much. I told him Mike's wife was going to be there, and she was going to make me nervous.

"Oh, sweetheart," he said, "I am so thrilled. You know you can trust your Auntie Andrew. I promise she will never come within ten feet of you."

Andy's gallery was jam-packed for Mike's opening, and within the first hour he sold every piece he had. I was glad he'd stuck with his impressionism but had used it in a completely original way to capture the smallest fragments of New Orleans streetscapes. Andy never had seen anything like it in all the years he'd been in business. "These aren't even all the usual suspects," Andy said as he floated from room to room. "I swear, I don't know a tenth of these people."

"So where are my fans?" I said.

"I just told you that to get you here."

"You don't know me as well as you think you do."

I stayed away from Mike because I was sure Avis would be near him, and I didn't want to see her in person. I wanted her to be an abstraction. But I could pick him out of the crowd from a distance, and his face was bright red, as if he was embarrassed. I didn't study his body language because I could already imagine he was thinking that he was a fraud.

"What am I going to do?" Andy wailed under his breath. "He's got nothing left. I can't even sell prints. What do I tell these people?"

"Oh, come on," I said. I pinched his cheek. It was cold and clammy. Andy was a nervous wreck. "He'll do more."

"But most artists with this kind of success quit their day jobs."

I did quick calculations in my head. But I had no way of knowing if Mike could quit his day job. It seemed to me that all doctors were stinking rich and had large houses and new cars and expensive wives, and Mike had a lot of those accoutrements, or at least he had the car and the wife. I personally couldn't imagine having to paint so someone like Avis could shop all day long. Actually, I couldn't imagine *having* to paint, period.

I told Andy I had a feeling that a lot of the cachet came from buying a painting by one's own doctor. These people looked to me like patients, though for the life of me I couldn't say what a patient looked like. Maybe it was something subliminal in their body language when they came close to Mike.

"What's a patient look like?" Andy said. I shrugged, but I knew I was right. I held up my index finger, letting him know I'd get right back to him.

I worked my way through the crowd over to the refreshments table. Andy wasn't the type to set out food and drink that would please a conscientious physician. Brie. Foie gras. Seafood dip. He didn't have beer, but he had heavy liqueurs. And of course a few harmless uptown offerings like white wine and strawberries. Andy had seen too many friends die. He liked living.

"I wonder what Dr. Rosenthal thinks of this food," I said to a woman who was holding a small plate and carefully spooning dip next to a neat stack of avocado slices. She was surprisingly slender.

"He tells me it's possible to be thin with fatty organs," she said.

"Oh, is he your doctor?"

"Isn't he yours?"

I told her he had been my mother's doctor, and that satisfied her, as if the only reason to be at this opening was to see what a man of science could do. But curiosity-seekers didn't spend money. This woman showed me the $3500 piece she had bought. I recognized it from the colors, his tomato-soup and teal, but this was a work he had done from childhood memory of a country cottage. A patch of neat garden. And a man I spoke to while he was spreading caviar on buttery crackers showed me his purchase, which was one of the three paintings I'd seen originally, the ones where Mike still seemed like a doctor who saw too much pus and blood all day, painting landscapes of red and ochre. The man was a diabetic in Mike's care, he told me, and he felt very much under scrutiny that night. Then he told me he was kidding, that Dr. Rosenthal might have been godlike, but even deities had better things to do than watch whether he behaved.

I was piling up my empirical evidence for Andy, and as I walked through the crowd, I heard a lot of comparisons of symptoms and treatments and much adulation, bordering on adoration, for Mike's diagnostic skills. "I swear, all I told him was where I felt pain, and over the phone—over the phone!—he told me I had helicobacter pylori! He sent me for lab tests, and what do you know? He was right. Now how can a genius like that be an artist, too? I had to bring Peter in to see this for himself. And of course, he's not just good; he's worth buying."

"He can't quit his day job," I told Andy.

His expression said a lot, I thought. I read him to be telling me, *So in ten minutes of cruising around you've figured out that a doctor still needs to earn a six-figure living. Imagine my surprise.*

"You know any of these people?" I said.

"Maybe three or four."

"Well," I said in my most pedagogical voice, "that means the rest of the crowd must be from his fan base. And the only way Mike's built a fan base is by being a doctor. He quits his day job, he loses his fan base."

"You want me to tell him you said that?"

Andy was good. The second he said that, and I knew the answer was no, I realized my logic was faulty. I didn't like to have faulty logic. My reasoning was that people came to buy his work because they liked him as a person. Mike wouldn't want that. I definitely wouldn't want anyone to buy my work because of my personality. I didn't want to come across as particularly offensive in public appearances, because the opposite of being appealing could affect how people saw my work. "I wouldn't buy her paintings; she's a real bitch." But if art didn't sell on its merits, then something shameful was going on. It could be something as annoying as what I saw as the cloying Christianity of Kinkade, or the greed of buyers after an artist's death.

I knew the value of good art was subjective and open to change on whim, and subjectivity was difficult for someone like me who wanted a purely objective world, but the least I could wish for was to slough off forces that had nothing to do with merit. And Mike needed Andy to sell his work for its merit. Not because patients thought the painter was a man of a certain magic, never mind that this man had studied nothing but facts as they were known at any given time.

The party didn't last terribly long, even though it was jam-packed. Andy was pink with pleasure, but he was going to have a lot of leftover food that was too shamefully extravagant to donate to a shelter and too unhealthful to eat for several weeks running. When the crowd started to thin out to the point where stragglers looked self-conscious because they'd already seen all the paintings, I figured it was time for me to leave. I didn't want to go but I thought Avis might still be there. More than one woman looked like her, with freshly round blonde hair. It wasn't possible to measure noses across a gallery, and women who were dressed well moved around too quickly and gracefully to freeze frame.

"Call me tomorrow," I whispered into Andy's cold pink ear, and I left before he could say anything. I imagined I saw Mike popping up over the crowd trying to get my attention, but I didn't turn to acknowledge him.

I WAS IN MY BED in the underpants that I slept in because I lived alone and could sleep in anything I wanted. I was lying with my eyes closed and trying to think. I was heavy-headed, the sort of sad I got when I was sorry for myself. Usually I was sorry for myself when someone hurt my feelings. I needed to think. I tried to think. I was there in my happy underpants. I didn't want anyone else in my bed. I didn't want to have anyone to talk to. At least not in my bed. It was only ten o'clock. It was not too late to have someone to talk to on the phone, though. I thought maybe that was what I wanted, someone to call on the phone. If my mother were alive, I could have called her on the phone.

I wasn't sure that her cutting into my loneliness would help my hurt feelings. Even if she told me why I had them. Who had hurt my feelings? Probably Avis. I lay there and thought about Mike's wife, who didn't even know I existed. If Mike knew what was good for him, he never would have bothered to tell Avis how this show came about. To begin with, he would have protected himself from her disinterest.

But my role had not been insignificant. Insignificant? What was I saying to myself? If I hadn't expressed my opinion to Andy, he would have thought of Mike as a dabbler. New Orleans was full of them, and Andy hated every one, especially straight white men.

So Mike hurt my feelings. He should have found a way to come over and say thank you. He should have found a way to clink his crystal glass that belonged to Andy and get the crowd quiet and tell everyone that the famed Cesca Price was in the room, and she had discovered him, and the night would not have been possible without her help. Instead he'd stood anchored to one spot, panicked and red-faced. He watched people die all the time. He had no reason to be afraid of anything.

I wanted my mother. Hell, I even would've talked to Tizzy if I could have found a way to cut her off from the leader of her herd. She knew all about men who couldn't see past themselves. I was thinking of calling Klea, because Klea, too, was making her choices with Seth in mind, when the phone rang.

In spite of my rationality, I told myself that whoever was calling was going to be important to me. Unless, of course, it was a wrong number. Superstition was rooted in brain chemistry, I had decided long ago.

Caller ID said it was Mike's cell phone. I was tempted not to answer, but if I didn't he might think I'd failed to get home, and in New Orleans that wasn't a fair impression to give anyone. Crime on the street was a real possibility. "That was so wrong," he said when I answered.

"Where are you?" I said.

"At the hospital."

"Oh."

"I'm checking on a patient so I can call you."

"Oh."

"Listen, not being able to be with you for even one second ruined the entire evening for me," he said.

I told him I was there, that I was moving around, that I was conspicuous, that the only time I was ever in conversation was when I talked to Andy, and I easily was pulled out of that.

"I was furious that she insisted on coming," he said.

I didn't know what to say to that.

"I swear, there has never been one time in all the years I've known Avis that anything I did was of interest to her. I'm talking about awards dinners and medical meetings in beautiful places like San Diego. But for some reason she thought being my wife tonight made her look good."

"It definitely was a great moment," I said. "You sold out almost as soon as the show started. Andy's never had that happen before."

"You mean he wasn't just saying that?"

"Andy does not bullshit. Particularly with a new artist. He was hoping you'd have an uphill climb; I could tell. But he actually joked about your quitting your day job. I promise; if you were waiting tables, he'd have told you to start painting full-time."

"Wow," he said, sounding like anything but a doctor.

I could feel myself getting sad again. "So," I said, "I was getting ready to go to sleep when you called." He already had had a good night. He didn't need to extend it by calling me.

"Could I come over?"

"I don't think so."

"Are you upset about something?" he said.

"I shouldn't be," I said. "Let's talk soon." Then I hung up.

CHAPTER NINETEEN

EVERYWHERE I TURNED, people close to me were getting what they wanted. I liked to think that my wisdom and ability to forget my own expectations played a role most of the time. This was especially true for Ronald, who was building his selfish little empire, sad soul by sad soul, out there across the parish line where I didn't have to know about it unless I talked to Tizzy on the phone and heard her not bother to struggle with herself. There was so much money that Ronald never knew how much she was squirreling away in 529 accounts and trust funds for Gracie and Levi. I suggested she might siphon off some large chunks into a Tizzy fund so she could escape when the day of Ronald's downfall inevitably arrived. "Oh, I'm way ahead of you," she said. "JesusCleanup has a pension fund that's so convoluted Ronald will never find what I've socked away."

I enjoyed the peace, of not struggling with my brother, my daughter, even Mike, because they were filling up their lives without taking anything out of mine. They were too busy to upset me.

Then I got an e-mail from PBS, and next, to my surprise, I read about myself in the *Times-Picayune*. New Orleans liked nothing better than a local who got a blip on the national scene, and my interview was going to air on Friday. The paper had a file photo of me from five years earlier, and I looked terrific.

It was airing in prime time, and Mike made a point of coming over to watch with me. I was grateful, because it would have been pitiful to see it alone, and I came right out and told him so. He knew better than to ask why I wasn't watching it with my family. I was going to get a DVD from the network, but I was recording it anyway.

In the first two minutes, I knew I was going to be sorry, not for the evening but for a long time. I had forgotten that the interview was two days after I'd gone to court with Ronald, and in spite of all my brushing up on art theory, all I had on my mind that day was what a numbskull and thief I thought my brother might be. Tevor Souriante was doing what a journalist did: he slipped family conflict into his interviews. And in the process I was on television calling my brother a charlatan and a crook. I had not known the camera was already rolling when I was at my angriest. "How did he get that out of me?" I said to the set.

"Well, I sure never did," Mike said.

The phone rang the second it was over. I picked up. Ronald's voice said, "You're going to be sorry you were ever born," and then I heard a click.

"That was short and sweet," I said to Mike.

RONALD HAD A NEW LAWYER. Tom Leyden. Ronald was a wealthy man now, and even though all of his congregants surely lived in outlying parishes, Jefferson and St. John and St. Charles, Ronald finally had become a man to be reckoned with in the City of New Orleans, so he had a dignified attorney at Liskow& Lewis in One Shell Square. Dignified attorneys didn't do frivolous lawsuits, and I would have thought they wouldn't be wild about representing a man who was something of a television cartoon, but evidently going after Cesca Price was classy enough. Once again I was served papers, and once again I called Mr. Alverson.

"You did libel him," he said.

"Isn't libel supposed to be erroneous?" I said.

"What's he doing, promising eternal life?" Mr. Alverson said. "I'm good, but not that good."

"I admit I wasn't sure then, but I've got a lot of evidence now that he probably doesn't believe in God," I said. "I mean he says Jesus works for him, but only for him. He's got to be a big phony." I wondered how I could work in suspicions of murdering my mother.

Mr. Alverson could see he had his work cut out for him.

I waited until I knew no one was at home at Ronald's house, and I left a message on the answering machine. "It's Cesca. If you were smart, you'd drop this whole thing. I guarantee you not one person in your entire congregation has even heard of PBS. But if you do this, I promise every single one of them will know I'm going to find a way to prove to the world you're a big fake. Not to mention there's a lot more I could tell them. Think *string beans.* You just watch that money dry up. I win any way you look at it, buddy."

A couple of hours later Mr. Alverson phoned. "I don't know what you said on your brother's answering machine, but Tom Leyden phoned and gave me a message from him. Basically he said, 'Bring it on.' Did you two fight a lot as children?"

"No," I said. "We just confounded each other pretty intensely."

Evidently our shared history was a drama that the media found endlessly entertaining. Channel 12 put an announcement in the paper that it was replaying the Tevor Souriante interview because it had generated a lawsuit. Channels 4 and 6 took clips from the beginning of it and did news reports. I was asked to do interviews but very maturely turned them down on advice of counsel and on the basis of plain old common sense. Ronald, on the other hand, saw an opportunity to vindicate himself in front of everyone who'd ever avoided him in his first fifteen years of life, as well as to reassure all those who venerated him now, and he went on all the morning shows on the local channels. I used my DVR and my fast-forward feature to catch him in action. It was for my own amusement. Mr. Alverson said I should have recorded Ronald on DVD. Why? For evidence. I had his old service on DVD. I could show where he was lying. Not enough. I should audio-tape, or video-record Ronald from my TV set. He was surely incriminating himself. He claimed that once JesusCleanup started being religious, his business expanded ten-fold, and wasn't that proof of his commitment to God? "See?" he would tell an interviewer, "I was a man of God long before my mother died."

I wondered at that moment whether I could bring in the entire televiewing audience of the metropolitan region to testify against him. Surely logic played a role in a courtroom.

The one witness Mr. Alverson wanted, of course, could not be made to testify because she was married to the man who was suing me. I thought that was no problem. Tizzy was long overdue to get a divorce. But with my Klea rule in place, I wasn't going to come right out and tell anyone that it was time to act; I was going to wait for her to come to her own conclusion. With me trying not to be direct. Of course, I'd been waiting for Tizzy to get a divorce practically since her wedding reception. She'd lived a religious life, and she'd become Elizabeth, and I'd waited, and she'd become Tizzy again, and now she had money for independence, and I had to wonder how long it would take for her to come full circle, unchanged except for the matter of children.

There was no harm in calling her and saying, "Mr. Alverson sure wishes you could be a witness on my behalf."

She hesitated. That could have had many meanings. But I was talking to her on her office phone, so I gave it a practical one. "I've had the same thought," she said finally.

"And?"

"I know what you're thinking, Cesca. I always know what you're thinking, especially when you're not saying anything."

"And?"

"I can't exactly rush into a divorce for somebody else's benefit."

"Probably a better idea than doing it for your own reasons. Then you'd have somebody else to blame."

She laughed. "I've been kind of figuring that if I got a divorce, and my life went to hell, I'd already have Ronald to blame for the rest of my natural life."

"I don't know about you, but I kind of blame Ronald for your life ever since you met him."

"Thanks a lot."

"Hey, I can say that," I said. "I lived with him most of the years before you did. He wrecked the good thing I had going on with my mother." I started to feel sad because I'd just hit a truth that could make me so angry I'd want to squeeze Ronald back to a zygote. So I shook my head, no, until it was gone.

Neither Tizzy nor I knew the law. But, she said, she knew what was right. Like me, she didn't see a whole lot of wiggle room in what was right. So if I told Mr. Alverson to go as far as he could in subpoenaing her, she would do her best not to be Ronald's cohabiting wife by the time of the trial. "And I know very well that Ronald gave you the go-ahead to take your mother off life support when the subject of her money was put on his table," she said. "In case you've forgotten, I remember."

I wanted to ask about the Thanksgiving food, but Tizzy was the one who cooked it.

RONALD PHONED ON MONDAY morning. I was in my studio, so I let the answering machine pick up. I had a new message. "If you are calling before noon, I'm sorry, but these are my studio hours, and I can't be disturbed. Please leave a message, and I'll call back in the afternoon. Thank you." I had the machine in the studio because I would interrupt if it was someone important or someone I needed.

Ronald started screaming. "Your studio is a playroom, Cesca! You can answer the phone, and you know it. I hope you're happy. The service yesterday was a nightmare. Donations were down maybe 80 percent. Attendance was all right, but only because every single person was there to talk to me afterwards. I didn't get out of there for probably two hours. Over and over, 'Is what they're saying on TV the truth?' 'I read something terrible in the paper. Tell me the truth, Reverend, please, tell me the truth.' Two hours! It's fine they showed up, but you want to tell me how in the name of all that's holy I'm going to pay for that church?"

I checked Caller ID. He was using his cell phone. I considered leaving a message on his land line right away, saying quite simply, *Cesca who can't balance a checkbook told you so*, but I thought silence would be better. It wasn't just that silence always had been the cruelest weapon against Ronald. It was also that getting into a dialogue with him was like arguing with the Jabberwock, only never slaying him.

I dug out my cassette recorder and recorded Ronald's message. Half of it was about a drop-off in donations and what Ronald was going to do about paying for the church. It seemed to me that the rest expressed annoyance about the congregants' skepticism, which to me translated into a possible loss of revenues. Evidence. If I wasn't careful, I might find a litigious corner of my brain. The law definitely played into my need for truth. Even if most attorneys played fast and loose with it.

At 12:30 the phone rang again. I was sure it was Ronald and almost ignored it. But it was Mr. Alverson. "Leyden tells me your brother says you're not returning his calls," he said.

"My brother is trying to run up your bill," I said.

"I told him to answer that if he loses this suit, he'll be charged for legal costs," Mr. Alverson said. "I also reminded him that contact between litigants is generally frowned upon in a civil case."

I told Mr. Alverson that I would definitely give him a hug when I saw him the next time. He said he would consider taking something off his bill if I did so.

It was possible to pay all kinds of people to take care of me. But occasionally people did it out of goodness. I might find some more goodness.

AVIS LIKED THE FACT of Mike's art, but she did not like the process. "It's like babies," Mike said. "She never wanted to be awake until they were clean and dressed." Mike preferred oils to acrylics, and any room he used smelled wonderful to him but terrible to her. Painting also was messy, no matter how hard Mike tried to conceal what he was doing. To Avis an unfinished canvas was an eyesore. A palette that did not look as if it came straight from the store was unsightly. And what was this with canvas on the guest-room floor? Or sketches propped up against the wall? Yes, she knew, the door was closed, but she knew this room was in her house, unused all day and left so awfully sloppy, and she could not be comfortable. It didn't matter that some of the most famous men in history had had studios in Paris that looked just like this. It was her house. She wanted it converted back into a guest room. Klea rule: wait to see what he will do, despite a strong desire to tell him to tell her to go fuck herself.

He was wondering, given that he had nowhere to paint, whether he could rent a corner of my studio.

Rent?

The worst sadness, the sadness that comes from hurt feelings, started to well up in my heavy head.

We were on the phone, and he couldn't see me, but he could hear my silence.

He apologized. "I know you need your privacy," he said. "That was presumptuous of me."

I still said nothing.

"I'm sorry I said anything. I take it back. I'll think of something else."

"Why would you think I'd want rent from you?" I said finally.

CHAPTER TWENTY

PRICE VS. PRICE WAS NOT the same kind of civil trial that the last *Price vs. Price* had been. We had a courtroom of our own, with a seating area for press and spectators. What happened wasn't going to create legal precedent, but it was going to set personal precedent, religious precedent, even, and in truth, Ronald and I were interesting. A suit for five million dollars in damages was attention-grabbing when it involved just two people. Neither of us would be beloved if we lost. I wasn't sure how heroic either of us would be if we won. But I hadn't gone into this to be judged in public. Actually I hadn't gone into this for any reason except that I had no choice.

Ronald started out not playing fair. He used Levi and Gracie as his first witnesses. Tom Leyden was clever. "Did you grow up in a good Christian home?" "Did your father have one set of rules in your house and another one in his church?" "Are you allowed to say bad words?" "Do you pray before you eat?" I saw their faces. Especially Gracie's. She was a reluctant witness. "Well, sure" and "I guess not" were her kinds of answers. Levi stuck with, "Uh, huh" and "uh, uh." Leyden didn't care. It was his expression that counted. Triumphant. He was interpreting for the jury. A jury, Mr. Alverson assured me, that had been through a *voir dire* that was so nuanced Ronald's lawyer would never know what hit him. Three of them had names like Miller that didn't sound Jewish, but were.

For Ronald and his bottom-line attorney, the issue was impending financial disaster. Ronald was suing me for libel, yes, but for libel that would result in the collapse of his empire. He was asking for projected loss of income in the millions. Mr. Alverson mumbled to me when he heard the opening argument, "*Res ipsa loquitur,*" and I knew I couldn't laugh. In due time, Mr. Alverson would come out and say that monetary damages spoke for themselves. If this was all about money, wasn't Ronald into his alleged profession of faith in the almighty dollar? Mr. Alverson had told me beforehand that he didn't often get a kick out of the practice of law, but the wordplay alone was going to keep him entertained for the duration of this trial. "I hope the satisfaction that comes from success will play a role," I said. "Oh, yes," he said. He had pure blue eyes that looked all the happier against the backdrop of pure white hair. I was glad haircuts weren't as important to him as to Tom Leyden.

Mr. Alverson didn't cross-examine Levi because Levi was too grumpy, and he had been told beforehand that Gracie was my little protégé, and Gracie had uncommon good sense, so he went for her. "So you said your father practices Christianity at home?" Mr. Alverson said.

"I guess so. We pray."

"According to your father, what does Christianity say about the woman in the family?"

I could see Gracie get the tiniest smile on her sweet little round face. "Well, according to something in the Bible somewhere, the man is the head of the woman. So everything my dad said to do was what my mom had to do. I thought that was stupid. I guess my mom finally figured it out, because she got an apartment."

"Objection!" Leyden was on his feet, but Gracie already had made her point.

I checked Ronald out of the corner of my eye. He was failing to get Gracie's attention with an expression that said, *I'm going to make you cry.* She was looking straight at Mr. Alverson.

The judge had the last couple of sentences stricken from the record, but I would remember them, and I didn't see how anyone else could forget. Especially a jury made up of nine women and three men. I adored Mr. Alverson.

"Okay, Gracie," Mr. Alverson said, sounding like her best friend, "we'll stick to the facts at hand. How did your parents handle money when your mother used to live in the house?"

"She got a small allowance. She worked full-time for my dad. Can I say that?" She looked in the direction of Tom Leyden, as if he were going to attack her physically. She knew loving mothers were on the jury. No one said a word. "My mom ran the business, but she didn't get a salary, not really. At least that's what she told me if I asked for money."

Gracie could not have done better if she had been coached. She'd just given Mr. Alverson a chance to ask her if she donated to her father's church. No, she said. Everybody was supposed to give twenty dollars, and she never had that kind of money. No further questions.

In a shameful way, I enjoyed watching Leyden present his case. The man had upper-crust Trinity Episcopal written all over him. His form of religious observation surely consisted of listening to astonishing organ music on Sunday mornings when he chose to go, then milling around with people much like himself, careful not to stray into the ghetto that was mere inches from the venerable old church. Having to consider faith or belief never crossed his mind. It would be crass. To have to question people on the stand so they looked sincere about their commitment to Jesus Christ and God and the Holy Spirit, whoever all of them were, was embarrassing and distasteful. I could tell he was worried word would leak out to his social peers that he was sounding sincere about this religious foolishness. Clearly he'd had to look hard at his New Testament, which he'd probably had to order from Amazon because he couldn't imagine walking into the Garden District Book Shop and asking for one. It would have come with an Old Testament attached.

"I watched Reverend Price's service on television on a recent Sunday," he said to a woman on the stand. The witness was named

Mrs. Koppel, and she was wearing a floral-patterned dress that had pastels only in a few of the flowers. "He was saying that the Bible is the revelation of God's word. Does he help you understand this?"

"Oh, my, yes," Mrs. Koppel said. "Reverend Price knows his Bible back and forth, inside out and upside down. Before I came to his church, I had so little guidance in my life. But now I have the Reverend to interpret the Lord's word for me."

Leyden announced that he had a video he would like to introduce into evidence at that time. He then played the first two minutes of Tevor Souriante's interview with me. I tried to keep my face neutral, but I couldn't help what color it was.

"Here's this brother who says he wants a couple million dollars to be some sort of evangelist," I was saying, "but I know he'll be bilking people out of their money so he can get rich. Well, extremely rich, because anyone with any sense would be happy with what our mother left him."

"Okay!" Leyden said, shutting off the recorder like a pianist at the end of a rhapsodic performance. Mrs. Koppel was still on the stand. "I trust you have seen this interview." Yes, Mrs. Koppel had seen the interview—at least, those two minutes. I knew very well that Mrs. Koppel wasn't interested in art theory and had skipped the rest. "And as a member of Reverend Price's church, how were you affected by what Miss Price said?"

"Oh, my, I got to say that my faith was shaken terribly," she said. "Nobody knew what to think. This is the reverend's sister and all. I don't want to go to a church where the preacher don't believe in nothing but money."

"So are you saying that what you saw on that video might influence you to leave Reverend Price's church?"

"For sure," Mrs. Koppel said. "He's asking us to give twenty dollars every week, see? He says that makes us very 'invested' in our church. 'Invested' is his exact word. So I'd like to think this is a man who truly has accepted Christ as his personal Lord and savior. I got to think Reverend Price is a man of God who will tell me what has been revealed through the Holy Spirit, but what am I to make of the things this woman says on television?"

When it was his turn, Mr. Alverson started with a simple question. Was Mrs. Koppel still a member of Ronald's church? Oh, yes, of course.

He could have left it at that as far as I was concerned.

But he had another matter on his mind. Poor, sincere Mrs. Koppel never knew what hit her. "So," he said, "do you speak with this Reverend Price and have him quote Scripture to you to solve your concerns?"

"Why, no, I'm just in the congregation."

"So he's just reading to you from a script? Or maybe he's speaking from notes?"

"Well, he's talking from the pulpit, yes."

"And for all you know, the only Bible passages he knows are the ones he throws out at you, right?"

Mrs. Koppel pulled her puffy little self up and thrust her breasts out in a threatening way. "The Reverend knows dozens and dozens of quotes from the Bible. Even the Jew part that we got from before Jesus. He builds our faith."

That was all Mr. Alverson needed.

WE STARTED WITH TWO SURPRISE witnesses for Ronald. Tizzy shouldn't have been a surprise, but the church woman was.

The church woman was Karen Kohler, the woman to whom I'd given twenty dollars and begged not to return. Evidently after I walked out of church that day, her head turned a good 270 degrees on its stalk; she was completely confused. Tizzy had seen her and scurried over, not knowing what I might have done. That was how Karen failed to disappear into a cheaper, more sincere church. Tizzy had told her that I probably wanted her to stay in touch some because she would be needed to perform an act of goodness.

Mr. Alverson called her first. Yes, she was on disability. Yes, she wanted a good church near her house. Yes, this reverend had out and out told the congregation that the church was just starting up and needed each and every one of them to donate twenty dollars each and every week. And what had she done? She had saved up from her grocery money. She was helping to build her church.

How did she get down to court today? Leyden asked. In a taxi. Did she pay for the taxi? No, she didn't. Mr. Alverson had sent her a voucher. No further questions. Karen stood up. Her clothes were ironed, but they weren't new, and they didn't fit. She looked as if a ride in a taxi was a treat she deserved. In fact, I bet the jury was hoping she'd get a nice lunch out of the deal.

It was time for the only witness who counted right now, in my opinion.

Mr. Alverson called Tizzy Price to the stand. Tizzy. That's how she stated her name.

He asked her what her current marital status was. She said she was married but separated from the plaintiff. And she planned to divorce him. Was she testifying of her own free will? Oh, yes.

Mr. Alverson asked Tizzy to describe for the court how JesusCleanup had come into existence.

"Well, it was sort of by accident," she said. "Our business was doing crime-scene cleanup, which we got a franchise for because it seemed like a good business to do in New Orleans, you know?" She looked around the courtroom and got the laugh she expected. "But I'm here to tell you that in New Orleans you don't have very well off victims, so we weren't doing all that well. And then one day this particular guy on our crew just happened to say a little prayer after he did a site that was really sad, I think it was where a kid got shot in a drive-by or something, probably in Jefferson, and the word got out that we were Christian or something, and Ronald said, 'Holy s-h-i-t, we're on to something; we're making a pile of money, Jesus is sure taking care of *me*,' and we changed our business to JesusCleanup, and we got all *religious.* We don't clean up after Jews and Muslims, but they don't get shot too much, at least not in this part of the country."

"So Mr. Price changed the business for monetary gain," Mr. Alverson said.

Leyden objected, but he was overruled, and Tizzy said, "Pretty much," looking straight at Ronald as if to say, *Bet you never dreamed this day would come.*

Mr. Alverson said he'd like to ask her if a similar thing had transpired in the formation of Mr. Price's church. He'd like to take her to the day her mother-in-law passed away. Well, the day before. Tizzy nodded agreeably.

"Could you tell us about your husband's involvement in the decision to turn off his mother's life support?"

Tizzy had the jury on the edges of their seats. "My sister-in-law, Cesca Price, had medical power of attorney, but she was being fair. She was asking for Ronald's input in the decision. You see," Tizzy said patiently, "the decision was a little complicated because Mrs. Price wasn't completely brain dead, but she was pretty much a vegetable; excuse me, in a vegetative state, and it's a matter of judgment whether to let her die. Which of course was what Mrs. Price would have wanted. Anybody who knew her would've known that. Anyway, Ronald went on about how turning off life support was murder, and Cesca left not knowing what she was going to do. So I just plain old lost my patience, and I apologize for this, but I said to my husband, 'Look, you know you've just been waiting for your inheritance so you can buy your church, so why don't you just cut out all this Christian bull-s-h-i-t and tell Cesca to pull the plug?' And do you know he called her cell probably thirty seconds later and acted all holy and said he'd go along with her decision?"

Leyden objected to Tizzy saying he acted holy, but if that was all he could find in that long story, Ronald wasn't looking too good. I hoped the next topic would be murder by mushroom soup and hollering, but I had a feeling that Mr. Alverson wasn't going to try to pretend he was on *Forensic Files* in a city where most labs were in recovery from drowning and most minds were chronically waterlogged. Which was too bad, because I had a hell of a countersuit. Instead, he let Leyden cross-examine.

Leyden asked whether he understood correctly that she was the estranged spouse of the plaintiff. Tizzy said that if that meant that she was separated, then yes. She opened her mouth to say more, then shut it. And had she also said she planned to divorce Mr. Price? Yes. Then the lawyer went for what he thought was Tizzy's soft underbelly. "You will have nothing to lose in a divorce if Mr. Price's church is closed, is that correct?"

"He didn't tell you we mortgaged our house to make a down payment on it?" Tizzy said.

Leyden froze. "Ah, okay." This clearly was news to him. He was getting a fresh lesson in truth.

"Now as to what transpired between you and your husband the day before your mother-in-law passed away, can you give me any evidence of previous behavior that would have led you to make such a statement to him?"

"Just ask my kids. Every time my mother-in-law was a cheapskate, Ronald said, 'More for me. Another pew for the church.'"

Leyden shrugged his shoulders and said, "Now, come on, we all say that sort of thing about our parents."

Mr. Alverson objected that he was arguing with the witness. I didn't object. It made Leyden look like a jackass.

Leyden kept trying to prove Tizzy was a liar. Making up a story about Mama's life support. Pretending that Ronald prayed over murder sites only because it paid well. "Would you consider yourself an honest person?" he said to Tizzy. I could feel Mr. Alverson getting ready to jump, and I grabbed his arm so he would stay still.

"It's because I'm an honest person that I'm getting a divorce," Tizzy said. "I got tired of doing things I didn't believe in just to please my husband."

Mr. Alverson had been planning to call me to the stand, but he decided I would be overkill. He told the court he had no more witnesses.

Leyden looked as if he was considering calling Ronald. It seemed it occurred to him that he could ask many questions to which he would not know the answers. He decided not to call any more witnesses. "Wait!" Ronald hollered to him, doing himself no good. The lawyer ran over fast, as if he could stop air from escaping from a small balloon. Everyone in the room, the judge, the jury, the press, the gawkers, bailiffs, Mr. Alverson, and I, all watched in silence, as if we might hear, while Ronald turned bright red as he whispered and pounded his fist on the table in front of himself. He wasn't praying. He probably wasn't obeying the third commandment.

"I'd like to call Ronald Price to the stand," Leyden said finally.

Once Ronald had returned to his normal blood pressure, Leyden asked him to please tell about when he became a Christian.

Not one person in the courtroom could find a dishonest word in what Ronald said then. He grew up in a wealthy, secular family. He admitted, with all the shame he could muster, that he was deeply hurt when his father, on his deathbed, said that he was glad his children were all right because he was leaving his entire estate for his wife to use in her lifetime. He needed her to feel taken care of. All Ronald had felt, he said, was hurt and abandoned. "My father didn't take care of me."

And then, he recounted, "As I failed and failed to make ends meet, something mystical happened. As the court knows, one man prayed at a crime scene, and it was as if God through Jesus had come to take care of me. In a way that my father had not. It was that single prayer by that one man that had changed my life." This was not Ronald of the pulpit. This wasn't even the Ronald I'd known all my life. Or even a Ronald who wanted my money.

"I went from a non-believer to a believer. God was my new

father; Jesus would take care of me," he said. "Everything I did after that day was based on my new beliefs. Yes, I admit, I was insatiable when it came to money. I mixed having money up with feeling powerful. And loved. And *venerated.* And I knew that was sinful. But it had nothing to do with my faith. My faith was pure: anyone who attacked me was just not able to see what had happened to me. Though I try to understand. I'm honestly a man of God. Very flawed, but I'm trying to prove my faith. I promise that to all of you. Money is an important measure to me. But God is more important." His voice was almost a whisper.

No questions, Mr. Alverson said.

"Damn," I whispered. I didn't need to watch Ronald's eyes. Either he was telling the truth, or he was the best liar in the history of the world. I wondered if anyone else could tell.

We were going to have a slightly late lunch. But only slightly. Mr. Alverson was calling another witness.

And that was when Ronald Price saw Herbert Coston for the first time the way he really was. He'd had no idea Herbert was waiting in the hallway. Herbert did a lot of waiting in hallways, but this time he was feeling all right.

It took only two minutes.

When Herbert said, "So, see, far as I'm concerned, praying only good for two things, keeping my mama happy, and maybe keeping ghostses out the room," Ronald burst into tears.

"Damn," I said again. Any other time, I would have enjoyed seeing him cry.

Mr. Leyden had no questions.

I WASN'T FEELING TRIUMPHANT during lunch. All I could find to eat were a bag of dried cranberries and a can of apple juice. I knew my belly was going to make me aware of it all afternoon, but I was too hungry to care. I popped those cranberries and tried to smile at Mr.

Alverson, who evidently had great genes and no conscience because he put away a cheeseburger dressed and dripping, using up two dozen paper napkins in the process. "They couldn't even bother to find someone who walked away from the church because of your allegations," he said to try to cheer me up, covering his full mouth with a fistful of napkins. Mr. Alverson was an old bad boy, and I had to admit I enjoyed him enjoying himself.

"We kind of dropped the bomb on Hiroshima," I said.

"Hiroshima rebuilt," Mr. Alverson said. "This is civil court."

I told myself I was going to have to think about conscience when I had some time. Right then, I was just going to save myself five million dollars. Though maybe I owed Ronald something.

It was too bad that Mr. Alverson had to go first with his closing statement, but he was a hard act to follow. Ronald was suing me for an enormous sum. It was all projected losses; he was claiming I had destroyed his reputation, and all he had to rely on to make a living was his good name. Mr. Alverson tried as hard as he could not to appear to be having a good time as he spoke to the jury about how absurd this lawsuit was.

"The burden of proof is on Mr. Price to show you that his sister has maliciously lied about him in a public forum," Mr. Alverson told the jury. "She says he runs a crime-scene cleanup business where crews pray for profit—and we've proven that it's true. Unless they pray to scare away ghosts and their mamas. But that's beside the point. She says he wanted his mother to die right away so he could get his inheritance to buy a church—and we've proven that's true, too. This is not defamation and slander. This is a statement of facts. Mr. Price is using piety to make money, and Ms. Price has stated that fact in a television interview. She cannot be sued for stating the truth."

Tom Leyden did what he had to do, which was to ignore the facts we thought were important. Ronald was a good Christian, a true, honest leader of his church. Leyden reminded the jury of a tape he had played of one of Ronald's services where Ronald was giving a sermon on how sins could be forgiven through the death and resurrection of Jesus Christ. I wondered what was going on in Leyden's mind, because men like him did not particularly care for religiosity. He could say such words, but only in a group response, or maybe in a hymn. "Here is a man who runs a true Christian home, who has dedicated himself fully to a congregation of devout followers, and a jealous sibling wants to destroy everything he has worked for. He will have an uphill battle of biblical proportions to recover from this onslaught, and she deserves to pay damages for her vindictive attack."

Next to me, Mr. Alverson let out the tiniest snort of derision that I was sure only I could hear. It carried many messages, not the least of which was, *Don't forget three of them are Jewish.*

I listened to both sides, as if I were a juror. They both were right, technically. I needed to be a Ronald. I needed to focus on money. I needed to win. This was a child's tug-of-war over five million dollars. It had been coming for a long time.

The wait seemed interminable, even though afterward I would look at my watch and realize it was only an hour and a half. Mr. Alverson and I sat on a hallway bench, he fat and full, I far too aware of apple juice and cranberries. I could see Ronald a good ten yards down the corridor talking with Tom Leyden. Ronald's expression was one I'd never seen on him before. He was trying to nod with enthusiasm as Leyden talked energetically. Leyden was spending his forty percent in his mind. Leyden was on contingency. Ronald owed Leyden hope. So Ronald was nodding fast, but his face wasn't thoroughly enjoying his three million. "What's Leyden get if he loses?" I said to Mr. Alverson.

"Maybe streetcar fare," he said. "I'll give it to him myself."

I tried to reach around his shoulder to hug him, but my arm didn't go that far. I hugged as far as I could. I wasn't sure how I felt about Ronald, but I knew I wanted Leyden to walk away having wasted his time.

I slipped off to phone Mike. This was his afternoon off, and he was in the studio. He found it difficult to take something for nothing, especially from a woman, but he was learning. Sharing work space with me was a first step for him. And probably an only step.

"It's going to be soon," I said.

"Your voice is shaky," Mike said.

I hadn't known that. I asked if he'd still be there, and he said he hoped so. I told him my victory might be pyrrhic, that if I won I'd keep my money, but I might ruin an honest man.

"Your brother?"

"After all this, I think maybe he's not faking."

"Lucky you don't have to tell your mother," he said.

I didn't know if Mike and I would see each other. Unpredictability was good. Ambiguity also was good, especially since we did a lot of painting and talking. We planned to go on like that forever. At least I did.

The bailiff finally called us in. I held Mr. Alverson's arm so we could let Ronald and Leyden go past us and enter first. I wanted Ronald to be confident. Win or lose, I wanted him to be confident. "Why'd you do that?" Mr. Alverson whispered to me.

"Because Leyden thinks he's won something."

The judge gave nothing away. The jury gave nothing away. The clerk walked back and forth with a lot of papers. I was trembling now, and I hunched over so I could fold my hands together in my lap. Mr. Alverson leaned over and whispered. "Sit up real straight so you win no matter what. But you're going to win or you don't have to pay me."

I sat up.

Ten seconds later the judge made the announcement. The jury had found in favor of the defendant.

"Five million saved for you, a chunk of real change for me," Mr. Alverson whispered out of the side of his mouth.

I giggled with relief, forgetting to care who saw.

Before the courtroom could empty out, I asked Mr. Alverson to see if the judge would let me speak. He said that would never happen;

I should just stand up and talk. I figured I had about ten seconds. For the first time I could remember, I felt bad for Ronald. He probably already had pocketed his three million in his mind. He probably already had expanded his ministry, bought a new house and cars, maybe found a beautiful girlfriend. It seemed that Ronald thought God and mammon could co-exist beautifully. In fact, dollars were the measure of Jesus's love, just as they'd been the measure of Daddy's.

I also felt good for myself in a perverse way. My brother could be as religious as the day Herbert prayed—never mind why Herbert prayed. Mama never would know. Even though it meant my brother wasn't rational, at least he wasn't a phony. He was greedy, and that didn't make him at all the humanist my mother had wanted us both to be, but he was honest. If an uptown rich man could be, and I thought it was remotely possible.

I stood up. "I just want to tell my brother that I hope we can put this behind us, and I wish him a good future," I said loudly. I meant it. This was going to be the beginning of peaceful times between us. I would respect him, if he would respect me. That was a truth. I looked at him expectantly.

"When you believe I'm honest, we'll get along just fine," Ronald said.

"When you believe I'm a good person, we'll get along just fine," I said back.

What we needed was for our mother to come back, but I didn't say that. If I did, I expected he'd look up at the ceiling, and I'd look, too, before I had time to think.

CHAPTER TWENTY-ONE

IF MY MOTHER HAD been around, she and I would have talked about whether sacraments and holidays existed for partitioning out the year so that people could make sense of time. Of course we wouldn't give any validity to the events themselves, but we'd try to sort out whether the mind needed cycles for figuring out meaning. I would say we had seasons, and she would counter that not everyone had seasons, especially us, and I would say back that we had months, and she would argue that months were artificial constructs, and eventually we'd talk about astrology, and we'd start laughing.

Without my mother, I faced Easter and took it as a milestone that surely would be useful. Never mind its Christian meaning, or even its proto-meaning from Passover; it was coming just far enough past Christmas for my family to have to show itself for what it had become in the interim. I wasn't sure of much, but I did know that my mother and Shellonde would not be at the table. Klea, Seth, Ronald, and Tizzy had to be figured out one at a time, then maybe re-figured out.

It would be spring break. "New Orleans is a much cooler idea than Florida," Klea said. "But I'm not bringing Seth if he has to have another total trauma."

I told her I could not guarantee a deathless vacation, but I would do my very best.

"Sorry," she said. "That wasn't very nice."

Ronald wasn't the next person I called. Easter at his house always meant a dead pig, and at all times I was perilously close to buying myself a micro-mini as a pet. Now I could find a way around him. The universe was divided once more, with ham and Jesus comfortably on one side and his estranged wife and dreams of micro-minis on the other. I called Tizzy.

I told her Klea was coming for Easter. "I guess you can figure my kids will eat once at Ronald's," she said. "Probably get trichinosis from him trying to cook. But I'll do something, too. Just heavy on the chocolate and light on the resurrection."

I BROUGHT A HUGE bottle of Absolut 100. No salad, no dessert. Klea knew she might have to be the designated driver going home. "I don't care," she said when we got in the car. "It's obviously going to be worth it."

Tizzy had a wonderful apartment. I'd been wrong about her having been the one who chose the décor in the house she'd lived in with Ronald. That house had been sleek and costly and had taken no risks. This apartment had the deep, dark, happy colors of my most exuberant paintings—almost a full 64 Crayola box. When we walked in, she said, "I'll buy when the divorce is final, but why not enjoy myself now?" I thought of two of my paintings I wanted to give her and one of Mike's new ones I would buy for her. Nothing I'd ever done had hung on one of Ronald's walls.

I realized I could get the Rodrigue out of storage. For myself, though it would look great in here.

I proffered the black vodka bottle. "This won't match the room," she said. "We'll have to kill it."

I followed her into the kitchen. It was then I realized I finally was going to get the answer to my question. I wasn't sure I wanted it.

All the dishes were covered with aluminum foil.

"Tonic? Sprite? Water? Ice?" Tizzy held a glass tumbler in one hand and the vodka bottle in the other.

"Go for tonic," I said.

Gracie and Klea walked in. I could hear low-timbre sounds from the next room that meant Seth and Levi were going to have a language all their own for the rest of the day. "On the rocks for me," Klea said.

"But I can already tell you you're going to be driving home," Tizzy said.

"Seth!" Klea called out. I tried to give her a stern look. "Hey, he's driven in midtown Manhattan," she said.

"On the rocks it is," I said.

I took a long draw on my drink, felt it hit, reached tentatively for the nearest covered dish.

"You're going to like it," Gracie said.

I pulled my hand back. I sensed a promise of Twenty Questions, and Twenty Questions almost could bring my mother back.

"I'm going to want to eat it?" I said.

Gracie nodded eagerly.

"So this dish is vegan?" I said.

"They all are!" Gracie said. "Well, all except one, and we decided on shrimp because even when you look at it, it just sort of looks like a little pink vegetable, so you won't feel too bad."

"Hey, I got it on my first guess," I said.

Gracie looked at me as if I were pretending to play with a kindergartener. "Not really," she said.

TIZZY DIDN'T NEED TO speak to get Gracie out of the room. The expression on her face said, *I'm doing this*, and when Gracie didn't move, Tizzy added a tinge of scowl. Klea leaned back against the dishwasher, ready for her reason not to be lying on a Florida beach. I tried giving her a *Get out* expression, and she gave me a slightly goggle-eyed *Not on your life* look right back. Evidently rules ran out with age and geography, or so it seemed when I was matching her ounce for ounce.

Tizzy whipped the foil off a dish with the panache of a magician playing to the back of a small arena. Lying there was a salad of spinach, pecans, dried cranberries, and some kind of white cheese. "Tofu," she said. "Oh, yes," I said.

She moved to the next dish. It was red beans. I loved red beans. I just never went to the trouble to cook them. And canned red beans had lard in them, last time I looked. "Rice, of course," she said, lifting the foil off a large bowl, then quickly replacing it.

"All vegan," I said.

Tizzy put a spoon into the red beans, filled it, offered it to me to taste. "I sent Gracie out for a reason," she said.

My tongue wasn't numb yet from the vodka. The red beans were just the way I'd have cooked them. With real garlic and real onions and no Tony Chachere's and a little pepper and no salt. No salt.

"No salt," I said.

"That's what I wanted you to know," Tizzy said. "No salt. Never. Unless I'm told to."

CPSIA information can be obtained
at www.ICGtesting.com
Printed in the USA
LVOW11s1752191017
553023LV00032B/36/P